R

GRIZZLY KILLER: WHERE THE BUFFALO DANCE

GRIZZLY KILLER BOOK V

LANE R WARENSKI

D1261766

WOLFPACK
PUBLISHING
— EST 2013 —

Grizzly Killer: Where The Buffalo Dance
(Grizzly Killer Book V)

Lane R Warenski

Paperback Edition
Copyright © 2018 by Lane R Warenski

Wolfpack Publishing
6032 Wheat Penny Avenue
Las Vegas, NV 89122

ISBN: 978-1-64119-343-6

Dedicated to the Memory of Bryce C. Anderson 1930-2017
A man of the Highest Integrity, a dear friend, who enriched
the lives of all who knew him and a Cowboy that is still
Riding the High Country

GRIZZLY KILLER: WHERE THE BUFFALO DANCE

JANUARY IN THE HIGH COUNTRY WEST OF THE GREAT divide is always a cold and dangerous time. Hunting and trapping had frozen to a stop with the bitter cold and deep snow over a month earlier as the long brutal winter gripped the land. Zach Connors and his Ute Indian partner Running Wolf sat by their fire on the first of several mornings that the wind hadn't been blowing. They had just finished shoveling the drifted snow from the front of their buffalo hide lodges and around their outside fire ring.

Their teepees were made in the traditional Shoshone way by their wives. Sun Flower and Raven Wing. Both women were Eastern Shoshone from the village of Charging Bull from up by the Wind River Mountains. While Zach's second wife Shining Star, was Running Wolf's sister. They were Ute from the village of Stands Tall on the south slope of the rugged Uintah Mountains.

Jimbo, Zach's huge dog and Luna, Running Wolf's white wolf had been out hunting since first light. The deep snow and bitter cold didn't seem to bother them much, but Ol' Red, Zach's big Kentucky mule, and their horses were suffering from the bitter cold and the lack of food much more than any of the others were.

After they had the fire going they used their shovels to clear the path leading out to the big meadow. They had worked every day clearing snow so the horses could get to the dry frozen grass beneath the four feet of snow, but it was a lot of work and never seemed to be enough. The cold hungry horses and Ol' Red seemed to graze it down to nothing faster than Zach and Running Wolf could clear the snow.

With the blue sky and promise of clear weather, they both hoped they could get a large enough area cleared that their small herd could get enough of the dry but still nourishing grass.

Looking south, Zach still marveled at the beauty of the peaks towering thousands of feet above them with the crystal clear air so pure it looked as though he could reach out and touch them.

This was the fifth winter Zach had lived here on the banks of Blacks Fork on the north slope of the Bear River Mountains, or as Running Wolf's people call them the Uintah Mountains. He and his Pa had come west in late 1824 with William Ashley bringing supplies for the very first Rendezvous and had decided to stay and trap for a season or two. His Pa, Captain Jack had run into a grizzly while checking his trap line one morning that first fall after the Rendezvous and Zach buried him on a creek he now called Grizzly Creek about twenty-five miles from where they had made their home.

Zach Connors had become known as Grizzly Killer throughout the west and had proven time and again that his medicine was strong. The Shoshone and Ute both consider him, Running Wolf, and their families, members of their tribes, but in making friends with some he has made enemies of others. While The Blackfeet, Arapaho, and Cheyenne had all felt his wrath and each time his medicine had proven to be more powerful than his enemies.

Zach was a big man standing over six feet and weighing well over two hundred pounds. He was powerfully built and although he'd had to fight to survive this wilderness he didn't like violence. He had killed to protect friends and family but to most that knew him he was a gentle, caring man, but all knew he was not a man to cross.

The smell of roasting elk and freshly made coffee carried on the slight breeze out to where Zach and Running Wolf were shoveling snow and made Zach's belly growl, letting him know just how hungry he was. It was only a few minutes later that Jimbo came running out to let him know to come in and eat.

Sun Flower met them standing by the fire and the smile on her beautiful face still sent chills all over his body. Shining Star was sitting there as well, nursing their nearly two-year-old daughter Morning Star, whom Zach's good friend Grub Taylor had once call the "Purtiest woman I ever saw, red or white." Zach smiled back at his two beautiful wives and thought as he had so many times before he had to be the luckiest man in the mountains.

Raven Wing stepped out of her and Running Wolf's teepee carrying their son Gray Wolf wrapped up in a rabbit fur blanket. Little Gray Wolf squealed and reached out for his father when he saw him and Running Wolf took the infant who was only a week older than Morning Star and spun him around until he was laughing right out loud.

Sun Flower was cutting off strips of the elk haunch that had been roasting for the last three hours as Zach and Running Wolf sat down. This was the last of their fresh meat. They had plenty of dried buffalo and elk to last them through the rest of the winter but this was the last of the fresh meat. Running Wolf had shot it just before the first heavy snow pushed the big game away from their mountain home and out onto the flatlands where the snow wasn't nearly as deep.

Winter was a time of year that mountain men couldn't trap the valuable beaver, the streams and ponds were all frozen over. Zach and Running Wolf did trap some but now it was mink, martin, and the occasional bobcat. Most of the winter was spent shoveling snow and stripping cottonwood bark so Ol' Red and the horses could eat, and then there was the never-ending task of gathering firewood to stay warm.

The small fire the women kept burning in the center of the teepees kept the air inside warm even on the coldest of nights. They had lined their teepee with buffalo and elk hides around the outside and stuffed grass behind the lining for insulation. The floor where they sat and slept was piled with furs and the door was covered with buffalo hide as well. The smoke from the fire was vented by adjusting the smoke flap. The flap was attached to a movable lodge pole but once it was set it only needed to be adjusted if the wind shifted when storms came in.

The winters were long and cold in the high country but it was a time of togetherness as well. Zach and Running Wolf were away much of the fall and spring trapping and hunting. The winter was the season they all stayed close to home.

Zach had learned to love his life in this wild and dangerous land. He loved the rugged beauty, the wild animals, and the way of life of the Indian people. Running Wolf was his brother in every respect except blood and

Zach would gladly give his life to protect any member of his family. He understood well the dangers of the wilderness, for he had witnessed firsthand what a grizzly had done to his father. He had nearly lost his beloved Sun Flower twice, once to an Arapaho arrow and just last year she was taken by a roving band of Cheyenne. It had been a long hard fight to get her back, but even with its dangers and hardships this had become his home and he never wanted to leave.

January turned into February and then March. The snow was deeper now than it had been but the days were much longer and warmer as well. The spring storms would come and pile up the snow as the clouds backed up against the high peaks of the Uintah's. By the end of March, the days were warm enough that the spring thaw had started.

By the first week of April, they were trapping once again. The streams had thawed and the beaver were active again. Zach and Running Wolf were both experienced trappers by now and their fall season had been a good one. They both knew if the spring season was as good they would have no problem resupplying for another year at the Rendezvous.

This year the Rendezvous was again being held east of the great divide up on the Wind River, just a short day's ride from where Sun Flower and Raven Wing's village normally spent the winter. They had all enjoyed their time last summer with the Rendezvous being nearly next door to the Shoshone village of Charging Bull. This year it was planned for just a ways downstream from last year's site. The Rendezvous, however, was still nearly three months away and there was a lot of trapping to do before the beaver lost their winter fur.

As not to completely wipe out the beaver population close to their home on Black's Fork, Zach and Running Wolf had decided to make a trek over to the Bear River and run their trap lines there. They planned on being gone for about a month so the whole family would go along.

The Bear River was only about twenty miles from their home but it was impossible to travel through the rugged mountains and foothills in a straight line. With this being the first major trip of the season, Running Wolf started working with the pack horses that hadn't been used since early fall, several days before they planned on leaving. Although it would still be a few weeks before the horses put the weight back on they had lost through the long cold winter; they could feel the season changing just like everyone else and were feeling wild and free. It took Running Wolf longer than he figured it should to catch them and then convince them to carry a pack saddle with loaded panniers.

Ol' Red and Running Wolf's pinto had been ridden throughout the winter and every day since the trapping had started, so they were both just fine with the daily work. Ol' Red had been Zach's mount since the first winter he had to spend alone in the Rockies. After the grizzly had killed Zach's Pa, a band of Shoshone had stolen Zach's horses along with Ol' Red and the big mule's sister Jenny but Ol' Red being a rather cantankerous mule hadn't stayed with the Shoshone and after killing at least one of them had run back to Zach. Ol' Red wasn't as fast as the horses but he had more bottom than any Zach had ever seen and had more than once outrun the smaller Indian mustangs because of his untiring strength.

With the meadows starting to open up, the game was returning and fresh meat was welcomed by not only Zach but the rest of his family as well. One afternoon while working two of the pack horses three or four miles north-west of their home, Running Wolf came across a small herd of elk. He didn't hesitate as he shot from the back of his pinto dropping a yearling just before it entered the trees. The lead pack horse wasn't expecting the flash and loud report from the .50 caliber long rifle. Running Wolf hadn't even brought the rifle down from his shoulder when the pack horse bolted away. The lead rope had wrapped around Running Wolf's wrist as he had quickly raised his rifle to shoot and when the horse jumped and ran he pulled Running Wolf out of the saddle and broke his arm. The frightened horse didn't stop and Running Wolf was dragged behind as it tried to run away from the heavy load.

It was over two hundred yards before Running Wolf got the rope off his wrist and after rolling to a stop he laid there in pain and watched as the horse kept running back toward the big meadow that had become their home. Running Wolf slowly sat up, the pinto and other pack horse were still standing where they were when he fired. He could tell he was hurt but he wasn't sure how badly. His arm was twisted and each time he tried to move it back into place the pain in his shoulder was excruciating. By the time he got to his feet he had beads of sweat across his brow and was breathing much harder than normal.

Running Wolf knew then his shoulder had been dislocated by the violent jerk from the pack horse, being thrown to the ground and then being dragged as far as he had. He also knew he had either a dead or wounded elk down inside the tree line below him and it could be some time before he was missed by anyone in camp. Not being able to use his left arm at all he decided he would try to get mounted and take it easy getting back to camp for help.

Running Wolf was shaking by the time he got seated in the saddle. He remembered the awful pain he had experienced when Grizzly Killer had set his broken leg that day when they had first met one another but he believed his shoulder right now hurt worse than his leg had then. By the time he had his Cheyenne Pinto turned and on a slow walk back toward camp, Luna appeared in the trail in front of him. She stopped, looking into Running Wolf's eyes for only a second then turned and disappeared through the brush. The other pack horse followed along behind Running Wolf just as if he was still holding the lead rope even though it was hanging free.

Running Wolf was in so much pain when he got to the far side of the big meadow he wasn't sure he could go on. As the Pinto carefully walked out into the open he saw Luna and Jimbo running towards him and only a hundred yards behind the big dog and wolf were Grizzly Killer and Raven Wing.

Beads of sweat covered his brow and were running down his cheeks as he slowly brought the pinto to a stop. A moment later Ol' Red came running up alongside the pinto. Zach was on the ground before the big mule came to a full stop and it only took a quick glance for him to tell Running Wolf was hurt. Raven Wing knew immediately his shoulder was hurt, even if she hadn't known her husband as well as she did she could see that by the way he sat his horse. Before Running Wolf could say a word Raven Wing shouted, "Grizzly Killer, it is his left shoulder."

Zach carefully lifted Running Wolf out of the saddle making sure he didn't bump or move his left arm. From the look on Running Wolf's face, Zach had no doubt about how much pain he was in. Zach remembered the day he'd set Running Wolf's broken leg after the Shoshone War party had shot his horse out from under him. Running Wolf never made a sound that day even when Zach could feel the broken bone grind back into place when he pulled and twisted his foot.

Zach asked, "Brother, does it feel busted inside?" Running Wolf shook his head just slightly then said in a weak and shaky voice, "I think it is just out of place, but I can't move it at all, you are goin' to have to do it for me." Raven Wing stood behind her husband supporting him as Zach got into position. She told Running Wolf to take three or four deep breaths and then hold it. Zach watched and as he let out the first breath he then grabbed Running Wolf's arm and quickly pulled it out straight. He figured by doing it before Running Wolf was expecting the pain he would not be all tensed up and it would be better for both of them. There was a loud pop as his shoulder snapped back into its socket. Running Wolf's knee's nearly buckled and Raven Wing struggled to hold him up.

Only moments after the shock of what had happened was over a huge smile formed on Running Wolf's face as he looked up at the worried expression on Zach's face and said, "The pain is gone." He turned around and hugged Raven Wing but winced as he reached around her with his injured arm then smiled and said, "Guess I'll just hold you with one arm for a couple of days."

Running Wolf slowly worked his arm and although he could move it okay it was still very tender. He then told them he still had an elk to take care of but Zach told him to go back to camp that he and Jimbo would go get the elk.

After Running Wolf had told them what had happened, Raven Wing said, "Luna knew when you got hurt, she was watching little Gray Wolf when she suddenly jumped up and ran across the big meadow. A little while later she came back to us and it was plain to tell she wanted us to follow her."

Running Wolf dropped to his knees and the white wolf came right to him, licking his face. The bond the two of them shared had become as strong as the bond between Zach and Jimbo, or as the Indians call him, the Big Medicine Dog.

THREE DAYS LATER JUST AS THE SUN WAS NEARING THE western horizon, Zach and Running Wolf topped the ridge and looked down onto the Bear River. The three women each leading two pack horses, were just behind them. Zach waited until their wives reached the top then said, "We will go down to the river and camp tonight." Not another word was spoken, just a couple of slight smiles acknowledging they had heard him.

Running Wolf looked upstream, he was remembering the day nearly five years ago that had changed his life so completely, the day he had met Grizzly Killer. Zach too remembered that day as Ol' Red slowly followed the game trail off the steep ridge toward the river. Running Wolf had been crawling through a meadow that fateful morning, his leg severely broken.

A band of Shoshone warriors had happened upon Running Wolf, and as the Shoshone and Ute's were mortal enemies, they had tried to kill him. The Shoshone shot his horse out from under him and Running Wolf's leg was broken in the fall. Not knowing he was injured and his bow was broken with the daylight nearly gone, the Shoshone had decided to wait until morning to track him down and take his scalp.

Zach and Running Wolf both believed it was fate that led Running Wolf to where Zach was camped that morning. Zach smiled as he remembered that was the day he gained a brother. After Zach set the severely broken leg, he along with Jimbo helped Running Wolf fight off the Shoshone and during his recovery a tight bond was formed. Zach and Running Wolf had been together ever since that day that had changed both of their lives so completely.

For this spring the two men had decided they were going to set their trap lines up the west fork of the Bear River. It had been nearly three years since they had been there and they weren't aware of any other trappers in the area. As they reached the bottom of the canyon the sun was behind the mountains to the west. Zach stopped as he rode into a stand of quakies just before reaching the river.

They were only about a mile below where the water of the west fork runs into the Bear River. Zach could hear the rushing water while still quite a distance from it. There were thick willows through this area so the river was still out of sight but with the roar of the rushing water, he knew it was running mighty high. Zach hoped crossing it wasn't going to be a problem the next morning.

Zach helped Shining Star with the cradleboard and set little Star free. Both she and Grey Wolf had slept most of the day as the gentle rocking of the walking horses had lulled them. Now the toddlers were full of energy and wanted to play, but darkness was coming quickly and camp had to be set.

In only minutes, Sun Flower had a fire going and she started toward the river for water but Zach took their large coffee pot from her and said, "I want to see the river so I'll fetch the water." She smiled her beautiful smile and handed him the pot. The willows were so thick he had to fight his way through them which was much more work than he thought it should be. When he pushed his way between the last two big clumps he lost his balance and nearly fell into the torrent of ice cold water that only a day before was still ice from the melting snowpack in the high country.

As he looked at the rushing white water and looked up and down the stream, Zach could see the river could not be crossed in this area and hoped they would come to a crossing before they got up to where the west fork runs into it.

As Zach left the roaring water he thought about past springs and how this trapping season was so much more treacherous than the fall. With the melting snow, the streams all ran high and wild making the river crossings so much harder. This time of year even the small creeks could be dangerous with the water only a degree or so above freezing. He knew that in just another two or three months they would be able to cross the Bear River any place they wanted. Right now that was not the case, they would have to look for the right spot and even then it would be a dangerous crossing.

Zach walked back into camp and smiled as he saw a cup full of coffee beans roasting on the side of the fire. He went over to the buffalo robe that Raven Wing had spread out for Star and Gray Wolf to play on. As he sat down both toddlers came to him and he laughed with joy at the antics of the two cousins.

Darkness had fully engulfed the mountains by the time Shining Star brought Zach and Running Wolf a cup of coffee. After the beans were roasted she had used the handle of her tomahawk to crush them before putting them into the boiling water. The coffee tonight was bitter, with darkness coming they hadn't given the coffee beans time to roast completely, but it was coffee and even though bitter Zach enjoyed the hot brew. He still remembered sitting around a fire with his Pa sipping on hot coffee and making their plans for the next day.

Supper was boiled jerky and biscuits and as Sun Flower handed Zach his food she said, "Our supplies are running low, none will last 'til rendezvous and we could use a nice fat bear for the grease too."

Running Wolf commented with a little chuckle, "Finding a nice fat one this time of year might be a problem."

Zach answered, "It might not be fat but I'm sure we can find a bear in the next few days. They ought to be out of their dens and hungry by now."

The sky was clear and the stars shined bright as they crawled under the heavy buffalo robes of their bed. They hadn't bothered to put up a lean-to and although the slight breeze that was coming down the canyon was cold they were warm under the heavy robes. Star was nestled between Shining Star and Zach with Sun Flower on the other side. Running Wolf and Raven Wing had Grey Wolf between them on the other side of the fire. Jimbo was curled up on the foot of Zach's bed while Luna was lying right alongside Running Wolf.

A wolf howled in the distance and Luna raised her head, ears straight forward looking out into the darkness as the wolf howled again. Running Wolf could tell there was a longing inside her to run out into the darkness and find her own kind and he wondered why she never did. He had known since he was a small boy that the wolf was his spirit helper and throughout his life wolves had helped him many times. This white wolf that Grizzly Killer and Jimbo had saved from a bear as a tiny pup, he believed was his spirit helper and now she had become a companion and protector of his family as well. He truly believed Luna had special powers; she didn't have the size and power of Jimbo and she didn't have the training to do whatever asked like Jimbo did, but she was always there protecting and warning them of danger.

A bright shooting star streaked across the sky and Zach thought about the Indian belief that when warriors died shooting stars were their spirits going to the land beyond. He wondered if one that bright might have been a great chief or medicine man passing to the other side.

A pack of coyotes started yipping downstream and then Zach could hear the soft heavy breathing of Shining Star as she fell into a deep sleep. He was just starting to doze off himself when Sun Flower reached around him and pulled her naked body up tight against his. Their lips met and they stayed with arms wrapped around one another as they fell into a deep restful sleep.

Zach felt Jimbo get up then heard him and Luna leave on their morning hunt. Jimbo had always liked to hunt in the early dawn. Whether it was a rabbit, groundhog, grouse, or just a squirrel or two, Jimbo and Luna hunted for their own food each morning. They never turned down anything offered to them but they liked to find their own food as well. Zach figured it was just something deep inside that made them love the chase. He then smiled thinking that they were no different than he was, for he loved to hunt himself and had ever since he was just a young boy and his Pa had first taught him to shoot.

As the coming light chased the darkness from the land a

warm south breeze had started. They all knew that meant a storm was probably coming, but worse than a storm, the warm air would be melting the snow faster making the Bear River even more dangerous to cross.

They were on the trail riding upstream without taking time to build a fire as Star and Grey Wolf suckled on their mother's breasts while they rode following alongside the roaring river. It was only a few minutes when they passed where the West Fork ran into the Bear and although the river was much smaller above that, Zach felt it was still too wild to safely cross and he wouldn't take the chance with the women and children along.

Running Wolf suggested they continue upstream another five miles or so to where the East Fork ran into the Bear and only a couple of miles above that another river ran into it. If they could get above both of those the Bear River wouldn't be much more than a big creek. Zach nodded his agreement and headed east further away from the wild river. The trees, willows, and thick brush made the going slow.

A quarter mile from the roaring water the land opened up into large sage filled flats and they were making very good time but as the morning progressed the warm southern breeze was turning into a stiff wind hitting them right in their faces.

They reached the East Fork in just a little over an hour and then had to go nearly a half mile upstream before finding a suitable place to cross. Once they were all safely across it they continued on without rest as they all were worried about a spring storm hitting them.

Another hour and they were crossing the next stream running into the Bear. As Zach crossed this smaller stream he remembered the time he had trapped this one. The spring after he'd buried his Pa. That was the trip when he had found Running Wolf and he smiled remembering that morning once again.

They continued following the river upstream through meadows several miles long until they came to a crossing that they all felt was safe. By now storm clouds were filling the western sky and they all knew they would never make it back down to the West Fork before the storm hit. Where they crossed the Bear there was a small feeder creek only a couple of feet wide coming from a canyon to the west. Zach pointed Jimbo up that little creek and led the rest of them into this unknown area. The aspens were thick and the ground rocky as they made their way west out of the canyon of the Bear River. Both Zach and Running Wolf, although familiar with this general area, neither one had ever been in this small drainage before.

As the sky continued to darken Zach was looking for a place to shelter out of the coming storm. An hour later, they crested a rise and before them was a small lake, along the northwest side were scattered pines and quakies with plenty of grass and flat area to camp.

They stopped about halfway down the small lake and started to set up camp before the storm hit. It still amazed Zach how efficient the women were at setting up the large heavy buffalo hide teepees. He and Running Wolf were taking care of Ol' Red and the horses, they had them watered and were putting the hobbles on the horses when Zach looked up to see both lodges up and the women were putting all of their supplies inside.

It had been years since Zach had hobbled Ol' Red. The big red Kentucky mule never strayed far, he was always watching over the horses and was just as aware of approaching danger as Jimbo and Luna. He was larger than any of the Indian horses and had the strength to carry Zach's large body all day without tiring.

The wind shifted from the south, it was coming from the northwest and the temperature was falling fast. Zach felt a cold raindrop hit his face and then another. He looked across the lake and the heavy timber on the far side was becoming lost in the cold rain and snow mixture. Zach and Running Wolf both gathered an armload of firewood as they walked back toward the teepees. They could already smell the sweet pine smoke from the fires the women had started, and as Zach stooped down and entered his lodge the smiling faces of all three women and both babies made him warmer than even the heat of the fire. Running Wolf entered right behind Zach and when Gray Wolf saw his father the toddler reached out to him and tried to run, falling right on his little face. There was a slight hesitation, then the crying started. Running Wolf took two steps and picked up the crying boy, softly talking to him in his native Ute language as he wiped the tears from his child's eyes.

It was just midafternoon but with the storm, it seemed like evening already. They had left that morning without eating and all were hungry. Sun Flower started roasting more coffee beans while Raven Wing started on biscuits. The flour they had left from last year's rendezvous was now full of weevil and although the small crawling bugs didn't seem to bother anyone she still did the best she could at picking them out before mixing in the baking powder, salt, bear grease, and water. After a thick sticky paste formed she would drop them by spoonful's into a hot cast iron frying pan and cook them over coals on the side of the fire. Running Wolf and the women had never seen a biscuit before Zach first showed them. That was one staple he and his Pa had brought with them from their home in Kentucky.

Zach could still remember his Ma's biscuits right out of the big black iron pot that would swing on a rod over the fireplace inside the cabin. These frying pan biscuits made with bear grease instead of rendered lard weren't the same but they were still pretty good. Zach as well as his family all had become used to having them and they dreaded the times when they ran out of flour.

This time of year all of their supplies were running low. Even the green coffee beans didn't look like they were going to last until they could resupply at Rendezvous. Meat, however, was plentiful. They still had dried buffalo, although by now it was so dry and hard it needed to be boiled to make it soft enough to eat. In the spring the animals always returned to their mountain home and for Zach and his loved ones to have fresh elk, deer, bighorn sheep, moose, or bear they only had to take the time to go hunting. Porcupine, pine hens, and the snowshoe hares made fine meals along with squirrels and groundhogs if needed. Most of the time in the years Zach and been in the mountains meat had been plentiful.

There were times especially in late winter when finding meat was nearly impossible. Zach always remembered the Cherokee called February the starving moon for that was the hardest time of year to keep the people fed. Zach, just over a year ago had to travel many days from home to find game out on the plains to keep his family fed through the starving moon or as his wives' Shoshone people called it, isha-mea, the coyote moon.

Outside the wind whipped the wet heavy snow against the sides of the teepee, but with the small fire it was keeping the inside warm and the heavy buffalo hides keeping the storm out. Zach laid back on a buffalo robe with his little blue-eyed Star in his arms, they both went to sleep.

What none of them knew is the little lake was right in the center of the home range of a large silvertip grizzly and after coming out of his den after the long winter's sleep, he was hungry and cantankerous, out searching for any source of food he could find.

By the next morning the storm had blown itself out, but before it had stopped it left nearly six inches of the wet heavy snow behind. Zach looked out into the predawn darkness and shivered from the cold then turned and watched as his two beautiful wives climbed out from under the buffalo robe naked as the day they were born and slipped into their deerskin dresses.

Star was still sound asleep as Sun Flower added sticks to the small fire ring and blew life back into the fire. Jimbo had left when Zach first opened the entry cover to look out and with only a whine called to Luna. She joined him and the two of them were off on their morning hunt.

As the sky lightened large patches of blue showed through the grey clouds. Running Wolf stepped out of his teepee carrying a burning branch and used it to start a fire outside. Zach walked out to Ol' Red and the horses making sure they were all okay when movement on the end of the lake caught his eye. He watched as a cow and calf moose walked out of the trees and into the shallow water of the lake. He watched as the cow put her whole head under the water for longer than he thought was possible then lift it up with moss and grass hanging from her mouth. He knew they could use fresh meat but he figured they would find it soon enough without taking this very young calf or its mother.

As Zach walked back toward Running Wolf and the fire he could see Jimbo and Luna on a dead run back toward camp. Zach knew his dog well enough to know Jimbo had found something that he didn't like. Zach's eyes scanned the area behind the dog and wolf wondering if something might be chasing them but he could see nothing except the white of the snow and dark green of the pines.

As Jimbo ran into camp Zach could already hear the low growl coming from way down deep in the big dog's chest. Luna stood there beside him and then Jimbo turned and started back on his own trail. Zach and Running Wolf both knew instantly they were supposed to follow the big dog.

Zach checked the powder in the pan of his trusted Hawken then without taking the time to saddle Ol' Red he grabbed a handful of mane, jumped up on the big mule's back and started after Jimbo. Running Wolf was right behind him with Luna staying alongside him and his pinto.

Zach kept Ol' Red at a fast walk not knowing what they might be riding into. His eyes covering every inch of the country before them. Jimbo seemed impatient with Zach's slow speed running back to him several times then ahead again as he led them up past the far end of the lake and into the large meadows above. There were beaver ponds all through the meadow, every place where even a trickle of water ran the beavers had built their mud and stick dams. For a trapper, this looked to be the land of dreams for there must be dozens of beaver just in this one meadow.

Jimbo was now nearly two hundred yards ahead when

he suddenly stopped. Zach slowed even more carefully watching the area all around them. They were out close to the middle of this meadow with its small stream running through it. Patches of willows were growing along the creek but they were over a hundred yards from the forest on either side. Running Wolf with Luna still by his side was less than fifty yards behind Zach as he approached where Jimbo was standing.

Zach could hear the low growl coming from deep in the big dog's throat. He looked around one more time before sliding off Ol' Red. Running Wolf stayed mounted on his pinto, scanning the area for trouble as Zach approached his dog. Zach was over ten feet away when he saw the tracks of a big grizzly that Jimbo was standing next to. He noted where they were leading and pointed in that direction then turning to Running Wolf he said, "Big Grizzly."

They were now nearly a mile from camp and without hesitation Running Wolf spun his pinto around the kicked him into a full run getting back to the women and their children. Zach was only seconds behind him but Ol' Red didn't have the speed of the Cheyenne pinto and was three hundred yards behind when Running Wolf rode into camp. Zach breathed a sigh of relief when he saw Sun Flower and Raven Wing by the fire, and as he rode up Shining Star stepped out of the teepee into the bright light of the new day.

The women all knew something was wrong to see their husbands riding in at full speed. All three of them were ready to fight if necessary. When Zach rode in Running Wolf had already told them that Jimbo had found tracks of a large grizzly in the fresh snow only a mile or so up from the lake. Zach patted Ol' Red on the neck as he slid off and all three women were looking to him for what they were going to do. Zach looked at Running Wolf and said, "If you will stay here I'll saddle up and go see just where that Ol' bruin is heading." Running Wolf nodded but both Sun Flower and Shining Star stepped toward their husband with concerned looks on their faces.

Sun Flower was the first to speak, "Grizzly Killer you should not go alone."

He turned and looked into the beautiful dark eyes of Sun Flower and then Shining Star and said, "I am not alone, Jimbo will go with me. Besides, I will stay alert and keep my distance, but we need to know where the grizzly is going so we can stay far away."

They all could remember the last encounter they had with a grizzly. The huge bear had killed two of their horses and severely hurt Ol' Red. He had then torn through the camp of some Shoshone hunters killing two of them and hurting others. In fact, it was the Shoshone that first gave him the name of Grizzly Killer after he had killed a grizzly near his home on Black's Fork. He knew how hard they were to kill. If this was the big bear's territory then they would leave the beaver in the meadows above the lake and move on, but if he was just passing through they would stay here and trap for the next couple of weeks.

Zach could see the worry in the eyes of his wives but he knew this had to be done. Neither Sun Flower nor Shining Star said another word, although worried about his safety they didn't question his judgment.

Zach quickly saddled Ol' Red and with his usual silent hand signal sent Jimbo out in the lead. He set the big mule into the easy ground eating lope that he knew Ol' Red could stay with all day and was back at the grizzly's tracks in just a few minutes.

He followed the bear's tracks to the northwest, and for

now he was relieved they were heading away from their camp. The bear had walked along the edge of the thick timber for nearly a half mile then abruptly turned directly into the dense pine forest. Zach hesitated, wondering if the bear could be waiting for him just inside the trees, but Jimbo would know if it was near and he trusted the big dog not only with his life but with the lives of his family.

He had to work his way slowly through the thick pine and fir trees and over deadfall as he followed he grizzly's trail. By midmorning he figured he was only a mile and half from camp, he was on foot leading Ol' Red when the tracks finally lead out of the thick timber and into a huge open meadow. The clouds had moved on to the east and now with the warm spring sun shining in a bright blue sky, the snow was melting rapidly. The tracks were still plain to see and even if they weren't he knew Jimbo could follow the bear with his nose.

Although Zach couldn't see the stream out in the big meadow to his north he knew it was there from the number of willows that ran down through this large open meadow. The meadow was nearly a mile across and ran down along the creek for as far as he could see.

There was beaver sign nearly everywhere he looked, either dams with their ponds backed up with their mud and stick lodges sticking up out of the water, or the familiar aspen stumps scattered along the hillsides. Zach knew if they didn't have problems with the grizzly or any of the other dangers this wilderness offers, they would have a great spring trapping season.

Zach followed the bear further upstream, he passed more and more beaver dams to his left and then he came upon a high pointed hill. This hill wasn't covered with timber, in fact, it was mostly barren of any plant life. The color of the ground was different as well, it was much lighter than the surrounding hills with rock turning from yellow to brown.

It was close to midday and there were now large patches of ground showing where the snow was melting away. Zach figured he was nearly five miles from camp and the bear's tracks were still leading away. Jimbo came running back to him as if everything was alright, so for now, he figured the big bear had moved on. He was above the last beaver pond and stepped out of the saddle and walked over to the creek. He moved his hand in a circle over his head that was the sign for Jimbo to scout the area in a large circle all around him. He then knelt down to get a drink and something shiny caught his eye. He reached out into the icy water and picked up a gold nugget.

Zach knew nothing about gold, he wasn't even sure what he had picked up was gold but he thought it was. The nugget was the about as large as his thumbnail and being wet it sparkled in the bright sunlight. The only other gold he had ever seen were two nuggets Running Wolf had found before they ever met. He traded those nuggets for his long rifle and supplies. He had heard people say, "Gold is where you find it," but he sure never expected to find it just lying in a stream bed along with all the other pebbles.

He reached out into the cold water again, this time bringing up a large hand full of the rounded pebbles and dirt and carefully looked at each stone finding one more, smaller nugget. He rubbed the two nuggets and compared their weight to the other pebbles their size and could tell they were much heavier. He dropped them into his possibles bag then looked up at the yellow colored mostly barren hill above him. He walked back over to Ol' Red looked all around him again, then patted his big mule on his neck and said, "Well, feller I think I'm gonna climb up to those yeller rocks and look around a bit 'til Jimbo gets back.

Zach climbed over loose rocks and dirt that had sloughed off the hill sometime in the distant past for nearly a hundred yards, then came to a rock wall that was twenty or thirty feet high. The rock was a yellowish color with darker streaks of brown running through it. Near the base, there was something totally different that caught his eye. A narrow strip of nearly crystal clear rock running from the base up through the face for nearly six feet. The strip varied in width from only an inch to nearly three. He reached out and rubbed the clear stone then noticed some of it had broken off along with the rest of the rocks when the hillside had sloughed off.

He reached down and picked up one of the larger pieces of the crystal and he could see something was embedded in it. There were threads of gold running through it and as he held it up the sunlight reflected off these gold threads. Zach had never seen anything like this before and wasn't sure what it meant. He thought he had found gold but if nothing else he knew Sun Flower and Shining Star would like the beautiful crystals with the shiny gold threads inside.

Jimbo came running up to him wagging his tail letting him know the bear had moved on and all was clear. Knowing the others would be worried about him he put the crystal with the nuggets in his possibles bag and started back to camp.

These streams were rich with beaver, Zach knew they could spend the next month running their trap lines without ever leaving this area, besides he was excited to show the others what he had found on his Gold Hill.

Zach rode steady but easy for the five miles back to

camp. He stayed out of the heavy timber instead riding along the edges of the trees. He saw several moose in the many beaver ponds or in the willows near them. He didn't see any elk but their tracks were thick on several game trails he crossed. He saw one black bear on the hill clear across the big meadow which he figured was over a half mile away.

By staying out of the heavy timber he realized he was following a different stream than the one that ran into the small lake where they were camped. He crossed over the ridge separating the two creeks and twenty minutes later could see the column of the smoke from their fire. Jimbo ran on ahead as he usually did letting them all know Grizzly Killer was coming back.

Zach hadn't realized how hungry he was until he smelled fresh meat roasting on a willow spit over the fire. He had left without eating this morning and he had been in such a hurry he hadn't even taken any jerky with him. Running Wolf had taken a yearling moose just after Zach had left that would provide them with fresh meat for the next few days and jerky for much longer.

He was met with questioning looks from them all as he stepped out of the saddle. He smiled telling them the grizzly hadn't stopped, that he followed the bear's tracks for at least five miles and it appeared the big bear was just passing through this area heading somewhere else. Zach didn't say anything about what he had found or seen just yet. He was excited to be here and wasn't sure if it was the beaver or the gold he had found that made him feel this way.

Sun Flower brought him a cup of coffee that was so hot it burned the tip of his tongue as he tried to take a sip but he just smiled and sucked in cool air to soothe his mouth. He sat the cup down and walked over to where the two toddlers were playing and picked up Star and held her above his head then kissed her fat little cheek. He then picked up Grey Wolf and spun him around until he squealed with delight then set him back down on the robe.

Raven Wing and Shining Star were staking out the moose hide getting it ready to start scraping and Sun Flower announced the moose roast was nearly done. Zach picked up the coffee cup and sat down by the fire when Running Wolf joined him and said, "I know the moose is more meat than we needed but he was walking right into camp, I had to drag him a hundred yards out of camp to gut and hang him." Zach nodded and smiled knowing he would have done the same thing. Running Wolf asked, "How far you do figure we are from the West Fork?"

Zach looked up and said, "Between five and ten miles near as I can figure but after what I saw today I don't figure we need to move at all. There's enough beaver in this area to keep us busy this season." Running Wolf smiled trusting Zach's judgment completely.

They had set up this camp in a hurry to beat the rapidly advancing storm so some minor adjustments would be made, but they were all happy with this site next to the little lake.

Shining Star and Raven Wing had the moose hide stretched tight and staked ready to scrape when Sun Flower had finished a pan full of biscuits and told them the meat was done. As they walked over both Star and Grey Wolf came to their mothers.

As they ate Zach told them all of this area they were in, the huge open meadows full of willows with one beaver pond after another for mile after mile. He told them of the plentiful moose and of seeing the black bear, the many elk tracks and yes there was the grizzly but it appeared, at least for now, that he was just passing through this part of his range.

Zach didn't say a word about the gold he had found until after they had finished eating and were drinking the last of the pot of coffee. He then reached into his possibles bag and pulled out the quartz crystal with the beautiful threads of gold running through it. Running Wolf understood the value of gold for he had traded two of the yellow rocks he had found for his rifle and supplies at the first Rendezvous he had been to with Grizzly Killer in Willow Valley. To the girls, however, this was just a strange and pretty rock. Raven Wing thought the crystals had magic powers, for as the sunlight passed through it made the colors of a rainbow on the ground. She could remember Blue Fox, the old Shoshone Medicine Man, having crystals that did the same thing. She couldn't remember any of his having these shiny yellow threads in them. Then he pulled out the two nuggets, the small one first and then the larger. Running Wolf smiled knowing how valuable the nuggets were but to the women they were just two yellow stones.

Zach explained how valuable these yellow stones were to the white men. That just one of the little pebbles was worth as much as ten or fifteen prime beaver plews. Raven Wing held the crystal, wondering about its power. Could she control the magic it possessed or did they need to return it to mother earth from where it had come?

THE NEXT MORNING ZACH AND RUNNING WOLF LEFT the women to make modifications they wanted to camp while they set their trap lines. Running Wolf set his in the series of ponds above the lake while Zach rode over the ridge to the north. He still had concerns about the grizzly but he knew Jimbo would let him know of any trouble that was near.

As Zach rode out into the very large meadow that he had skirted the day before, he couldn't get the sight of the gold nugget shining in the shallow water from his mind. He was not a miner, he was a trapper, he knew he could find and trap beaver in these ponds that went on for miles but the thought of gold was still on his mind. Could there be more of the shiny nuggets just lying in the stream bed? He believed the gold threads inside the crystal rock were gold as well but he had no idea how to get that gold and Raven Wing seemed concerned about the crystal anyway. He still didn't understand all of the Indian beliefs and superstitions but he respected them, and if Raven Wing or any of the others weren't comfortable with him having the crystals, gold or not, he would leave them be.

It wasn't long before Zach found an active beaver drag trail and waded out into the icy water. He pounded a stake into the soft mud deep enough he knew it would hold a beaver. He then set the trap and placed the trap's chain over the stake and put a few drops of the pungent castoreum on the top of the stake. He then walked out of the cold water to where Ol' Red was standing and looked at his beloved mule and asked, "Where did Jimbo get off to?" Just as he said that he heard a loud splash downstream and only a hundred yards below the beaver's dam Jimbo came out of the willows running at full speed and only ten yards behind him was the large cow moose with her head down charging after him. Zach figured Jimbo could outrun or at least outmaneuver the large moose but Jimbo was leading her right back to where he and Ol' Red were standing. He jumped up on his mule and sensing the urgency Ol' Red jumped and turned taking off at full speed before Zach had his feet in the stirrups or even had the reins in his hands. He came out of the saddle and landed flat on his back in the soft wet mud nearly knocking the breath from his lungs.

He knew the angry moose would be on him in only seconds so ignoring the pain and shock of the fall he rolled over and jumped to his feet just as Jimbo got to him. He didn't have time to run to the willows for what little protection they might offer and he wasn't sure his rifle would fire after the lock had been in the wet mud so he threw his arms in the air and yelled just as loud as he possibly could at the charging moose. She stopped only five or six yards from where Zach was standing wondering what this thing was standing in front of her. Just then Zach heard the cry of a young calf coming from the willows where she and Jimbo had come from. Upon hearing her calf call for its mother the moose turned and trotted back to her frightened calf.

Zach stood there and watched her disappear back into the tall willows, then assessed his predicament. Ol' Red was standing about thirty yards away looking at him like he was asking, "*What is the matter with you?*" He then looked down at Jimbo and he too looked at Zach as if asking, "*Did you really fall off Ol' Red?*" Zach was silent for a moment then said, a little louder than he intended, "Yes, I fell off!" Jimbo flinched at the sound of his voice and Ol' Red brayed as if he was laughing.

Zach was cold and wet and covered with mud. His rifle had mud caked over its action and was covered and nearly all the way back to its butt. Its frizzen had been knocked open and wet mud had replaced the powder in the flash pan and he couldn't even see the flash hole through the mud.

He had to stop to thoroughly clean his rifle and get what mud he could off himself and he knew he couldn't do either without a fire. He glanced back at the willows where the moose had disappeared one more time then walked over to Ol' Red and stepped up into the saddle. A few minutes later he was at the edge of the forest starting a small fire burning just inside the tree line.

Running Wolf already had six of his twelve traps set, the first of them was less than a half mile from their camp. He marveled at this area, it was as rich in beaver as any they had trapped over the last five years. Standing there looking up at the towering peaks just to the south of them and the rugged beauty all around, he wondered what his life would have been like had he not met Grizzly Killer. He thought about the Ute village of Stands Tall where he and Shining Star were raised. Although Stands Tall had passed on to the land beyond, his son Two Feathers was now their Chief. It had been several years now since they had been to the south side of the Uintah's. With Rendezvous being to the north every summer, it seemed there was never the time to go south. He thought maybe this year after Rendezvous and the buffalo hunt there would time for a trip south before the cold maker closed the mountain passes with snow.

Running Wolf loved his life and his family and it was only on rare moments of reflection such as this that he felt a little homesick and wondered how his friends on the south side of these very mountains had faired during the winter. Then, a movement in the willows only a few yards from him caught his eye, bringing him out of the moment of thought. It was a weasel still in its pure white winter coat with only the tip of its tail staying black year round. The white ermine fur would soon be changing to the light brown of its summer coat. It had caught a field mouse and was running back to its den with the mouse in its mouth, where Running Wolf figured little ones were waiting for their meal.

This was the time of year the mountains were coming to life after the long cold winter. They were at the end of badua'-mea', the melting moon, as his wife called it while Grizzly Killer called it the month of April, and now there was new life starting everywhere in the mountains.

Running Wolf continued up through this shallow little valley until he had set all of his dozen traps and wondered how Grizzly Killer was doing. His belly growled with hunger and he knew the women would have fresh moose roasting over the fire, but he wanted to see the area Grizzly Killer had told them about. So ignoring his belly he headed north away from the creek and beaver ponds to find the area where his partner would be setting his traps.

He rode through the thick timber and just like Grizzly

Killer the day before ended up on foot leading his pinto around and through the thick trees and deadfall. When he came out of the timber and onto the edge of the huge meadow, he looked up at the yellow colored hill and could see the area that Grizzly Killer had described where he had found the crystal stone.

Running Wolf knew Raven Wing was uncomfortable about Grizzly Killer removing the strange stone from its resting place. She didn't know what magical powers the beautiful crystals may hold. She had told him after they had crawled under the robes last night that it was like some of the magical healing stone Blue Fox had used, but that he had never taught her how to use their power. Only this stone with its golden threads through it she believed held even more magic than the ones Blue Fox had and she didn't know if she dared try to use it. Running Wolf believed his wife to be much more than just the healer Blue Fox had taught her to be. Even though Raven Wing herself didn't really believe it, everyone that knew her believed her to be a powerful shaman. He had told her to take the stone into the woods and ask the One Above what should be done with it.

Running Wolf wanted to see where the strange crystal had come from but he knew there would be plenty of time for that. Right now he wondered where Grizzly Killer was and if he had his traps set yet.

He rode downstream expecting to find Grizzly Killer but he had traveled nearly a mile and had seen no sign of him. At first, he wondered if Grizzly Killer might have gone upstream setting his traps but that didn't seem likely. He then caught just a faint smell of smoke and he knew he was too far from it to be the fire from camp. He left the creek and headed back toward the forest and the faint smell of wood smoke seemed to get a little stronger. Although still only slight, he knew it could mean trouble. He quickly checked the prime in the pan of his Pennsylvania made long rifle and took the pistol he looped over the saddle horn and stuffed it in his belt, then he continued slowly forward studying every shadow or hiding place before him.

He hadn't gone more than a hundred yards when Zach stepped out of the forest. Running Wolf was so tense expecting trouble he had his rifle nearly to his shoulder before he saw the movement in front of him was Grizzly Killer. Zach instinctively dove back into the trees when he saw Running Wolf's rifle coming up and hit the ground hard. Jimbo was sitting there watching and as Zach looked at his dog he could see that laughter in his eyes again.

Running Wolf dismounted and walked forward with a big grin on his face. Zach was just getting to his feet when Running Wolf said with a chuckle, "Well, least we know you haven't slowed down any." Then he noticed what looked to be all of Zach's traps still hanging off the side of Ol' Red's saddle and he knew something had happened.

Running Wolf stood by the fire warming and drying his wet legs as Zach finished cleaning and reloading his Hawken. Then with a smile and more than a little embarrassment Zach told him what had happened. It made it even worse when Running Wolf stated in the form of a question, "You really fell off Ol' Red?"

They worked together over the next few hours setting the rest of Zach's traps. Since both of them were tired and hungry they headed straight back to camp. Jimbo ran on ahead as he always did to let the women know their men were coming back. Luna met him while he was still three hundred yards from the teepees and with just a quick greeting she hurried on to meet Running Wolf while Jimbo went on to camp.

Zach could smell the meat cooking even before he could see their camp and his belly growled from hunger at the smell loud enough that Running Wolf started to laugh. Then Running Wolf's belly growled just as loud and they both laughed at one another.

They rode into camp and the first thing Zach saw was the two toddlers playing on a buffalo robe alongside the fire. It always brought a smile to his face watching the little ones play. Running Wolf took care of Ol' Red and the Pinto giving them each a good rubdown with dry grass then turned them loose with the rest of their herd.

Shining Star had cooked the biscuits in their frying pan nearly three hours ago and had kept them warm covered with one of the wooden bowls Zach had carved out of dry cottonwood. Both Zach and Running Wolf noticed Raven Wing was quiet as they all sat around the fire and ate. A pair of loons landed on the far side of the lake and their cries echoed across the water as one more sign spring was finally here. The male started his courtship dance across the water and Sun Flower especially enjoyed watching them dance and listening to their echoing calls.

After they all had eaten their fill, Shining Star and Raven Wing picked up the little ones and after partially chewing pieces of the warm moose meat they would feed it to the babies, teaching them to chew their food. After that, they nursed the rapidly growing little ones. Only seconds after Raven Wing started to nurse little Grey Wolf, she cried out and jerked Gray Wolf off her breast. The teeth marks were plain to see around Raven Wing's tender nipple as she started scolding her little boy in her native Shoshone tongue.

Running Wolf couldn't help but chuckle lightly as he said "Maybe you shouldn't teach him to chew just yet," at that they all laughed except Raven Wing she didn't think it was at all funny. After she calmed the crying little boy and then let him finish nursing, they sat around the fire enjoying each other's company. Zach was holding Star while Running Wolf was holding little Grey Wolf and it wasn't long until both babies were asleep. They took them inside their warm lodges and covered them with their rabbit fur blankets.

When Raven Wing came back out of her lodge she was carrying a small bundle. She sat down next to Zach and slowly unwrapped the gold-streaked quartz crystal. Once she had the crystal completely unwrapped but without touching it she held it out for Zach to take then said, "Grizzly Killer, I took my husband's advice and today I spent much time alone with this stone asking the One Above what should be done with it. I believe it to hold much power but it was you that found this special stone and I believe it is you that must ask the spirit of the mountain if it is alright for you to take this stone from its resting place and use its powers."

Zach had been around Indian people most of his life. Many of his friends in Kentucky were Cherokee and he had lived with his mixed family of both Ute and Shoshone for the last five years. He was well aware how superstitious most of them were. Even though he didn't necessarily believe in all their superstitions he did have an enormous respect for their beliefs. He was aware people had been taking gold out of the ground for nearly as long as man had been on the Earth and he didn't believe there was anything wrong with the mining of gold or anything else. He didn't believe this gold streaked crystal held magical powers, but he did know Raven Wing and the rest of them truly believed it did.

He reverently picked up the crystal that was nearly three inches long and over an inch square. The top of it came to a point with several flat sides but the bottom was broken with milky colored impurities. The golden threads inside ran in different directions even in the milky white color of its base; it was truly a beautiful crystal whether or not it had magic powers.

Zach looked his sister-in-law directly in the eyes and nodded. He took the softly tanned leather strip she had wrapped it in and reverently rolled it up again. He then walked out of camp and out into the forest. He was only a couple hundred yards when he came upon a group of quakies in the middle of the thick pines. There he knelt down and prayed. He thanked the Lord for his life and for his family, for his happiness and this land he had grown to love so much. He then asked for wisdom in making the decisions that were best for all of them.

He waited there on his knees until all the light had faded from the forest when suddenly he knew what to do. He hadn't heard a voice and he hadn't had a dream, if fact he had no idea where this thought had come from, it was just there and it felt right. He slowly rose to his feet and looked up into the heavens at the few stars that were visible through the bare branches of the quakies and said thank you.

When Zach walked back to camp everyone was looking at him with anticipation. He took the wrapped crystal and knelt down in front of Raven wing. He handed it back to her and said, "My sister, I asked the One Above, the creator of all things for guidance in the decisions that I make and I believe he has answered my prayer. We may use this stone and any power it may hold as long as it is used for good, we may take any of the gold or any of the crystal that mother earth has already released from her grip. We must not dig into the earth to take what she still holds onto.

Raven Wing smiled and nodded, they all could see the wisdom that was given to Grizzly Killer from the One Above. Raven Wing took the wrapped crystal and said as long as she lived the power of the crystal will only be used for good.

Zach could see the first light of day through the smoke hole of their buffalo hide lodge. He could feel the warmth and softness of the naked bodies of Sun Flower and Shining Star that were lying on either side of him. It had been a calm and restful night after he had eased Raven Wing's troubled mind about the gold-streaked crystal he had found.

Star began to fuss and Shining Star rolled away from Zach and picked up their nearly two-year-old daughter and laid her back down between Sun Flower and Zach. Sun Flower cuddled the little one, kissing her fat little cheeks as Shining Star stood up in the dim light of their lodge and slipped on her soft doeskin dress. She then took Star outside to clean her up and feed the rapidly growing little girl.

Sun Flower still didn't understand why she hadn't given Grizzly Killer a child but then she smiled as she rolled up on top of him with her naked body and kissed him, thinking she would keep trying. They made love, then laid there holding one another until they could hear the others getting the fire started and moving around camp.

Zach had nearly quit wondering how these two beautiful women loved each other and shared him with no apparent jealousy at all. After the five years they all had been together, he accepted having two wives but he still didn't understand how they did and figured he never would. He loved them both dearly and would gladly give his life for any member of his family. Star had become the joy of his life. He never tired of watching her learn or seeing the light in her sky blue eyes as she discovered something new. Her skin was dark but her hair was brunette not the shiny black of her mother's. Her eyes she got from her father and stood out in contrast to the color of her skin.

Zach watched with delight as Sun Flower stood up and slipped her dress down over her naked body, then he stood in the warmth of the lodge and dressed. He stepped out of the teepee and saw Shining Star holding her daughter, standing alongside her brother with Grey Wolf in his arms, pointing across the lake. They were showing the little ones a cow moose with a very young calf. Zach figured it was the same ones that had been at the lake when they first arrived.

The trapping seasons, both fall and spring were always a lot of work, but Zach felt no pressure to hurry this morning. Their trap lines were set so close to where they were camped he knew they had plenty of time to check and reset them today. As they ate more of the moose that was cooked the night before Zach thought about the two gold nuggets and he didn't really understand why but he wanted to go back and look for more. He knew his Indian family didn't understand the value of gold, in fact, money of any kind was meaningless to them. They had learned the value of the beaver, for it was the beaver plews that they traded for the supplies they all had learned to enjoy so much.

Trapping beaver and the coming of the white men had

made their lives so much easier than it had been before. By trading furs to the white men they now had metal knives and axes, cooking pots and pans, metal plates and cups. They had the wooden barrels to store the precious flour, cornmeal, baking powder, and salt. It was the white men that brought the bright trade cloth and other foofaraw and gewgaws they loved so much. They also brought the powder, lead, and guns that they now depended on for hunting and defending themselves with.

Most tribes in the west didn't feel threatened by the coming whites because they were so few in numbers. A few hundred or even a thousand white men were scattered all over the west but there were tens of thousands of Indians. One thing most Indians, and whites as well, did not understand was the differences in their cultures and those differences led to conflicts and in some cases a severe hatred of one another.

Zach Connors had always been different from most white men, raised in the small community of Pottersville, Kentucky in a good Christian home. Most of his friends as he was growing up were Cherokee Indians from a village not far from his Pa's homestead. Zach had spent a large portion of his life with Indian people and he understood the differences in their beliefs much better than most white men. Just like with mining for gold, his own beliefs were completely different than the beliefs of the Indians but he had learned to respect theirs and that had made him one of the most respected men in the mountains. So many of the white men didn't honor the Indians beliefs, they thought they were just wild and cruel savages to be taken advantage of or eliminated and Zach feared the future as more and more of this type of white men came west.

As Running Wolf was bringing up Ol' Red and his

pinto, Zach checked Sun Flower's .36 caliber squirrel gun, making sure it was ready to shoot. She had become a very good shot since he had given her his Pa's squirrel gun when they first were together. He then checked the old Harpers Ferry rifle that he had taught Shining Star to use. He turned to Raven Wing and she picked up her bow and showed him it was ready and within easy reach if trouble were to come. Zach still had the thought of the grizzly that had passed through the area in his mind.

Zach and Running Wolf rode out together but at the end of the lake they split up, Zach turning off and climbing up over the ridge before he had to go through the very thick timber.

Just after the women watched them ride away, Sun Flower and Shining Star headed for the closest stand of willows. They were cutting long branches to tie into hoops to stretch the beaver plews on that they knew the men would bring back. Raven Wing stayed in camp scraping the moose hide and watching the little ones play.

Three hours later Zach had three beaver and had reset the three traps. He was thankful the day was sunny and warm. After wading in the icy water the warm rays of the sun felt mighty good on his aching legs. Jimbo as always was scouting the area as Zach set his traps. The big dog would come back to where he was every so often making sure he was alright but Jimbo loved to explore new areas and was out of Zach's sight most of the time.

Zach and Running Wolf met where Zach had built the fire the day before and once again they built another to dry their cold wet legs. Both men carried extra moccasins so they could change into dry ones after the traps were all checked and reset. They had five beaver to skin between them and for one day that was great. They both knew once they started taking beaver from an area the trapping would slow way down, but this area was large enough they could probably trap here for the rest of the spring season.

It was just past midday when they had the beaver skinned and the pelts rolled and tied on behind their saddles and they decided to ride up to the gold hill and Zach would show Running Wolf where he found the nuggets and crystal.

It took less than an hour, just letting Ol' Red and the pinto set their own pace. Jimbo once again was well out in front leading the way. Zach was relieved, it appeared he had been right about the grizzly for Jimbo didn't seem to be able the smell any sign of the big bear.

They stepped out of their saddles and hiked the hundred or so yards up the hill to where the vein of quartz showed on the rock face where it had sloughed off. There were more crystals lying there loose below the vein but none of them were the size of the one Zach had picked up before. Running Wolf and Zach both knew the crystals would be precious to Raven Wing and they picked up each one that was lying on top of the ground. Zach didn't count them but he figured there were over a dozen of them. One he picked up had specks of gold in it and another had some gold around the base of the crystal right on the outside of it.

Zach figured there would be many more just under the surface of the dirt but he didn't think Running Wolf would be okay with disturbing the ground at all. They went back down to the creek and Zach pointed out where he had found the nuggets and in the next hour, the two of them had picked up a dozen more of the pure gold pebbles. One of them was nearly double the size of the largest he had from before. It was nearly as big as the whole end of his thumb.

Zach now figured spending time here would be more

profitable than trapping the beaver for just in the last hour they had picked up more wealth than a full week of trapping would give them. He did worry some just what Raven Wing and the others would think about taking the nuggets from the stream bed, but for right now he was excited about this newfound wealth.

As they rode back toward camp he thought about bringing their families up to this area and they all could look for nuggets in the stream. Running Wolf didn't say anything for a few minutes after Grizzly Killer mentioned the women but after he thought about it he said, "What do you think of moving camp up here, it would not be much farther to travel for the trapping and we would be right here where the gold is all of the time."

Zach looked at Running Wolf with a bit of a surprise on his face and asked, "Do ya figure Raven Wing will be alright with being right up here by this gold hill?"

Running Wolf slowed his pinto right down and turned toward Zach and said, "I believe when she actually sees how the hill broke apart spilling the clear stones and gold out upon the ground she will think just as I do, that mother earth did that for us to find and use. The great bear would not have led you to this place if you weren't supposed to find it and if we weren't supposed to use it. Yes, my brother, I figure Raven Wing will be excited to see where the magic stones come from."

It was a little over five miles back to their camp and it was only a half hour later when they saw Luna running toward Jimbo. After a quiet greeting, the white wolf continued on to Running Wolf and Jimbo ran on into camp letting the women know they were coming in.

Zach smiled at the sight he saw, Raven Wing and Sun Flower were both on their knees rubbing the brain and warm water mixture into the stretched out moose hide and the little ones were once again playing on the buffalo robe. Shining Star was sitting by the fire using its heat to help her bend the willow branches into the hoops they needed to stretch and dry the plews on. All three women stopped for a moment and smiled at their men coming back but the toddlers were so involved with one another they totally ignored their return.

After Ol' Red and the pinto were unsaddled and cared for, Zach and Running Wolf laced the plews onto the willow frames that Shining Star had already finished. While the men were finishing lacing the plews onto the frames, Raven Wing stopped working the moose hide and went over to the fire and she and Shining Star finished preparing the meal they had started earlier in the day.

That morning the women had walked down to the end of the lake and wading in the frigid water they had pulled up cattail shoots. It was still a few weeks too early in the year for any new growth but by peeling the dead brown leaves back from each stalk they got down to an edible core. They had cut up the cattail shoots into their black iron pot, then nearly filled the pot with moose and water. It had been slow cooking over hot coals for several hours now and was ready to eat. In minutes the two women had biscuits mixed up and Raven Wing reminded the men they were running low on bear grease. She sat the frying pan on a bed of coals that Shining Star had flattened out next to the pot of their simple moose and cattail stew.

While Raven Wing was cooking the biscuits Shining Star mixed a big hand full of flour with a little more bear grease and slowly stirred the mixture into the stew. By the time the biscuits were cooked the stew was slowly bubbling in a rich thick gravy.

Shining Star set two of the light brown biscuits in a wooden bowl and then filled the bowl with the stew, and as she handed Zach his meal she said, "We have used almost all of the bag of salt. It will not last much longer so I didn't use much of it in the stew."

Zach smiled and said, "One day we may not be able to get it at all, we will get used to eating without it." They all had gotten accustomed to the supplies they traded the beaver plews for at Rendezvous each year and although Zach and the rest of them knew they could get along without them, none of them wanted too. Especially the flour, salt, and baking powder for the biscuits that had become such a large part of most of the meals.

Zach and Running Wolf had enough powder and lead cached to last them several years but the perishable food supplies never seemed to last all the way to the next Rendezvous. Zach looked at Running Wolf as he said, "After we check the traps in the morning, we'll try to find a bear, least that way we can resupply the grease." Running Wolf nodded but had a questioning look, wondering when Grizzly Killer was going to show them the gold and talk about moving camp.

The sun wasn't far above the western horizon as Zach reached in his possibles bag for the gold nuggets, but before he pulled them out Jimbo and Luna both jumped to their feet growling and barking at the lodges. Both Zach and Running Wolf jumped up with rifles in hand just as a skunk came from between the two lodges.

The skunk was snarling and vicious and with one look they all knew something was wrong with it. Zach had heard of skunks and other small animals getting hydrophobia. If anyone or any animal got bit by one of them it meant a slow and agonizing death, but he had never seen one before now.

He yelled at Jimbo and Luna to get back as Sun Flower, being the closest, grabbed both toddlers by an arm and got them out of the way. Running Wolf fired but the skunk was rapidly coming toward them. He was trying to hit it in the head away from the terrible scent glands, but his shot missed its mark and the heavy lead ball tore right through its back half sending the sickening smell through the air to all of them and soaking into the soil as well.

From the time Jimbo first growled at the rabid skunk to when Running Wolf killed it was only a few seconds, but in that few seconds, their campsite by the lake was destroyed. Even Jimbo and Luna backed away from the sickening smell. Zach could see a white foam on the skunk's mouth and he knew they were lucky no one had been bitten.

Without anyone saying a word the women started taking down the lodges and it still amazed Zach how fast and efficient those three small in stature women could bring down the large heavy teepees and then put them back up again.

Zach and Running Wolf helped pull the heavy buffalo hide teepees away from the dead skunk and its smell, then he started saddling the horses. In less than an hour, they were moving camp. Zach told Running Wolf to take the lead that he was going to bury the skunk so no other animals could get to it. Although Running Wolf and the women didn't understand the term hydrophobia they had all heard the tales of the terrible death that came from being bitten by one of the rabid animals.

Running Wolf and the women had only traveled about two miles when Zach had caught back up to them and as he rode up he brought a slight hint of the smell with him. A drop or two of the oily scent had got on the spade he had used. He had been where the scent was so strong he couldn't smell the faint odor but Sun Flower and Shining Star let him know to bring up the rear and to stay back there a ways.

Running Wolf led them up to a spot just a couple of hundred yards downstream from where the mountain had sloughed off and the vein of quartz was exposed. There were tall pines surrounding a grassy flat area with the hill to the north and the small clear stream bordering on the south. The sun had dropped behind the mountains to their west by the time the women had both teepees up. Zach and Running Wolf had the horses all unsaddled and the packs emptied by then as well. They found a shaded tree about a hundred yards further downstream where they hung the moose quarters hoping it would stay cool enough there to keep at least for a few more days.

Zach still worried about what Raven Wing was going to think about the additional crystals and nuggets they had found but for now, they were all much too busy to talk about it.

ELY TUCKER STOOD BY THE FIRE TRYING TO WARM HIS
cold aching legs and wondered how much longer he was
going to be able to live this life that he loved so much. It had
been a full year now since that murdering white trash group
of Matt Tillman's had walked into their camp and shot him,
leaving him for dead. As much as he didn't want to accept
it, the wound still bothered him and had slowed him down a
lot more than he would admit. He had no desire to go back
to the so-called civilized world back East, but this year the
work seemed so much harder and the water so much colder
than it ever had in the past; he really wondered how much
longer he could go on. He watched his lifelong partner,
Grub Taylor, walking back to camp knowing Grub was only
a year younger than he was. Grub walked with his head
high and his back straight and Ely wondered just how he
held up like he did. Their other partner Benny and his
woman Little Dove were still out setting his trap line and
the thought of what else the young couple might be doing
put a smile on the much older mountain man's face.

Grub walked up to the fire shaking his head and said,

"I's don't know how ya can get yer traps out faster than I just did. How long ya been back here anyhow?"

Ely smiled at Grub as he answered, "If'n you had the know-how of this here ol' coon ya wouldn't have to ask that."

Grub grumbled under his breath as he said, "We been out here together fer over ten years now, I's think I knows just as much as you 'bout trappin'."

Ely smiled and answered, "Now, If'n that were true you would've been back here just as quick as me."

They then both chuckled and Ely asked, "Have ya seen any sign of the kid and Little Dove?"

"Nary a track." Was Grub's reply. Ely unconsciously rubbed his aching right shoulder and the movement didn't go unnoticed by Grub.

Then Ely said, "No tellin' what those two is doin', I's don't figure they're in any hurry to get back."

Grub smiled and said, "Yer right 'bout that pard, I's know I sure wouldn't be in any hurry if'n I had a girl like Little Dove with me all the time." The two old trappers laughed but they both still worried some about their young partner Benton Lambert.

Ely wondered why they would be concerned though after what Benny had done last year. They knew he was a man fully capable of taking care of himself and Little Dove. After Ely had been shot, while Grub took care of his closest friend and partner, Benny had tracked the four men that had shot Ely for nearly two hundred miles and taken their plews. He saved Little Dove along the way as a Blackfoot war party attacked and killed everyone else in her Shoshone village. He then helped Grizzly Killer in a fight with those same Blackfeet and after that, he and Grizzly Killer caught up with the men he was tracking and recovered their plews.

Ely and Grub both knew Benny had become a man to be reckoned with but both of them were so much older they couldn't help but still think of him as a kid.

GRUB HAD BEEN RIGHT, Benny wasn't in a hurry to get back. Little Dove had gone with him this morning because she hadn't wanted to be alone. Benny was moving his trap line onto a different stream for he had nearly trapped out the one he had been working. This day however, Little Dove wasn't the playful distraction she usually was. She had dreamed the night before about her mother and father and the last time she had seen them in their village. It had been just a little while before the Blackfeet had attacked and she seemed sad and quiet as Benny had set his traps. He knew something was wrong but didn't know what it was.

Grub, Ely, Benny, and Little Dove had spent the winter in the Shoshone village of Charging Bull. Ever since Benny had saved Little Dove a year ago she had stayed with him. Although both of them were still in their teens, the wilderness had made them grow up fast. They were living as man and wife and everyone that knew them liked them both.

Little Dove was a cousin to Sun Flower and Raven Wing. The village of Charging Bull was where the only relatives she had left lived, except of course Sun Flower and Raven Wing who lived with Grizzly Killer in the mountains far to the south.

After the Rendezvous broke up last summer, Grub knew Ely was still weak and needed much more time to recover. After hunting buffalo with Grizzly Killer and Running Wolf on the plains south of the Sweet Water last fall, Grub had suggested they talk to Chief Charging Bull about staying with the Shoshone through the winter. Benny was nervous about living in a village full of people he couldn't understand or talk to but Little Dove loved being with her people. Grub pulled Benny aside and explained living in the village would be much easier on Ely as he recovered from the terrible wound in his chest.

They had trapped the upper reaches of the Popo Agie through the fall but as the winter set in the deep snows of the high country drove them to seek shelter in the Shoshone Village and Charging Bull welcomed them as family. Grub and Ely had been with Grizzly Killer, many other trappers, and Ute Indians when the Blackfeet had attacked Charging Bull's village. It was on the east side of Sweet Lake at the first Rendezvous that was held in 1827. Charging Bull and the rest of the Shoshone people had considered Grub and Ely good friends ever since that day.

Benny and Little Dove were nearly inseparable as the long cold winter dragged on. Benny, Little Dove, and Grub hunted together much of the winter providing meat not only for themselves but for many of the village seniors. Grub delighted in teaching the young woman to shoot and he was even more excited than she was the day she made her first kill. It was a fat bull elk, and Benny and Grub proudly displayed its head outside their teepee. The four of them still lived together in a teepee that Little Dove along with her aunt White Feather had made. White Feather was Sun Flower and Raven Wing's mother and was very happy to have a young woman back in the family.

It had taken Ely a long time to recover from the terrible wound on the right side of his upper chest. Towards the end of last summer, after nearly five months Grub could tell it still hurt Ely to shoot his heavy rifle. He had improved through the long winter but Ely wasn't the same. He was a little slower to move and the cold seemed to bother him more than usual. Now the spring trapping season was underway and although Grub knew Ely's shoulder still bothered him, he was amazed Ely was still trapping right along with himself and Benny. He hoped the coming warmer weather would help Ely feel better and help his body finish healing.

After Benny set his last trap they moved downstream a mile or so and he stopped in a clearing along the stream. He built a fire under a large pine to dry his cold wet legs then motioned Little Dove to come and sit with him. She had taught him the Shoshone language and being in a village where nothing else was spoken for several months Benny had picked it up fast. At the same time, he worked with her on English and she could now speak it to the three men as well.

She was silently staring into the flames and he could tell she was in deep thought, when suddenly she looked up into his grey-blue eyes and asked, "Do you ever miss your mother and father?"

The question took Benny by surprise. He slowly nodded his head and said, "Ya, I miss 'em all the time. I wish I could go see them and my brothers and sisters, but they are so far away."

She looked puzzled and asked, "Why can't you go see them? If my mother was still alive it would not matter how far away she was I would go see her."

Benny had never even considered the possibility of seeing his family again. Now Little Dove's simple statement made it seem possible. She then looked down at the ground and asked, "Is it because of me you won't go see them?"

Although she meant nothing more than her wanting to know, that statement hurt him. He wondered if he had done something that would make her think that. He reached down and ran his fingers down her cheek and under her chin then gently raised her head until their eyes met then he said, "Little Dove, I love you, I want to be with you and no one else. If I ever go back to see my family I want you to be with me. I want them to know that I am happy living here and you are the reason." She had tears in her eyes as she raised up and kissed him.

Benny had meant everything he said to her. He did want to see his family and he wanted them to know Little Dove. He had not been raised with the prejudices so many people seemed to have against the Indians. He had heard the horror stories of Indians torturing and killing and he knew many would kill anyone not from their tribe, but for himself other, than the Blackfeet he had been treated with respect by the Indian people. On his Pa's farm back in Missouri they had traded many times with Indians and he had found them to be honest and truthful, more so than many of the white men in the area. He was sure his family would accept Little Dove with open arms, but he wasn't so sure about many of the others back there.

GRUB HAD a fresh lamb roast cooking on a spit over the fire as Benny and Little Dove rode into camp. Ely was by the fire with a pile of willow limbs he was tying into hoops to stretch their plews on. Both men looked up and smiled at the two of them and for a brief moment, Grub was just a bit jealous of Benny. He shook that thought off nearly as fast as it had come to him. He didn't want a woman, not one permanent anyway, but seeing how happy Little Dove and Benny were together did make him wonder about the choices he had made in his life.

Benny had thought about what Little Dove had said as they rode back to camp. He knew if he really wanted to see his family again he would have to make the time for that trip. It would take at least sixty days each way if there wasn't any trouble, plus the time spent there. It would take five months and there wasn't that much time after Rendezvous before winter set in, let alone before the fall trapping season. He realized if he was ever going to go he would have to leave in the spring, taking his plews with him to sell in St. Louis so he could resupply for the next year there.

Ever since Benny had become partners with Grub and Ely the thought of going back home had never entered his mind. That is until Little Dove had said what she did today, now he couldn't get it from his mind. If her mother was alive it would not matter how far away she was she would go see her. Were his mother and father still alive? He had no reason to think they weren't but the truth was he really didn't know.

That night around the fire Benny was much quieter than normal and Ely could tell something was bothering him and asked, "Benny, whatcha got on yer mind boy, ya ain't said ten words all evenin'?"

Little Dove sitting by his side knew he was thinking about his home and leaned against him as he raised his head toward Ely. He was silent for another couple of minutes then asked, "Did you or Grub ever go back home after you left?"

Ely looked down into the flickering flames and with a look of regret and said, "Naw, we never did, we never heard a thing 'bout home after we left." The only sound around the fire then, was the fire itself with its pine logs crackling sending the red-orange embers into the air above it as all three men were now deep in thought.

A wolf's howl from the ridge above them broke the silence and then Benny asked, "Do ya ever wish ya had?"

Grub who was usually the light-hearted one of the three said, "Only when I think about it."

Then Ely responded, "After all these years I still wonder what happened to my Ma and Pa and older brother and wonder if they did the same 'bout me."

After another period of silence, Grub asked, "Are you thinkin' 'bout home Benny?"

Benny looked up and said, "Yes I am. Little Dove got me to thinkin' 'bout home today. I sure would like to see Ma and Pa one more time and to have 'em meet Little Dove. I want 'em to know I's happy and I found the life I was meant to live, but I figure Pa knew all along I wasn't cut out to be no farmer." The mood stayed solemn around their fire for the rest of the evening, each man lost in his own thoughts and memories.

The next morning Little Dove had coffee beans roasted and crushed and was just adding them to the coffee pot full of water when Benny stepped out of their teepee. She turned and smiled at him and just that simple look made Benny wonder why he would ever want to go back home. He was truly happy living here in the Rockies with Little Dove and his two older partners. Grub and Ely stepped out into the crisp early spring air just a few minutes later and smiled at the smell of the boiling coffee. Grub was about to ask Little Dove where Benny was off too when he saw him bring the horses up from the creek after watering them.

Since they had lost what baking powder they had in early winter to rodents chewing through the leather bag making a hole large enough the precious white powder was scattered to the wind, they had been making bannock instead of biscuits. The unleavened skillet fried bread was nothing more than flour, grease, a little salt, and water. It was flat and heavy and took some time for them all to get used to it after they had been eating the fluffy biscuits, but it was a good way to use the wheat flour and cornmeal they still had. After a breakfast of the bannock bread and leftover lamb from the night before, they all headed out to check their trap lines.

Again today, Little Dove joined Benny riding out enjoying the beautiful spring day. They rode side by side where they could but as Benny started into the timber she had to drop back to be able to follow him through the thick trees.

The scent of the pine was strong as they pushed through the dense pine forest, climbing to the ridge top before dropping down into the canyon where his traps were set. The chatter of the squirrels and squawking of the jays let them know that just by walking through the forest they were disturbing it. Benny came out of the trees just yards before reaching the top and he continued until his sorrel mare was standing right on the top. There he waited for the moment it took Little Dove to catch up. She rode up alongside him and they both enjoyed the majesty of the Wind River Mountains with their snowcapped peaks towering above. Just below them were a half dozen bighorn sheep grazing on the exposed grass that would very soon be turning green with the changing season.

Benny reached out, took Little Doves hand and looked into her obsidian dark eyes. It had been a full year now that they had been together and he had never been happier. He was living a life he truly loved with a girl he had grown to both love and depend on. She had taught him the Shoshone language and with living in a Shoshone Village all winter he'd had plenty of practice. She spoke some English when they met but with her living with the three white trappers she now spoke English nearly as well as any of them.

As Benny looked at the breathtaking view before them he squeezed Little Doves hand, looked into her eyes and said, "I never want to live nowhere but in these mountains with you." She smiled at him and silently thanked the One Above for bringing her such a man. She knew her life was much better than it might have been. Many Indian women were treated as nothing more than the property of their husbands but Benny treated her as his partner. She did feel like she belonged to him, after all he had saved her life, but she had grown to love him deeply and wanted nothing more than to please him. She was aware she had made him sad in asking about his home and mother and father. Even today he wasn't talking to her as much as usual and she could tell he was still thinking about his family that was back in the land where the sun rises. Little Dove didn't want to see him sad but she didn't want him to have any regrets about his parents either.

Benny started off the ridge toward the stream and beaver dam where his first trap was set. The sheep below scattered as he headed toward them, all but one ewe. She took a few steps but stopped then hunched up her back as if she had just been shot. Benny and Little Dove both stopped to see what was wrong and watched as her sides started to convulse. A couple of minutes later the front feet and head of a little lamb appeared from between her rear legs and another push and the tiny lamb was on the ground.

Benny glanced over and Little Dove was smiling watching the birth. They were not more than fifty yards away from the ewe as she turned and started licking the helpless little newborn clean. It took only minutes before the lamb was standing on wobbly legs as its mother continued to lick the little lamb dry.

Movement in the trees caught Benny's attention just as a Black Bear charged at the ewe and her lamb. He didn't have time to think he only reacted, bringing his rifle up to fire not knowing whether he had enough time to stop the charging bear from reaching the ewe and her newborn.

BENNY'S SHOT CAUGHT THE CHARGING SOW RIGHT ON her right shoulder, spinning the bear around. The bear was now confused and biting at the painful wound that had shattered the bone. She slowly laid down, mortally wounded as Benny reloaded with all the speed he could muster. Less than a minute later his second shot found her heart and her pain was gone.

Benny and Little Dove didn't move right away, they sat there on their horses and watched the ewe lead her wobbly legged lamb toward the trees. Little Dove was smiling, knowing Benny had just saved the tiny lamb and probably its mother as well.

After the ewe and lamb were out of sight they rode down to the dead bear and got off their horses to take care of this unexpected kill. When he rolled her over to start skinning and gutting her, he stopped and stared at her teats bursting with milk. He looked up at Little Dove who started looking at the trees from where she had charged hoping to see the cub or cubs the bear had left behind.

Benny wondered if he had done the right thing as he

started the process of skinning her. By saving the newborn lamb he had cost at least one cub its life maybe two or even three. He wondered were the sheep and lambs life more important than the bear and her cubs?

His thoughts were interrupted by Little Dove's voice as she said, "I will ride down through these trees and see I can find her little ones." Although she knew the chances of finding them were slim and the chances of her being able to save them if she did were even slimmer; she felt like she had to try.

Benny watched her disappear into the trees not far down the hill from him and felt bad all over again for the cubs he knew could not survive. He thought just how cruel this wilderness could be, but this was the way of nature. For one animal to survive another must die. Just like the bear, wolf, cougar, and coyote, he too had to kill to eat. It was the same now as it had always been, the way God intended it to be. He again thought about the little lamb on its wobbly legs trying desperately to keep up with its mother and figured he would do the same again. He would not be able to watch and do nothing while a defenseless newborn of any kind was killed.

He had the bear gutted and skinned by the time Little Dove rode back up the hill to him. The look on her face let him know without saying a word she had not found the cubs. She had lived in the Rocky Mountains her whole life and Benny had grown up right on the edge of the wilderness on his Pa's farm forty miles northwest of St. Louis. They both understood they could do nothing to change what had happened and neither of them was sure they would want to.

After hanging the bear carcass in the closest tree they continued on down the canyon to the creek and Benny's trap line. He had set his ten traps on slides leading into the numerous beaver made ponds that extended up this creek for a couple of miles. The first trap they came to had not been touched so Benny moved it to the other side of the pond, putting more of the strong smelling castoreum on the stake.

The next two traps were the same and again Benny reset them in different locations on the same ponds. The fourth one was successful, a large beaver with beautiful thick prime fur was caught and had drowned in the water by the stake. While Benny was resetting the trap Little Dove skinned the beaver, rolled up the pelt, and tied it behind her saddle.

Benny had caught two beavers and reset all but three of the traps; he was satisfied those three would be successful where they were. He was wet and cold, his buckskin leggings were soaked through with the icy water. Little Dove insisted they stop and build a fire. Benny was carrying an extra pair of moccasins just like Grub and Ely and taught him to. It made for a more to. He was just going to change out of his wet ones when Little Dove started to gather wood.

She had a small but warm fire started in just minutes and reluctantly Benny slipped out of the cold wet skins. She smiled at the goose bumps on his stark white skin as he stood there enjoying the heat from the fire. She set his wet leggings over a branch above the fire to help them dry then knelt down and started to rub his cold skin. As she rubbed along with the heat of the fire the goosebumps started to disappear but something else started happening as well and they made love right there next to the fire.

Nearly an hour had passed when Little Dove pushed her naked body away from him, stood and slipped her dress back on. Benny reached up and felt his leggings, they were drying but the tops were still damp and cold. Little Dove took them from over a branch and started to walk toward her horse with them, Benny asked, "Where ya goin' with them, I got to put 'em on and we gotta head back." She just kept walking until she reached where they had tied the horses. He watched as she rolled the still damp leggings up. She then reached into her saddlebag and pulled out a brand new pair of leggings that she had been working on for the last couple of weeks while he was away from camp trapping or hunting. They were made from elk hides she had tanned herself and were as soft as any leather he had ever felt.

The soft dry leggings felt mighty good on his still chilly legs and as she tied one side up onto the waistband that held his breach cloth he tied the other. The smile on his face warmed her heart. She loved doing things for him and once again thought how lucky she was to have the One Above lead this man to her.

Grub and Ely were sitting by the fire, each was lacing a plew onto a willow frame as Benny and Little Dove rode into camp. Ely noticed immediately the rolled up bear skin behind Benny's saddle and the two beaver pelts behind Little Dove's. He didn't say anything right then but he was mighty proud of Benny. After only two years he was already a better trapper than many who had been in the Rockies longer than he had.

Benny unsaddled Little Dove's horse and dropped the bearskin next to it as he started to get a pack horse ready. He figured he had time to go back up and get the bear carcass and be back before dark. While Benny rode out leading the pack horse Little Dove staked out the black bearskin then unrolled the two beaver pelts and with her sowing awl started punching the holes around their perimeter to lace them onto the willow frames. As she did she told the two older trappers of the birth of the lamb and why Benny had shot the bear, but how bad they both felt that there were bear cubs out there without their mother and they were sure to die.

Even the two old mountain men hated the thought of the cubs starving to death or being eaten by wolves or a cougar. Even a male bear would kill and eat the cubs if they got the chance, but such was life and death in the wilderness. Many things about this vast land seemed cruel and harsh but there was a lot to love about it as well.

With Ely's help, Little Dove had the plews laced good and tight onto the willow frames and was scraping the bearskin when Benny rode in for the second time today. Grub went out and helped him hang the bear next to the yearling lamb. With what was left of the lamb and now the bear they had enough meat to last them for a while, in fact with the warming weather they may have to make jerky or the meat may spoil before they could eat it all.

Although Benny hadn't said anything about his home throughout the day, but his family had been on his mind all day long. Like Little Dove, he didn't want to have any regrets about the choices he made in his life and he knew if he never saw his parents again he would regret it until the day he died.

Although he never wanted to be a farmer like his Pa and rarely saw things the way his father saw them, he had always felt loved and he loved his parents as well. His childhood had been happy, even though being the oldest he'd had to grow up fast. There was never a doubt in his mind both his parents loved him and his brothers and sisters. Although Benny's childhood had been a lot of hard work it had been happy for the most part. The only things he had really hated was the work of farming; it was never done. He didn't mind the hard work, trapping was hard work but it was work he enjoyed. Clearing fields and then plowing them he found boring and as he grew into his teenage years he swore to himself he would never be a farmer. So he'd left home at only sixteen years old and went to work on the riverboats and barges moving goods up and down the Mississippi.

The men he encountered on the river were a hard drinking, hard fighting lot and Benny soon found he didn't like the life on the river just as much as he didn't like farming, so the first chance he got he came west to try trapping. His first winter in Jackson's Hole he met Grub and Ely and with their friendship he'd found the true happiness he'd been missing. Grub and Ely taught him trapping and the skills to survive in the wilderness. They thoroughly enjoyed the young man's company and by the next spring offered to make him their partner.

Their partnership had suited all three of them, Ely especially, but Grub as well liked teaching Benny the ways of the wilderness and its people. They found him to be a quick learner and very interested student. Benny was young and energetic and he made the two older trappers feel young again themselves.

As they all enjoyed the warmth of the fire that night it was plain to see Benny was still in deep thought. He finally looked across the fire and asked his two older partners, "Did y'all ever go back to the settlements after ya come to the mountains?"

Grub was the one who answered telling Benny, "Fer the first couple of years we had to take our plews all the way to the settlements and we spent near half the year makin' that dangerous trek. Then in '23 Andrew Henry built his Tradin' Post up on the Big Horn River just south of the Yellerstone so fer the next couple of years we took 'em there.

Then in '25, William Ashley started bringin' the supplies to Rendezvous' in the summers and we ain't left the mountains since then."

Benny didn't say anything for several minutes as he stared into the flames then he asked, "If I was ever goin' back to see my folks when would I have to leave in order to get back in time for the fall trappin'?"

Grub and Ely looked at each other before Ely answered saying, "Benny that is a mighty long and dangerous trip to be takin' by yerself. Whether ya go by way of the rivers and float or go overland along the Platte ya have to go through weeks and weeks of Injun country an some of them critters ain't to fond of white men bein' in their land." Benny nodded he understood and no more was said about it. Benny couldn't get it from his mind even though he didn't say any more about it, the thought of seeing his parents again weighed heavily on his mind.

The next morning the three trappers each headed out alone to check their trap lines. Little Dove stayed in camp to work on the bear hide she had staked and partially scraped. She watched Benny ride out of sight then added a little more wood to the fire and stepped into the teepee to get her knives. The four green plews from yesterday's catch were leaned up against the side of the teepee drying and she hoped they had another successful day.

She thought of her mother as she still did nearly every day as she brought out the three knives. She had been only a small child when she was first taught to scrape all the fat, flesh, and tissue from the hides making them ready to rub in oils from the animal brains that both preserved the hide and helped make them soft. As a child, they had used a sharpened shoulder blade from a buffalo instead of knives. She thought how much easier the white man's tools had made her life. Now she used a blade lashed to a long curved rib from a buffalo like a draw knife. Although she didn't know what a draw knife was she knew that is what Ely and Grub call it. What she did know was using this knife she could scrape a hide in just a fraction of the time with a lot less work than it used to be.

After the hide was scraped Little Dove took their two heavy black iron pots down to the tree where the bear was hanging to get what fat she could to render for their grease pouch. In the spring most of a bears fat reserves were depleted from the long winters sleep and with a young mother as this one appeared to be, her cubs had depleted even more of her fat. Little Dove found just one of the pots held all of the fat she could trim off the carcass.

Back at the fire she added just a small amount of water to the pot then moved a bed of coals to the side and set the pot on them to slowly melt the fat. Rendering it into grease or lard would take nearly all day long so while the heat from the coals started the process of melting the fat she started on the bear's hide once again. She had the skin scraped or fleshed as Ely and Grub called it, so it was time to start with the brain and warm water mixture.

She put the bear's brain along with a few cups of water in their second pot and heated it up until it was warm to the touch. Once she was satisfied with its temperature she used her hands and mixed the brains and water into an oily slurry. She then used a rough stone and rubbed the skin down smoothing it out and getting it ready to accept the oily mixture.

Little Dove went back to the fire and stirred the melting fat before starting the process of tanning the bear hide. Although she was young she had been doing this work for years. Starting at the center she poured a small amount of the oily mixture onto the hide then started rubbing it into the raw leather. She rubbed in every direction just like her mother had taught her.

Even though it had been a year since the Blackfeet had attacked and killed everyone in her village she still missed her family. When Benny was with her she didn't think about it that much but on days like today when she was alone with her thoughts and doing the tasks that her mother had taught her, she missed her. Tears rolled down her cheeks and mixed with the oily slurry as she worked all the harder trying to rub her pain away.

Little Dove worked a little over half of the mixture into the hide stopping only long enough to stir the melting fat once or twice an hour. It was midafternoon when she finished and laid an elk hide over the top of the bear hide to keep it from drying out while the oil finished soaking in. Tomorrow she would do it all over again with the remaining brain slurry then would come the hard work of pulling and stretching the hide over a log until it was soft. Once she had the hide soft enough to be a comfortable sleeping robe she would then smoke it for the final preserving process. Just like keeping meat from spoiling, smoking the hide not only helped to preserve the leather it also discouraged insects from making it their home.

Again today Ely was the first to make it back and again his trap line had yielded one prime beaver. She went to get the plew from him but he told her, "You don't have to do my work, Little Dove."

She pulled the still damp pelt from him and with a determined look said, "It is not work if I choose to do it, you take care of your horse and I'll stretch this beaver skin onto the willows." He smiled and nodded then walked his horse out to the others.

Little Dove was just finishing lacing the beaver plew onto the willow frame when Grub came in, but today his trap line hadn't caught a thing. He smiled and nodded at her and told her to make sure it was good and tight as he led his horse out to the others.

She checked on the rendering pot and smiled seeing the fat had all melted. The coals had cooled enough that the grease was just starting to set up and she got the pouch and started spooning the thickening lard into it. While she was doing that Grub started more of the lamb to roasting.

The sun dropped behind the towering peaks just west of them and she wondered why Benny had not yet returned. The sun was not only reflecting its golden orange glow off the clouds but off the sheer granite cliffs making the mountains appear to be made of pure gold.

The light was now fading and still no sign of Benny. Ely could tell Little Dove was worried and was about to tell her Benny could take care of himself when they all heard a crack and then the pounding of hooves as Benny came riding in. At first, he didn't say a word he just ran to the fire and kicked it out not taking care to save the cooking meat. Ely reached for his rifle as Grub jumped up, then Benny said only one word that sent fear through them all, "Blackfeet."

As Zach walked back toward where the women had their teepees set up he could smell the sweet scent of burning pine from the fire they had already started. He still wondered what Raven Wing was going to think about them picking up more gold and crystals and had decided he wasn't going to say anything about it until after she saw the quartz vein and how it had been exposed by the sloughing off of the hill.

Running Wolf took care of the pack horses that had carried the moose while Zach stood there just outside the ring of warmth from the fire and smiled at Shining Star and Raven Wing sitting and nursing their babies. He walked over to Sun Flower and although she no longer seemed to have the sadness of not having a child of her own, he could still tell there was a longing in her that nothing else would fulfill. She didn't understand why the One Above was keeping her from having Grizzly Killer's child, but just as her mother had told her, she believed when it was time, she would.

Running Wolf came back from the horses just as Grey

Wolf was satisfied with a full belly. He sat down next to Raven Wing and took their rapidly growing child from her. The little boy reached for the three eagle feathers that Running Wolf had tied in his hair and that made Zach think back to the time when Running Wolf had named his little boy. Bear Heart, the child's grandfather and father to Raven Wing and Sunflower had given the infant an eagle feather that day. That feather was held with the little one's sacred medicine pouch by Raven Wing and would be until he was old enough to understand just how special it was.

Running Wolf looked across the fire to where Grizzly Killer was standing with Sun Flower. He had a puzzled look on his face, but just a slight shake of his head Zach let Running Wolf know this was not the time.

In the high country, the air cools mighty fast after the sun has set and with the cooling air a gusting wind had started up that sent chills through them all. Shining Star and Raven Wing took the little ones inside their warm lodges and only minutes later Running Wolf joined his wife.

Sun Flower leaned against Zach, enjoying his warmth as well as the warmth of the fire. She had noticed the silent nod between Zach and Running Wolf and finally asked, "Is something wrong my husband that you and Running Wolf do not want us to know about."

Zach was taken back by her question, then he smiled knowing he could never keep anything from her or Shining Star; they knew him too well. He thought for a minute as he looked into her beautiful dark eyes then said, "We will take a short walk and I will show you."

She wrapped an elk robe around her shoulders and he led her by the hand along the creek until they reached where the hill had sloughed off. She followed him, not questioning his wisdom but curious as to where they were going when she realized this is the place he and Running Wolf had described to them, this was where they had found the crystals.

The moon was nearly full and was now a couple of hand widths above the horizon just as a cloud covered its bright light. Although now they couldn't see much, Zach knew right where he was going and stopped after only another twenty yards. A quick glance at the sky and he knew it would be only a few minutes for the light of the moon to once again be upon them. He explained, "This is where we found the crystal, and in the creek below is where we found the gold." He then reached in his possibles bag to show her they had picked up many more and continued to explain, "I didn't want to say anything to Raven Wing until she could see for herself how the mountain had given us these treasures and we only took what it had given us."

Just then the light of the moon flooded over the hillside and the quartz vein sparkled in its light. Sun Flower was in awe of what she was seeing and so excited she said "we must not wait we must bring Raven Wing right now," and she turned running all the way back to camp.

Being careful not to wake either of the babies she got her sister and Running Wolf out of their lodge. She was so excited she was speaking her native Shoshone instead of English. Shining Star joined them and they all could see how excited Sun Flower was. She told her sister, "You must come and see what the mountain has given us." Raven Wing looked back at the lodge and Running Wolf told her and Shining Star to go and see and that he would stay and make sure the little ones were safe.

It took but a few minutes for them to reach where that small portion of the mountain had slid down to the creek.

They had just started up the hill again when they could see what looked like a light coming out of the hill. The light from the bright moon was reflecting its light off the quartz vein and even Zach marveled at how it looked like the light was coming from inside the mountain. The reflected light had a profound effect on all three women, but for Raven Wing, she was stunned and silent. At first, she was frightened by this strange light but then said almost as if to herself, "There is a light inside the mountain." Zach then showed her the light was just the reflection of the moon by standing where his body was shadowing the quartz vein.

Raven Wing then walked forward, reached out and touched the narrow band of crystal that was exposed and as she did another large piece of the quartz broke off in her hand. She stared at the nearly four-inch long crystal she was now holding and then looked up at the others in amazement. Sun Flower said, "The Mountain has given that crystal to you my sister, it knows that you will use its powers wisely." Raven Wing never said a word she just stood there staring at the crystal and the way the light from only the moon danced through it. This was truly a powerful sign that they were supposed to use what the mountain had given them.

Raven Wing never let the crystal leave her hand that night and she never slept either. She sat by their little fire holding the mystical clear stone and praying until she heard her sister starting the outside fire, then only a few minutes later little Grey Wolf was awake and hungry. She let him fuss then start to cry while she prepared a special piece of softly tanned doeskin and carefully wrapped the crystal, placing it next to the one Grizzly Killer had given her in her medicine kit.

When she picked up the hungry child and exposed her

breast she winced as he vigorously started to nurse, then said in Shoshone, "You take after your father little one, I think it is time for you to start learning to eat on your own." Even as she spoke those words she knew the child would have to suckle for at least another year before he would be able to eat enough to grow into a warrior as great as his father and Grizzly Killer.

After a breakfast of roast moose and biscuits, Zach opened up his possibles bag, laying out the dozen or more crystals he had picked up the day before. Before he took out the gold nuggets he said, looking right at Raven Wing, "These crystals were lying on top of the ground below where the mountain placed the large one in your hand. I believe the mountain also placed these there for us to use." All three women reverently picked up one of the crystals and they marveled as the light from the morning sun was transformed into the colors of a rainbow as it passed through the clear stones. They all could see the magic these stones held in the colors of the rainbow.

Zach was silent as he watched his wives and even Running Wolf marvel at the power these little clear stones held, he then said, "Shining Star and Raven Wing, pick a good clear stone to place in Star's and Grey Wolf's medicine bag, that they may hold their entire lives.

Shining Star turned and watched Star sitting on the buffalo robe that was spread next to her then knelt down next to the child and let her play with the magic clear stone while she went inside and retrieved the sacred medicine pouch she had prepared for her. It already contained a small tightly wrapped bundle of sage and another of sweet grass. It also held a small portion of the child's umbilical cord that she had saved and dried over a fire of the sage. Star was only a week old when Shining Star had sewn this small pouch together. It was then that she had taken a pinch of sage and another of sweet grass wrapped them tightly with sinew and placed these along with the dried umbilical cord in the pouch.

Although she had not said anything about her beliefs to anyone, not even her husband, she believed her little girl would become a Medicine Woman as great as she believed her aunt Raven Wing was. She believed Raven Wing would teach Star just as Blue Fox had taught her. Shining Star knew that Raven Wing had never believed herself to be a great Medicine Woman, but that did not change the fact that she was. Everyone that had been helped by Raven Wing believed it. Even Blue Fox the great Medicine Man of the Shoshone had said so.

Shining Star knew deep within herself that when the time was right, Raven Wing would start teaching her little blue-eyed girl. After all, Morning Star was the daughter of Grizzly Killer, the greatest warrior these mountains had ever known.

Sun Flower had gone to the creek for water this morning and had seen one of the yellow pebbles while filling the coffee pot, and it was nearly as large as her thumbnail. When she picked it up she noticed it was heavier than the other pebbles, it was irregularly shaped and had some black on it as well. She took one of the crystals that had just some tiny specks of gold inside of it and the gold nugget she had found and held them next to each other as she walked to Grizzly Killer. She held out her hand and said, "My husband, this pebble spoke to me in the stream this morning, it came from inside the mountain long ago. It has been waiting for me to find it so I could give it to you. It and the clear stone that was its mother is for your medicine bag. It will give you and only you the power it holds."

Zach knew very well how deeply religious and superstitious his wives were, although he didn't really believe the way they did he truly respected their beliefs and would do nothing but honor them. He took the small medicine bundle that he wore around his neck along with his famous grizzly claw necklace and opened the small pouch and watched as Sun Flower placed the nugget and quartz crystal inside. After closing it up and placing it back around his neck he reached out and hugged Sun Flower, then dropped to his knees and showed the women the dozen other nuggets of varying sizes he and Running Wolf had found.

He explained to them the value white men place on the yellow pebbles. He told them Running Wolf had bought his rifle years ago with only one pebble. He told them these pebbles were worth more than all the beaver that lived along this stream. If anyone ever found out this gold was here, many, many men would come and dig this mountain away. Then Sun Flower asked, "But why Grizzly Killer, why do they put more value on gold than they do our sacred mother earth?"

Zach didn't know how to answer her, he looked into all of their faces searching for a way to make them understand then said, "Most white men believe they own the land and all that is in it. They do not believe the way you believe."

Running Wolf then spoke, "A man can't own the land. That is like owning the air or the wind or the clouds. We live on the land but no man can own it."

Zach looked at him and answered, "They think they do. In the land toward where the sun rises beyond the great river where I was born. There the white men own the land

and they take what they want from it. If they care for it and plant it with seed, the land will give them food and they can raise their cattle, sheep, hogs, and goats."

Shining Star then asked, "What is cattle and hogs? Sheep and goats already live in the mountains above our home."

Zach now realized that being isolated in these Rocky Mountains, his family knew nothing of the world that was moving westward toward them, and moving west it was. His father had been a part of the settlers that had moved into Kentucky and Tennessee from the east. Even now, St. Louis was a large city, and towns and settlements were going up even west of there. Although the Rockies were still a long ways away, he knew that settlements would one day come here as well and he feared for the Indian's way of life.

Zach wanted his family to be prepared for the eventual settlement of this land. The only way he figured he could make them understand how many people were back there was to show them. The white man's world was unlike anything the Indians could imagine and Zach believed that would eventually mean trouble, trouble that the Indians would not understand and therefore could not defeat. There are just too many whites and eventually, he knew they would vastly outnumber all of the Indian people.

Zach sat down and looked at the gold nuggets, still wondering how he was going to make them understand. He finally looked up and said, "What would y'all think if instead of goin' to Rendezvous this year we went all the way to St. Louis and traded our plews and gold there to General Ashley? Then you will see the land of the whites and maybe then understand the things I tell you."

No one made a sound until Star started to cry, Grey Wolf had just taken the rawhide chew Sun Flower had made her to help with her incoming teeth. It was Sun Flower who spoke first as Shining Star was picking up the crying child, she said, "I have always wondered about the land and people where you come from Grizzly Killer I would like to go there."

Next Raven Wing said, "Grizzly Killer, you have told us many times how far away the big river and the city where all the white men come from. How long will it take us to get there, and when will we leave?" She asked that as if it had already been decided and they all anxiously awaited his answers.

He again wasn't sure how to answer them, in fact, he still wasn't sure he even wanted to go. Yet he had made the suggestion and he figured there would at least be a debate about it, but the debate seemed over so he asked each one individually if they wanted to go. The only one that even hesitated was Shining Star, and even she nodded yes then said, "I too want to see the land where you came from Grizzly Killer, but I go where my husband goes, my home is wherever he is. If you go to the land where the sun rises that is where I shall go."

He smiled at her then at his other wife; Sun Flower had always been the bold and adventuresome one. By now he believed Sun Flower would stand up to anything, although small in stature, she seemed fearless in the face of nearly anything and she seemed more excited than the rest of them to go.

GRUB GRABBED THE COFFEE POT AND POURED IT OVER the smoldering and smoking coals. Ely was just heading for the horses when he asked, "How far is they boy, how much time we got?"

"Last time I saw 'em they was just on the other side of the creek where all my traps is set" Benny replied," then continued, "They ain't wearin' no paint so I figure they're just huntin' but they is sure to find my tracks that leads right back here."

Grub grumbled under his breath then said, "Don't matter none they ain't wearin' paint, if'n theys find us we is gonna be in fer a fight." Ely saddled his and Grub's horses then Little Dove's while Benny was helping her take down the heavy buffalo hide teepee.

Grub was working on getting the sawbuck saddle trees on their pack horses. By the time he led the pack horses into camp Benny was ready to lift the heavy buffalo hide teepee onto their largest and strongest horse. He was part draft horse that Grub had traded for at last year's Rendezvous, and looked to be four or five hundred pounds heavier than the Indian ponies they all rode. Grub had taken to calling him Sampson because of his unbelievable strength and extra-long mane and tail. He was a dark sorrel and had pure white socks on three of his legs and a white blaze down the center of his face. It seemed the big horse could carry any weight they could pack on him.

By the time Grub and Benny had the heavy teepee loaded and tied down, Little Dove had everything else they had ready to load. Within minutes the panniers were all filled and their drying plews still tied in the willow frames were tied on top of two of the pack horses.

Ely led the way into the dark forest knowing, full well they were leaving all of their traps and the meat still hanging in the tree. They didn't question what to do, they all knew they must leave the area until the Blackfeet were no longer a threat. They stayed off the trails so the traveling was painfully slow. It was dark and difficult to see in the thick forest, Ely knew the horses could see much better than he could so he let his mare pick her own way. The moon was just peeking over the horizon as they topped the ridge heading south, and with its light Ely hoped to make better time.

They figured the Blackfeet would wait until morning before following Benny's tracks back to camp, so the only lead they would have would be the ground they could cover in the dark tonight. Benny was bringing up the rear, then it was Grub and Little Dove with the five pack horses in between Ely and Benny.

By the time Ely figured they had covered five miles the night was half gone and he knew they had to make better time. The next ridge they crossed, he turned and headed east going down out of the mountains. They came upon a well-used game trail and followed it down to the stream in the bottom. The nearly full moon was now overhead and in the open meadows along the creek they started making much better time.

After covering another five or six miles Ely stopped to give the horses a break and let them drink if they wanted. Benny asked, "How far you figure it is back to Chargin' Bull's village?"

Ely just stared at him for a few minutes then said, "I's figure yer right Benny that's gonna be the safest."

Grub turned to Benny and said, "We's at least two good days to get there."

Then Ely added, "I sure hate loosin' all our traps, that'll mean trappin' fer this year is done."

Grub said, "I know what ya mean pard, but traps is easier to replace than yer hair."

They pushed hard through the rest of the night and well into the morning, not stopping until they were out of the mountains and into the broad valley of the Wind River. Once they reached the river, Ely figured they had covered well over twenty miles, most of it had been through the rugged mountains and they as well as the horses were exhausted. Ely led them just a little further downstream to a thick stand of cottonwoods, where they stopped for a few hours of rest.

Benny volunteered to take the first watch; they all knew if the Blackfeet caught up, this stand of trees would be the first place they would head for. The horses needed rest though and there just wasn't time to try and find a place that would be difficult for the Blackfeet to find. After two hours sleep Grub relieved Benny and two hours after that Ely took the watch.

Six hours after they had stopped they were loading up again. Knowing the safest place to be was back in the village of Charging Bull, they followed the river south. They had just started out again when Benny told Grub he was going to ride up on top of a bluff and check their back trail. Grub looked behind them, then nodded, thinking it would be best to know if they are being followed or not.

The bluff was nearly two miles behind them over against the mountain. It was steep and rugged and Benny left his horse at its base. It took him longer than he figured it should to fight his way to the top. His horse was nearly two hundred yards below now. Looking south he could not see his partners and Little Dove as they were lost in the distance and bends of the river. It was only about a mile from the bluff to the creek they had followed out of the mountain and he knew if anyone else was following that creek or their trail he could see them easily.

Knowing he could catch the others before dark, he decided to watch their back trail, at least for an hour or so. The majestic Wind River Mountains towered over him to the south and west and the miles wide valley of the Wind River disappeared into the distance to the northwest. Benny's life was normally so busy he didn't have a lot of time to just sit and enjoy this vast untamed land, but even at a time like this, he marveled at the size and beauty of these Rocky Mountains.

Benny still wondered about home and seeing his parents one more time but he didn't want to leave these mountains. He thought about what Little Dove had said, but she didn't know how far or dangerous a trip like that was. He remembered the weeks it took crossing the endless plains where you could travel day after day and couldn't tell you had moved. There were constant worries about Indians and crossing the land of the Osage, Pawnee, Sioux, Rees, and the hundreds of miles right through the heart of the Cheyenne nation.

He had just about talked himself out of ever making the trip when movement caught his attention. A moment later he focused in on what it was; it was nine riders following their trail out of the mountains.

He had only been sitting there an hour at the most so these Blackfeet were less than two hours behind Little Dove and his partners. He was in near panic as he raced back to where he had left his horse, going down the south side of the bluff at a dead run and one time jumping off a boulder that was ten feet high. He landed on the steep hill and rolled, protecting his rifle with his arms as he did. He was out of breath and bruised when he reached his horse but didn't even slow down as he jumped into the saddle without using the stirrup. His horse was running full out before Benny's feet found the stirrups and he kept her on a dead run for over half a mile before slowing to a fast gallop. He figured the horse could keep this pace until he caught up with his partners.

It was nearly an hour later when he finally saw Little Dove and the others about a half mile ahead. He could feel his horse straining to keep up this pace and he could see the white lather covering her neck and sides. Only a couple of minutes later Little Dove heard the pounding hoof beats and turned to see her man waving at them.

Ely stopped and rode back to where Grub and Little Dove were holding the pack horses as Benny came riding in. One look at Benny's horse and they all knew trouble was following. Benny was still in a panic and his words came out a much louder than he intended as he shouted, "There's nine of 'em and they ain't much more than an hour behind us." No one said a thing, Ely turned back to the front and kicked his mount into a lope. He set a pace he knew even the heavily loaded pack horses and Benny's tired mount could handle. He figured there were about two hours until sunset and hoped he would find a suitable place to hide before then.

Suddenly Ely came to a stop, turned and came back to Grub. He looked at Grub and said, "You figure you could take them pack horses you got and backtrack a ways up this here river then lead them out onto the other side a ways then make yer tracks disappear and catch up to the rest of us."

Grub smiled and said, "Sure enough pard."

Ely nodded then said, "We will go on down the river and I won't climb out 'til I can hide our tracks goods." Then he pointed to a tall stand of pines right at the base of the mountain and said, "Once you make your tracks disappear you can pick up our trail in those pines."

Grub thought about that for only a second then said, "That's just too close, you keep your trail hid good and I'll do the same and I'll meet ya in Chargin' Bull's village tomorrow." Ely frowned, he didn't like the thought of Grub being by himself if he had to fight, but he could see the wisdom in it and turned his horse and rode out into the river.

Benny watched with more than a little concern as Grub turned upstream, leading the two pack horses. He didn't like the idea of Grub riding away alone when the Blackfeet were so close behind them. He didn't say anything about his two older partners' decision, when it came to outsmarting an enemy he knew Grub and Ely were as good as any men alive, they couldn't have survived out here for over ten years if they weren't.

As they rode through the water staying as close to the

middle of the stream as they could, Benny thought of last year and fighting the Blackfeet with Grizzly Killer. He smiled thinking he sure wished Jimbo was with them now, that huge dog that the Indians called Big Medicine Dog, Benny figured was like having two or three extra men with them. Just then Little Dove said, "It sure would be nice if Grizzly Killer, Running Wolf, and Jimbo were with us now."

Ely heard her and turned in his saddle and said, "Well Missy, on that I agree with ya, I would take any one of them right now." Benny smiled knowing he wasn't the only one with that thought.

Grub hadn't gone all that far upstream when he came to a small creek running into the river from the northeast. He climbed out of the river, following that creek about thirty yards then stopped and stepped out of the saddle. He went back down to the river and purposefully did a poor job covering his tracks, making sure anyone that could see could still follow them. He wanted the Indians to think they were following a greenhorn or someone that didn't know what he was doing. When he found the right spot he would make his tracks disappear completely, but for now, he wanted as many of the Blackfeet following him as possible. He knew if they all followed him that Ely, Benny, and Little Dove would be safe. One thing he made sure of was the Blackfeet would be able to tell how many horses they were following. He was hoping that would give Ely, Benny, and Little Dove more time to get away.

Ely STAYED in the river for nearly thirty minutes before finding a good rocky bank as the river made a tight bend. He led them out of the water onto the rocks and motioned

Little Dove and Benny to continue as he climbed out of the saddle. As Benny rode by him, Ely handed him the reins to his horse and told him to head for the pines on the hill. He would meet them there after he made sure there were no tracks to follow.

Benny nodded then said, "Them Blackfeet could be gettin' close Ely, we was in that there water fer a long time."

Ely looked upstream, hoping Grub was alright then smiled at Benny and said, "Yes they could, so don't waste no time getting that little gal of yours away from here."

Ely spent the next fifteen minutes covering the tracks of their six horses, leaving the stream, then following along behind where Benny had led Little Dove towards the pines and heavy timber. He knew this was going to be another night riding through the thick forest and rugged country, but at least they were getting closer to Charging Bull's village as each hour passed.

Ely was sure the Blackfeet knew where the Shoshone village was as well as he did, and he didn't think they would get all that close to it. For that was also the Village of Spotted Elk the Shoshone War Chief and he was well known to the Blackfeet. He had defeated them on more than one occasion. Ely smiled, thinking the Blackfeet probably hated and feared Spotted Elk nearly as much as they did Grizzly Killer.

The creek Grub was following was nothing more than a trickle when he came to a large stand of cottonwoods. These trees were growing around the spring that was the head of the small creek. It had formed a shallow pond that was feeding water to the old trees all around it. Grub stayed well away from the pond, knowing the horses would sink well into the mud along its edge. He led the two pack horses through the cottonwoods in a very round-about way and then out the far side. Once out in the brush, he stopped and tied the horses and went back. This time he wasn't acting like a greenhorn; he now used every skill living a lifetime in the wilderness had taught him to cover his trail. He believed a good tracker would eventually find his trail but he hoped it would slow the Blackfeet down enough he could get away from them.

GRUB'S RUSE at the river had worked, even though the Blackfeet had split up with some going upstream and some down. The trail Grub had left for them to find was found fairly quickly. The Blackfeet laughed seeing his attempt to hide his tracks, but they could tell there were only three horses. They sent a rider downstream to get the others and soon all nine of the enemy warriors were on Grub's trail.

Once Grub was mounted and riding again he headed to the far side of the valley, still in a fairly round-about way. He backtracked and stayed on the hardest ground he could find. He knew the Blackfeet could follow but he wasn't going to make it easy on them. He also knew he was taking a lot of time going nowhere, making his trail this hard to follow.

Just before the sun dropped behind the mighty peaks of the Wind River Range he decided it was time to put some distance between him and the enemy. He patted his horse on the neck and asked, "Are ya ready girl, let's give em a run fer their money." His mare broke into a fast gallop with just the slightest pressure from Grub's moccasins. He let her set her own pace until most of the light was gone then he pulled her back into an easy lope and continued until the full night was upon him.

Out in this broad valley of the Wind River there wasn't much to slow him down. Grub kept his mare and the two pack horses at a fast walk after it had got dark. With the light from the rising moon he was able to let the horses go into a slow canter. By the time it was straight overhead he figured he was far enough ahead that he could give the horses a well-deserved break. He slowed them to a walk and turned back toward the river. By the time he reached the banks the three horses were cooled down enough to let them drink. After drinking their fill he let them graze for nearly a half hour and wished he had the food pack on one of his horses, he didn't even have a piece of jerky with him and it had been nearly two days now with nothing to eat.

Grub watched the horses graze and wondered if Ely, Benny, and Little Dove were okay. He had a sense that he was being followed, he couldn't really explain it, it was like the feeling you were being watched even though you couldn't see anyone but he just knew the Blackfeet were following him. He didn't know if it was all of them or if some had found Ely's trail. He smiled knowing he would hate to have to follow Ely if the man didn't want you to. He respected Ely's ability to track or to hide a trail more than anyone he had ever met, but still, the Blackfeet were a dangerous enemy.

In the dark Grub didn't really have a good sense of how far he had traveled as he mounted up again and crossed the river. He had zig zagged and taken such a round-about route at first he really didn't know how far he was from Charging Bull's village. He knew it didn't matter; he had to ride until he got there. He could feel the horses were starting to tire so he slowed down to a walk for a couple of hours then set them at a slow cantor once again until the moon dropped behind the Wind River Mountains to the west of him.

Grub figured it was just a couple of hours before daylight when he crossed the river again, letting the horses rest for another half hour. He was exhausted and he knew his horses were as well. He continued pushing, still not sure how far he had to go until the sky along the eastern horizon started to lighten. Over the next hour daylight washed over the land he could see he had made better time than he figured. He was going to be to the village in less than an hour.

Grub still wondered about his partners. Had they fared as well as he had? He knew traveling through the forested hills they wouldn't make nearly as good of time as he had been able to make. He hoped they would be to the village by midday but he knew there was just no telling when they would come in.

As he rode he was met by the two young men that were guards for the village. It was their job to sound an alarm when anyone approached. This morning it was Fox Who Runs and Broken Thumb. The teenagers recognized the old trapper and rode out to greet him. He sent them to get Spotted Elk at once.

Spotted Elk met him just outside the village and Grub wasted no time explaining about the Blackfeet. The concern was evident on Spotted Elk's face and within minutes he had seventeen warriors ready to ride. Grub asked if he could borrow a horse and go with them and it was Charging Bull that offered his. Broken Thumb took Grub's worn-out horse to unsaddle and care for as the Shoshone warriors along with Grub rode north at a gallop.

Two hours and twenty miles later they saw the nine Blackfeet about three miles ahead of them on a dead run back to the north. Spotted Elk sent half his warriors to follow them and make sure they left Shoshone lands or died here.

Grub and eight Shoshone turned and headed back just as Ely, Benny, and Little Dove rode out onto a rocky point about a mile south of them. Ely had Little Dove hold all the horses back in the trees and he and Benny crawled out into the open. They were checking to see if it was safe to come out of the timbered hills and ride along the river to the village. Ely saw the nine riders and thought for sure it was the Blackfeet but Benny's young eyes kept staring and soon he told Ely, "Look at that there one in front on the right."

Ely was straining to see but as they rode closer a smile started to form on older trapper's face. He turned to Benny and said, "Why would ya just look at that, nobody sets a horse the way that ol' partner of ours does and if I ain't mistakin' that's Spotted Elk ridin' next to him."

"That's the way I sees it." Replied Benny.

Ely burst out into a roaring laughter and a moment later Grub and the Shoshone all stopped as the sound of laughter reached them. Less than ten minutes later Ely, Benny, and Little Dove rode out of the trees and were met with the smiling faces of Grub and their Shoshone friends.

FROM THEIR CAMPSITE ON THE CREEK JUST SOUTH OF the Gold Hill, Zach looked downstream remembering back to when he and his Pa first crossed the vast prairie, the land where the buffalo dance. He could see in his mind the first huge herd of the great beasts he had seen as his Pa and he had crawled to the top of one of the thousands of rolling hills. Tens of thousands of the big humpback animals covered the prairie for as far as their eyes could see.

He turned back toward the fire where all the others were watching him. He smiled, being just a little embarrassed and said, "I was just rememberin' when me and Pa first saw the buffalo. I don't remember just how far out of St Louis we was, but it seems like we'd been travelin' for weeks when we could hear a strange sound comin' from over a hill. Me and Pa crawled up to the top and there was buffalo for as far as we could see. We just laid there on that hill and watched them buffalo dance. I remember not far from us there was two young bulls with their heads pushin' each other around and there were calves runnin' around and kickin' their hooves in the air as they played. Not far from us on the same hill was a pack of wolves watchin' the dancin' buffalo just like me and Pa was, waiting for one of them calves to run a little too far from the herd."

Zach shook the memories from his mind then said, "I figure this is April, the melting moon, so we best be leavin' soon. Let's plan on leavin' here in five suns. We'll spend two more suns at home getting ready for the journey then we'll head for the village of Chargin' Bull."

The next morning after telling the women to look for more of the golden pebbles in the creek, Zach and Running Wolf left to check their traps. Zach thought about just how fast their lives could change as he rode Ol' Red and watched Jimbo checking everything out in front as they headed to where his first trap was set. Just two short hours ago he wasn't even thinking about going all the way back to the settlements, but now, in only a week they would be on their way. He remembered how fast his life had changed when his Pa was killed by the grizzly and once again when he met Sun Flower. He had never even considered having a wife except maybe Emma Potter from his hometown. That thought made him pause as he wondered whatever happened to Emma. He hoped she had found the happiness that he had.

Zach had two beaver to skin by the time he reached his last trap and by then it was mid-afternoon. He wondered where the day had gone, he really couldn't remember even checking most of his traps. He had been lost in thoughts of the past all day, even Jimbo had watched Zach during the day looking as if he wondered what was wrong with his master as he had just stared out into the wilderness not moving for several minutes at a time.

As Zach approached camp he stopped one more time, he hadn't realized going back would cause the emotions he felt. He could see his wives and Raven Wing busy around the fire, then he saw Running Wolf carrying a bearskin and watched him set it off to the side. He smiled knowing that although they would be leaving these beloved mountains for a while, he would still be with his loved ones. He felt warm inside knowing Sun Flower and Shining Star and his little girl were waiting there for him. Then the sight of Emma's pretty face surrounded by her long auburn hair and green eyes flashed through his mind. Once again the promise he had made her, to return all those years ago returned to him. In all of his life that was the only promise he had ever made and not kept and it still haunted him. He hoped she had found happiness and had forgiven him by now.

Zach rode in and was greeted by smiles from them all. Sun Flower had found two more gold nuggets and Shining Star three, but it was Raven Wing that seemed to have an eye for seeing the heavy yellow pebbles in the running water of the creek. She alone had found a dozen. Most were small but three of them were impressive, being the size of her thumbnail. Zach glanced at Running Wolf with a questioning look as he was staking the bearskin on the ground. Running Wolf smiled and said, "This young bear was hungry enough to challenge me for my only beaver, but he ain't got a lot of fat."

Zach shook his head and said, "None of 'em do this time of year."

Zach was quiet as he skinned the two beaver. Sun Flower could tell something was bothering him as he handed her the two plews to lace onto the willow frames. Without saying a word he turned and walked back down to the creek. His mind was confused, he knew he needed to prepare his loved ones for the white men that were coming to their lands. Just a few short years ago, many Indians had never seen a white man, but now it was rare to find one that hadn't had some contact Zach just wasn't sure he wanted to go back there. These mountains were now his home and he loved it here; he had two women that he loved and he knew loved him. His life felt complete so why would he want to go back? He knew the answer before the question fully developed in his mind. He would do anything to protect his family and that is what he figured the journey back would do. By making them understand the white men, he knew they needed to see where and how they lived.

He hadn't thought of Emma for a long time until today, and it troubled him. He knew he still cared for her but he had made his choice and he didn't regret it at all. What he regretted was breaking his promise to return. He knew he would do it again, the love he felt for these mountains, Sun Flower, and Shining Star were much stronger than the promise he had broken to Emma.

Just then Sun Flower walked up beside him. Without saying a word she took him by the hand and leaned into his tall muscular body. He could smell just a hint of bear grease on her for she had been cutting what fat there was off the young bear and putting it into their black iron pot to render. He turned to face her, then picked her up and hugged her.

Neither of them had said a word for nearly a half hour until Shining Star walked down to the creek to join them. She too knew her husband and knew something was bothering him and she suspected it was going back to the land of the white man. Sun Flower smiled at her as Zach reached around Shining Star, bringing her tight up against him.

Shining Star was the first to speak when she asked, "My husband, why are you troubled about returning to the land where you were born?" It was unlike Shining Star to question Zach on anything, Sun Flower was the bold one, questioning nearly everything.

Zach smiled at them both then turned to the creek to watch the clear water as it rippled over the pebbles of the stream bed. Several minutes passed before he told them, "My home is here with you two and our daughter, but the east still holds many memories of my youth. It is where my mother is buried, it is where I learned the skills of the forest, but it is there I broke a promise to someone I cared about." The only sound around them was the creek gently tumbling over the rocks and both Shining Star and Sun Flower could tell Grizzly Killer was struggling to tell them the story. He hadn't spoken again when Raven Wing called down, telling them the bear meat was done.

The three of them walked back up to the fire and ate in relative silence. Running Wolf then told them the story of the bear he had shot while he was skinning the beaver he had just taken from a trap. He told them it felt like he was being watched, he stopped skinning two different times before he got the pelt off to look all around but he couldn't see a thing. The feeling he was being watched didn't go away and as he was tying the rolled up plew behind his saddle. Then his horse got all excited and knocked him to the ground as she took off just as the bear stood up from the willows only thirty yards from him. Running Wolf had dropped his rifle and was scrambling to get to it as the bear dropped down and charged. He had only seconds and he could see the animal was going to be on him before he could get to his rifle so he pulled the pistol from his waistband and fired. The heavy lead ball hit the bear right between his eyes, dropping him instantly.

Concern was showing on all of their faces as he said, "I must admit I was pretty excited as that bear hit the ground."

Zach added, "Sounds like you need to teach that pinto some better manners."

Running Wolf nodded and said, "We had a long talk about that coming back to camp. That pinto seems to be good except when it comes to a bear, then she goes crazy."

Raven Wing then spoke, "She will never be calm when she smells a bear, I believe she was attacked by a bear when she was very young and the fear will always be with her." Zach smiled at the wisdom of his sister-in-law. He didn't doubt for a minute that what she said was true.

Zach still hadn't told his wives what was bothering him and both of them wondered why he seemed to be having a hard time. He was lost in thought and just staring into the flickering flames of their fire as Shining Star put their baby to bed for the night. Sun Flower just finished cleaning up after dinner as Shining Star came back to the fire. Raven Wing and Running Wolf were in their lodge trying to get Grey Wolf down for the night, but the toddler was fighting sleep, and everything the two of them did just seemed to make him mad. Finally with both Running Wolf and Raven Wing lying under the robes with their little boy he starting to doze off.

Zach waited until Sun Flower sat down next to him, then started to tell them about his home and the girl he left behind. He wasn't sure how to tell them what he felt about going back because he really didn't know or understand it himself. Both women could tell he was struggling with his thoughts and Sun Flower remembered back to when he had taken Shining Star as his second wife, how her husband had struggled with that. He had told her then that it felt like he was betraying her to be with another woman. Although she didn't understand why, she did understand that it bothered him a lot.

Finally, Zach said, "I love you two more than life itself and I believe you both know that. I once loved another, or at least I thought I did, and planned to marry her when I returned to Kentucky, but I fell in love with these mountains and later the two of you. My love for both of you and this wilderness is stronger than what I had left in Kentucky and I knew I would never return. I have only broken one promise that I remember in my whole life; I promised Emma that I would return and I didn't. I guess that is the part that troubles me, I made a promise and did not keep it." Sun Flower slid a little closer to him but Shining Star looked up into his sky blue eyes and said, "You are returning now my husband so your promise is not broken, it was only delayed and if you still care for this woman the way you care for us there is room in our lodge for another wife."

At first, Zach was shocked at what Shining Star had said. Then he smiled knowing how little his wives really knew about the white man's ways. He knew that he would be looked down on for having two wives and even if he wanted another, no white woman would agree to be his third wife and live her life as an Indian. He smiled into the beautiful faces of Shining Star and Sun Flower and said, "No, I do not want another wife, I do not want another woman, you two make me happy, happier than I ever was back there. I love my life and I don't want it to change."

Sun Flower then said, "But Grizzly Killer, you said our lives will change when more white men come to our lands."

He nodded and said, "Our lives will change some, but that does not mean I want it to. You must learn the ways of the whites so you can live in their world as well as ours. I do not know how long it will take for enough white men to come to change the way we live, but I know they will and we must be prepared so we can teach our children." He went on and told them about his father bringing whites into the wilderness of Kentucky and Tennessee and how they eventually pushed the Shawnee and Cherokee from the land.

By now Running Wolf and Raven Wing had rejoined them by the fire and he told them about the first settlement in Kentucky, Boonesborough. He explained how at first the Shawnee had traded with the whites and were friendly, but soon so many of them came to clear the land and farm they started taking away the Shawnee's hunting grounds. There were so many whites they were killing all of the wildlife so the Indians were going hungry. Soon the Shawnee were at war with the settlers even though back then the Indians outnumbered them, their bows, arrows and war clubs were no match for the white man's guns and more of the white settlers came. Soon the Shawnee were defeated and the white man took over all of Kentucky and the only Indians that survived were the ones that learned to live with them.

Running Wolf said, "You make it sound as if the white men are an evil curse."

Zach understood completely how it sounded and said, "Most Indians think that, but there are both good and evil white men just like there are good and evil Indians. The whites are not all evil, they just don't believe in the ways of the Indian and that is why you must learn the white man's ways so you will understand them when they come into our land. If the Indian will not change to live in the world of the white man they will be destroyed here just like they were in Kentucky and Tennessee."

The mood was solemn around the fire as they all were deep in thought. Zach had painted a pretty dim picture of the future. Then he continued, "We may not have to change a lot but Grey Wolf and Star, and their children will. Ever since the white man first came across the ocean from Europe they have pushed ever westward and they will keep pushing westward until there is no more land. All throughout the past, people have had to change to survive and we will have to change as well. That does not mean that change is bad, it can be very good. Look at the metal knives you use now and the black iron pots and frying pans. Look at the flour and baking powder we use to make biscuits. All of these changes have been brought by the coming of the white man. The guns that we use to hunt and for protection, we wouldn't have them without the white man. If we accept the changes just as we have accepted using the tools, there is no need to be fearful of them. We must learn and embrace them for the good, for only those that resist will be hurt or destroyed."

When he finished speaking he hoped he had not discouraged them all, but he wanted them to understand the white man. He then smiled to himself realizing he was thinking like he was an Indian, not the blue-eyed, sandy-haired white man that he was. He had embraced the Indian way of life so completely he really felt like he belonged in an Indian village much more than in Pottersville, Kentucky where he was born and raised.

FOUR MORE DAYS had passed and they loaded up the pack horses to head back to their home on Black's Fork. Zach put all of the gold they had found in a pouch that Shining Star had sewn together for just that purpose and it felt like they had between five and ten pounds. Although Zach didn't know how much it was worth, he really believed it would be worth more than all of their plews from last fall as well as this spring.

Another four days had passed and they were now on the trail once again heading down Black's Fork for the village of Charging Bull nearly two hundred miles to the northeast. It was a little over sixty miles to the confluence of Ham's Fork with Black's Fork and loaded as they were, Zach figured it would take two full days. After that, it was a short fifteen miles to the crossing of the Seeds-Kee-Dee, then it was seventy miles of waterless plains as they made their way to the pass at the southern end of the Wind River Mountains. They had made this journey many times, but Zach always worried about the horses carrying heavy loads and going two full days without water.

EIGHT DAYS AFTER LEAVING THEIR HOME, ZACH WAS standing on a rocky point along the east side of the pass crossing the southern end of the Wind River Mountains. He had first been on this point a few years ago while taking a white girl named Lizzy to Charging Bull's village for help after he had rescued her from her white abductors. He was leading his family as they crossed the great divide and he was looking northeast toward the Popo Agie where he was sure he would find the village of Charging Bull. Although, like most Indian villages the Shoshone moved from place to place finding better grazing for their herds and to let the land recover where the village set, he felt sure it would be along the Popo Agie not far from where it runs into the Wind River.

For Sun Flower and Shining Star this was a homecoming. Their parents, Bear Heart and White Feather were there along with their brother Spotted Elk. Spotted Elk had become the War Chief of the village and was known as the great protector of the people.

It had been hard at first for Running Wolf and Shining

Star to feel comfortable in a village of what most of their lives had been mortal enemies, but Grizzly Killer had changed all of that. Even though they were still Ute and proud of their Ute heritage they both felt as much Shoshone now as they did Ute. Both of their parents were gone, passed over to the other side and with Raven Wing and Sun Flower being Shoshone Running Wolf and Shining Star had spent much more time with the Shoshone than they had the Utes in the last few years. The Shoshone as well treated them as family and valued members of their tribe even though they were Ute and lived in the land of Grizzly Killer. Running Wolf was known as the protector of Shoshone women and Shining Star had become White Feather and Bear Heart's daughter just as much as Raven Wing and Sun Flower. They all looked forward to seeing friends and family in the village.

It was late in the afternoon when they saw the faint smoke haze over the river letting them know they were approaching the village. Not long after that, they were seen by two teenage boys who instead of approaching them rode to the village. Just a few minutes later a group of ten warriors rode out of the brush along the river and stopped nearly three hundred yards away. Zach stopped, wondering why they were greeted by warriors, and said, "There must have been trouble for us to be greeted this way."

He had barely finished talking when two of the warriors started on a dead run toward them with the others galloping along behind. At first, Zach was alarmed but as they closed the distance he could see the two warriors racing toward them were Red Hawk and Buffalo Heart. Red Hawk saw Ol' Red was a mule and when they saw Jimbo they knew Grizzly Killer had come to visit. Zach had known them both since they were the young teenagers, standing watch around the village and horse herd. Buffalo Heart slid his pony to the stop and as his feet hit the ground the two hundred pounds of Jimbo jumped up on him knocking him down. Buffalo Heart was trying to get away from the licking tongue of Jimbo, who was as happy to see his old friends as the rest of them were. While Buffalo Heart was getting to his feet, Red Hawk was greeting Grizzly Killer then Jimbo saw him, only Red Hawk saw the big dog coming and was ready. He greeted Jimbo with an open-arm hug. Luna just sat back and watched Jimbo's antics as he ran around to each of the Shoshone. Jimbo was the Big Medicine Dog and they believed if the dog liked them it made their medicine stronger.

Spotted Elk greeted Zach and Running Wolf by extending his arm for a handshake the way Zach had always greeted him, then said, "Welcome my brothers, the village will celebrate your return." He then turned to his sisters and greeted them and then the little ones, amazed at how much the two babies had changed since he'd seen them last. Then he smiled and said, "Butterfly has just given me a son. He is just a week old and you will honor him by being at his naming tomorrow night."

Spotted Elk rode beside Zach and Running Wolf as they entered the village, he was proud to have such great warriors as his family. The entire village was out to greet them and to Zach's surprise Grub, Ely, Benny, and Little Dove were there with big smiles on their faces.

Observing proper etiquette Zach rode to the center of the village to the lodge of Charging Bull. His teepee was the largest in the village and had a nearly life-sized painting of a buffalo bull charging through the prairie grass on its side. Charging Bull stepped out of his lodge in full headdress and carrying his ornately decorated pipe. By these actions he was letting everyone in the village know how important he considered his visitors.

After the formal greeting of the Chief and smoking of the pipe was over, Zach and his family were free to mingle and greet their friends and family. After greeting his wives' parents he went right to Grub, Ely, and Benny to find out what they were doing in the village instead of out trapping. Concern crossed the faces of both Zach and Running Wolf as they were told the story of the three of them along with Little Dove running from the Blackfeet.

Grub and Ely sat by their fire and were shocked when Zach told them they were going back to St. Louis and wouldn't be back until the fall. Benny had completely forgotten about making the trip back to see his family. Crossing nearly fifteen hundred miles of hostile country with just him and Little Dove was just too great of a risk. When he heard Grizzly Killer was going, that changed everything. He didn't even think about it before he asked, "Could ya use one more gun fer yer trip."

Ely smiled at his young partner and said, "Now's yer time boy, if'n you is ever gonna go back home ya got no better chance than now." Zach and Running Wolf both smiled, they were very pleased to have Benny with them. He had proved himself to be a mighty capable warrior in their eyes and a man both trusted completely. Another gun meant the trip might be a little safer as well.

They spent the next week preparing for their trip. Red Hawk and Buffalo heart took Zach, Running Wolf, and Benny out to where they knew a small herd of buffalo were and they took a yearling bull. The four women dried the meat to take along, for they didn't know how plentiful the game would be along the way.

When Zach learned Ely, Grub, and Benny had lost all

of their traps he felt bad that he had left all of theirs in their cache on Black's Fork. Grub told them they figured they had enough plews from the fall to get through another year, they just wouldn't be able to buy all the extras at this year's Rendezvous. Zach smiled and gave them each a heavy gold nugget and said, "That otta take care of any extra's ya might want.

Grub's eyes were wide open along with his mouth as he felt the size of the nugget in his hand, then said, "We can't take yer gold."

Zach just smiled and said, "Yer not takin' it, we are givin' it and you ain't turnin' down a gift from a friend are ya?"

Ely shook his head and said, "That's mighty generous of ya," then he looked at Running Wolf and asked, "Is this from the place where you found them nuggets when you was with us?"

Running Wolf didn't even hesitate to answer like many would to protect his source as he told them, "No, Grizzly Killer found these clear on the other side of the mountain from there. We was trappin' up west of the Bear when he saw the first big ol' nugget just lying there in amongst the pebbles on the stream bed, 'tween us and the girls we picked up all of 'em we could find."

Grub said, "You do have mighty big medicine Grizzly Killer, that's fer sure."

Besides spending time with her mother and father, Raven Wing also spent several hours with Blue Fox, the old Medicine Man that had taught her to be a healer. Blue Fox was already convinced Raven Wing had great powers but when she showed him the crystals and he heard the story of mother earth opening herself up to give the crystals to Raven Wing, he knew her powers were going to be greater than any Shaman since the time of their grandfather's grandfather.

Blue Fox had never seen crystals so clear and pure and with the rare yellow metal inside, but he knew these crystals carried powerful magic with them. She tried to give him one but he refused, telling her, "These magic stones were given to you, my daughter, they might lose their power or it might turn to evil if anyone else uses them." Raven Wing held the sacred crystal in her hand, feeling its magic. After what Blue Fox had just told her, she was even more concerned about her guardianship of their power. She remembered what Grizzly Killer had told her after he prayed and vowed then and there she would protect the clear stones and only use them for good.

Once all the meat from the buffalo was dried and they were doing the final packing to leave the next morning, Red Hawk and Buffalo Heart came to Grizzly Killer and asked if they could go as well. They had already talked to Charging Bull and Spotted Elk making sure their absence wouldn't harm the village. They didn't know what to expect when they approached Grizzly Killer, but Zach smiled and turned to Running Wolf and Benny and asked, "What do you two think, could we use a couple more guns?" Zach knew their answer before either of them said a thing.

Running Wolf answered first knowing how exciting a trip like this was for the two nineteen-year-old men, saying, "Ya, I think we could use a couple more guns alright." Benny smiled and nodded; these two were about his age and he'd hunted with them a lot throughout last winter and although neither of them was married and kidded Benny about always wanting to get back to his teepee, they had become good friends.

Grizzly Killer watched those two as they were packing

to go. He remembered the first time he had met them, they were staked to the ground being tortured by five Arapaho warriors. The day after Zach, Running Wolf, Sun Flower and Raven Wing along with Jimbo had killed the five Arapaho, they buried Sees Far. He was their friend and Sun Flower and Raven Wing's cousin, his injuries from the Arapaho were too severe to survive. Over the years these two young men had become loyal friends and all were glad to have them along.

Zach knew St. Louis was going to be a shock to them all. It had been a shock to him the first time he and his Pa entered the city. He figured he had two full months to try and prepare them for what was there, but he knew hearing about it was a lot different than experiencing it.

Zach and Running Wolf were planning on leaving the next morning and by the time they had the packs ready for the horses and realized how many pack animals it was going to take, they talked to Grub and Ely about them taking all their plews to Rendezvous and trading for the supplies they would need for next winter. The old friends were happy to do it, but Benny told Zach he needed to take his plews or he would have no money once he got to the city. Zach smiled and said, "Ya don't have to worry 'bout that, Benny. We got enough to cover everything and that will be six less horses we got to worry 'bout." Benny wasn't going to take anything from his friends and told them that, but Zach countered back, "I know how ya feel and you can pay us back when we get back. Besides six fewer horses will make the travelin' easier and faster." Benny had no argument for Zach's logic and finally agreed. Grub and Ely would trade all their plews for a year's worth of supplies and leave it with Spotted Elk until they all returned. By doing that it would save packing the plews to St. Louis and packing the supplies all the way back.

Zach remembered losing 17 horses to a Crow raiding party while he was with General Ashley, bringing supplies out to the very first Rendezvous, and he knew if that happened again they could lose a years' worth of work. Zach was grateful he had friends he trusted like Grub and Ely that were willing to do that for him.

Around the fire that night, Little Dove asked how far it was, she had heard them say it was fifteen hundred miles but she didn't know how far that was. Zach stood up and picked up a stick and drew a line in the dirt. He started by their fire and drew a line all the way across the village, when he came back he told her the other end of the line was St. Louis and this end was their home on Black's Fork. He made a mark on the line about six inches from the end and told her, "This is where we are right now."

Zach knew his example wasn't to scale but it was the only way he could think of to let them all know how far and how dangerous the trip was going to be. Even Running Wolf and his wives were shocked at his example. Red Hawk stood up and walked along the line halfway through the village then came back with a look of disbelief on his face. Zach just nodded and said, "If we travel as far as the horses can go every day, it will take us two full moons to get there." Everyone was in deep thought when Zach said, "We should start early in the morning, we ought to get a good night's sleep.

THERE WAS JUST a faint light along the eastern horizon when Zach heard the village start to stir. Everyone was going to be up to see Grizzly Killer, along with his friends and family, leave to go to the land where the sun rises, the land of the white man. Only half the sun was showing above the horizon when all the goodbyes were said and Zach pointed south by east, telling Jimbo which way they were going. As the big dog took off, a little boy of ten or eleven years stepped forward and asked, "If you go to where the sun rises won't you burn up?"

Zach stopped and climbed off Ol' Red and knelt down by the boy and said, "We are only going in the direction of the sunrise, we will stop before the sun can burn us." The boy smiled apparently satisfied with the answer, so Zach mounted up and they headed south by east toward the Sweet Water River.

JIMBO WORKED THE AREA IN FRONT OF THEIR LITTLE column, staying at least a quarter mile in the lead. Zach and Running Wolf were next and then the girls each leading two pack horses. Because of the weight and size of their teepees they had left them in the village and had brought only buffalo hides as protection from the elements. Behind the girls and pack horses were Benny, Red Hawk, and Buffalo Heart.

They hit the Sweet Water about mid-afternoon on the second day of their journey. Zach was setting a pace he figured all of their horses could take without becoming tired or broken down by the time they reached St. Louis. He knew they needed to cover at least twenty miles a day to be able to make the trip in just two months. He pushed on downstream for another three hours before stopping for the night. They had seen several small herds of antelope and even a few deer along the river, but no buffalo.

The willows and cottonwoods were starting to bud along the banks and the prairie grasses were starting to turn green as well. It was now the first week of May, or Buhisea'-

Mea`, the budding moon, as the Shoshone called it. Ol' Red and the horses were all enjoying the tender new grass as well as the buds on the willows.

So far the weather had been good. The sun was warming the land, bringing life back to the mountains and prairie. After they had stopped for the day, Zach sent Jimbo to scout all around them, all though he thought they were safe for now, still well inside the lands of the Shoshone. The valley of the Sweet Water was broad and shallow, covered with short sage and prairie grasses. The only brush and trees were right along the river banks and even they were scattered.

Zach had forgotten about the constant wind crossing the vast prairie. This was the land where the buffalo danced and also where the wind always blew. When Zach came west it had been winter and even with the bitter cold the wind never stopped. As the sun set, the sky turned a brilliant yellow but quickly turned to flame red. The wind was becoming gusty and the sky, although clear to the east, was getting cloudy in the west. They ate jerky again that night and Buffalo Heart asked if they could hunt for fresh meat tomorrow. Zach smiled and nodded, knowing they all would enjoy it.

By morning the sky was dark and grey. The clouds looked so low you could nearly touch them. Raven Wing and Shining Star bundled the babies up tight to protect them from the coming storm and they headed out, all being grateful the wind was at their backs.

By mid-morning a cold rain started falling and by noon it was turning into a wet heavy sleet. Where they were along the river there were no trees for cover, so Zach pushed on. Even Ol' Red had his head down and was miserable in the cold wind and sleet.

Zach was nearly upon the cottonwoods before he saw the trees standing like ghostly sentinels along the river and he chastised himself for not paying closer attention. He stopped once under what little protection the budding trees provided and although it was just past mid-day they stopped for the night.

They were all soaked and cold, and starting a fire with the wet wood in the wind took much longer than normal. Little Dove and Benny held up a buffalo robe to block the wind while Sun Flower started the fire as Raven Wing and Shining Star changed the grass packing in the bottom of their babies' cradleboards. Zach, Running Wolf, Red Hawk and Buffalo Heart unpacked the horses and hobbled them all.

After the fire was burning good and hot they tied the buffalo robe between two trees to act as a windbreak for the fire. While the women started on coffee and boiled jerky, the men put up four small lean-tos for them all to sleep under. By dark, the wind had died down to just a slight breeze and the rain was now lighter but steady.

Zach's lean-to was barely big enough for Sun Flower and Shining Star with the baby between them so Zach spent most of the night sitting up, keeping the fire going. Jimbo stayed with him even though Zach tried to get the big dog to lay along the edge of their lean-to. Buffalo Heart tried to trade places with him sometime during the night but Zach refused. Instead, he made a pot of coffee and kept the fire burning with a heavy wet robe over his shoulders until the rain finally stopped a couple of hours before dawn. He then crawled under the robes with his wives and got a couple some sleep.

They stayed at their little camp along the Sweet Water until nearly noon the next day, spending the time drying out their wet heavy robes. Although still damp, Zach felt like they should make progress every day so a little after midday they were on the trail once again. He knew that as spring storms blow across the prairie, this had been a small one.

They had been traveling along the Sweet Water for nearly a week before they saw another person. Benny, Red Hawk, and Buffalo Heart had been out hunting and had seen a hunting party of seven Cheyenne. They had spotted the hunters before the Cheyenne seen them so they stayed out of sight and watched as the Warriors led their pack horses laden with antelope and deer northeast toward the Big Horn Mountains. That sighting let them all know they were now in Cheyenne territory, so from then on Zach rode a half mile in the lead off to the left while the other men took turns riding a half mile ahead and to the right. Jimbo spent most of his time nearly a mile ahead casting back and forth between Zach and the other point rider.

The following day they passed the rocky gorge of Devil's Gate and reached the massive mound of granite rising out of the flat prairie just north of the Sweet Water that later that same year, William Sublette would name Independence Rock as he stopped there on the 4th of July while carrying supplies west for the Rendezvous on the Wind River.

That night they camped on the river directly south of the rock. Zach knew they had not made good time so far, the storm had slowed their progress for two of the days and he knew they needed to cover more ground each day.

Just before the sunset that night Zach was standing just outside of camp, watching the long shadow from the huge rock stretch across the prairie to the east. Jimbo started his low growl that came from way down in his chest. Zach readied his rifle and stood there, rock-steady as his eyes covered the area before them. Soon movement caught his eye and a soft whistle signaled the others that danger may be approaching. A moment later three Cheyenne appeared out of the prairie. One of them saw Zach and raised his hand in the Indian sign language for friend and waited for Zach to respond. Zach waited for only a moment before signaling back.

As the three Cheyenne approached, Running Wolf and Benny stayed back to protect the women while Red Hawk and Buffalo Heart came forward with their rifles ready. At the same time, Jimbo vanished into the willows by the river and Luna sat on her haunches right in front of the two babies. The Cheyenne stopped when Red Hawk and Buffalo Heart stepped up beside Zach, the Cheyenne could plainly see they were Shoshone warriors and Zach could tell they were now nervous about coming any closer.

The Cheyenne that had made the sign for friend again then signed, *"Hungry, give us food."*

Zach hesitated not sure whether to trust them or not. It had only been a little over a year since he and Running Wolf had to rescue Sun Flower from a band of Cheyenne. He knew these were not the same ones and he couldn't turn anyone away hungry, not as long as he had food. He signed back, *"Welcome friend come sit by our fire."*

All three of the Cheyenne stared at Zach's grizzly claw necklace and the one in the lead looked around. Zach smiled inside, believing they now knew who he was and were wondering about the big medicine dog.

Sun Flower had picked up her rifle and Raven Wing her bow. It was Shining Star that put some dried buffalo jerky in a bundle and tied it with a rawhide string then stepped forward to give it to the Cheyenne. Shining Star remembered the Cheyenne coming into their home last year and taking Sun Flower and Raven Wing away after leaving her for dead. She still had bouts when the pain would come back to the side of her head where the Cheyenne war club had hit her. She had no fear as she walked forward, not with Grizzly Killer standing right by her. She handed the jerky to Red Hawk to give to the Cheyenne, for she would not give it to them directly.

The Cheyenne were on foot and Zach had seen no sign of horses as they approached. He began to wonder if they really needed food or if they were scouting them out in order to better plan an attack. Jimbo must have sensed the same thing for as the Cheyenne turned to leave Jimbo was right behind them. The one closest to him jumped, obviously startled, having never seen a dog that big before. Jimbo didn't move and neither did any of the three Cheyenne until Zach swept his hand slightly to the right, signaling him to move out of their way. Jimbo slowly moved to the right but keeping his head low and the hair down his back standing up. Zach didn't know what their motives were, but if they were planning an attack at least now they knew it was not going to be easy.

Zach watched as the three disappeared into the long shadows just as they had come and decided right then he and the others would post two guards tonight. Although he trusted Jimbo and Luna to warn them of any approaching trouble, he figured it would be safer if at least two of them were ready to fight at a moment's notice and they all agreed.

The three Cheyenne were part of a larger hunting party that were camped only a mile north of Independence Rock. The three that had visited their camp had been coming for water when they first smelled the smoke from the campfire.

It was then they left their horses and came forward on foot planning, not only to find out who was going through their hunting grounds but to see if they had horses to steal.

It was Buffalo Heart that was first to say, "Did you see them look at Grizzly Killer's necklace?"

Benny answered, "Yeah, I figure that scared 'em but not as much as Jimbo did."

At that, they all chuckled but then Running Wolf said, "They might be scared some, but they'll be comin' for our horses, if not tonight, sometime soon." They all nodded they understood and agreed, knowing they would likely have to fight in the near future.

That night passed without incident but they all knew they were just starting into the Cheyenne's vast territory. Although they needed to follow the river, Zach decided that they would travel south of the Platte a mile or two after they reached it sometime tomorrow. They would go to the river only after dark to water the horses each day.

It was mid-afternoon the next day when they came to the confluence of the Sweet Water and Platte Rivers. It was there they saw the first buffalo of this journey. They had thought that it was probably hunting along the Sweet Water that had kept the buffalo away from the river. They had been in buffalo country since leaving Charging Bull's village over a hundred miles ago without seeing any of the big humpback beasts.

Before they crossed the Platte, they stopped and watched the buffalo dance. They could see several newborn calves lying in the grass near their mothers while a couple of others were trying to learn to run. It made them all laugh as they watched the little reddish-brown calves try to make their legs work. There was a group of young bulls on a small rise just south of them and they all laughed again as the one standing right on top was being pushed off the top by some of the others.

With hundreds of buffalo across the river, they decided not to cross until they had moved on past this herd. So far they had seen no sign of the Cheyenne and the constant prairie wind had made it impossible for Jimbo or Luna to pick up on any scent that may mean danger. Zach still felt they were being followed even though he had seen no evidence that the Cheyenne were there.

It was late afternoon when they crossed the river and let all the horses drink their fill and filled all of their own water pouches. They then moved about a mile and a half south and camped on the open prairie. Zach had crossed this land before but it had been years ago, and then it was in the winter when most of the Indians were in their villages. This was spring and Zach knew very well that young warriors would be wanting to raid after being cooped up all winter. Even though the prairie was nearly treeless for hundreds of miles, the rolling hills provided some protection from the constant wind. They made their camp in the swale between two hills and then dug down into the ground so the flames of a small fire couldn't be seen. They waited until nearly dark to get a fire started so the smoke wouldn't be spotted. The dry buffalo chips they gathered for the fire burned slow and fairly hot, helping to keep the flames from showing above the prairie grass.

Still worried about the threat of a Cheyenne attack, they shortened the hobbles on the horses. Without any trees, they either had to try and ground picket the horses or keep them on short hobbles to keep them close throughout the night. Once again they posted two guards, changing about two hours after midnight.

They did carry some lodge poles they had cut in half so

they each could put up a lean-to if the weather got bad, but for tonight it was clear and with the setting sun the wind died down as well. They spread their robes around the fire and watched the stars become so bright it was as if you could touch them. They could hear both coyotes yipping and prairie wolves howling as they closed their eyes for the night.

Zach preferred taking the second watch, he always figured late night or very early morning were the most likely times for an attack. Tonight, it was Benny and Red Hawk that took the first watch and Zach and Buffalo Heart the second. This was Running Wolf's turn for a full night's sleep. Zach felt he had barely got to sleep when he felt Jimbo's rough wet tongue lick across his face. He was wide awake instantly and could hear the low rumble coming from his dog's throat. Shining Star gathered Star into her arms while Zach and Sun Flower pulled on their moccasins. Jimbo had already left the camp area when Zach checked the prime in his pan as he headed for the horses.

Running Wolf with his rifle and Sun Flower with her .36 caliber squirrel gun stayed right there to protect the women and children while Zach, Benny, Red Hawk, and Buffalo Heart were out with the horses.

Zach reached Benny only moments before Buffalo Heart and was told just where Red Hawk was posted. Zach had just started to move toward him from that direction when the stillness of the night was broken with a bloodcurdling scream. Only seconds later there was a bright flash then the boom of Buffalo Heart's rifle just twenty yards to his left. Zach heard the twang of a bowstring then a slight grunt as the arrow found its mark.

Zach moved toward where Buffalo Heart was supposed to be and he hoped it was his friend's rifle that had fired.

Less than a minute later Buffalo Heart spun toward Zach with his rifle coming up, the ramrod was still in the barrel. He saw it was Grizzly Killer before he pulled the trigger then said a little louder than he intended, "They got me in the butt."

Just then two shots right close together came from camp and Zach shouted "Benny, Red Hawk, stay with the horses" and he ran with all the speed he could back toward his wives and child. He covered the forty yards in seconds and found Running Wolf ready to fire again, Sun Flower had just pulled her ramrod from the barrel. When Sun Flower had fired Luna left camp, and Zach hadn't heard or seen Jimbo since the dog had woken him.

All was quiet for the next few minutes then Zach said, "Buffalo Heart has been hurt, I am going to get him now." Buffalo Heart hadn't waited right there where he had been hit. He limped on down to the horses and when Zach found him he was standing guard right next to Ol' Red.

A few minutes later both Benny and Red Hawk met them and stayed with the horses while Zach helped Buffalo Heart back to camp. Way off in the distance they heard what sounded like a dogfight that lasted for just a few seconds, then once again all was quiet. It was too dangerous to build the fire back up so they just waited, all watching and listening until the morning light started to wash over the prairie.

BUFFALO HEART LAID ON HIS BELLY UNTIL IT WAS light enough for them to see how bad he was wounded. His pride was hurt more seriously than his body. The chipped stone tip of the Cheyenne's arrow had penetrated only about an inch through two layers of buckskins, his breach-cloth and leggings before hitting his skin. Raven Wing told him he was lucky his leggings were made from buffalo and not antelope or they might have had to cut the arrow out.

Jimbo and Luna both came back as Raven Wing was stitching the inch long and inch deep wound that was high on the right side of Buffalo Heart's butt. Luna's white face was red with dried blood, as was Jimbo's, but it didn't show up on his dark gray fur like it did on hers. As daylight fully came they found two Cheyenne dead and two other blood trails leading away from their camp. They hadn't succeeded in getting a single horse.

They moved on toward the rising sun without lingering at all, they wanted to be gone from this place if the Cheyenne decided to return. Buffalo Heart led his horse as much as he rode him for much of that day, although neither was comfortable for him.

Zach figured they covered a full twenty-five miles and hoped the Cheyenne would not follow, although he knew if they wanted revenge, the distance would be nothing to them.

The Cheyenne didn't follow and Red Hawk and Buffalo Heart figured it was the powerful medicine of Grizzly Killer and Jimbo that had stopped them from attacking again, although several of their warriors said they wanted to. Even those that did were not really sure they wanted to go up against the medicine of Grizzly Killer and his big medicine dog again. They believed his medicine was so strong that even a wolf was following the big dog now, and a Cheyenne war party would not follow.

The Cheyenne, Black Horn, was the keeper of the sacred arrows. The four arrows, two for man (warfare) and two for buffalo (hunting), were used only in ceremony and Black Horn told them their medicine was weak and they must dance to honor their dead and be blessed by the sacred war arrows that their medicine would once again become strong before they could defeat such a power enemy.

The warriors all followed Black Horn and they carried their four dead north to the river where they found enough wood along the river banks to build the burial scaffolds they needed to honor their dead. They set the scaffolds in a row on a little hill north of the river and from there headed north to their village which was located in the foothills at the southern end of the Big Horn Mountains.

Zach was now following the North Platte around the north end of the Laramie Mountains. He remembered these mountains from the cold and starving journey he and his Pa had made with General Ashley in the winter of 1824-25. It was in the Laramie's that he had finally found game plentiful enough to feed the brigade of twenty-five men that Ashley had hired to take the supplies west for the very first Rendezvous. As they rode around the Laramie Mountains Zach remembered hunting out on the open plains. At times they found enough buffalo, antelope, deer, and elk to feed the men but at other times they were forced to eat their horses and mules, hoping to trade for more with the next friendly Indians they found.

Zach thought back to the first time he'd seen Laramie Peak, just after passing what many trappers were now calling Scott's Bluff. Just the top of the peak could be seen as they were still a hundred miles away, but seeing that peak let them know the seemingly endless prairie was finally giving way to the Rocky Mountains. Scott's Bluff had been the first major landmark after nearly a thousand miles of grass-covered rolling hills as they crossed the great prairie. He remembered General Ashley telling them of Jacques La Ramee, a French Canadian fur trader that was one of the first white men to come to this area and how he had disappeared many years before. It was La Ramee that Laramie peak and the Laramie River were named after.

Ten days later, the Laramie Mountains were well behind them and they were approaching Scott's Bluff. They hadn't seen any other people since the Cheyenne had tried to steal their horses but they kept a double guard on each night anyway. As they approached the giant rocky bluffs towering nearly eight hundred feet above the flat prairie, Zach saw a smoky haze on the horizon. He figured there must be an Indian village camped at the Bluff and stopped, not wanting to get any closer until he found out what tribe they were and if they were hostile.

After moving a couple miles off the river, Zach and

Running Wolf left the others to see who was camped at the Bluff. They moved even farther from the river as they approached but they were spotted long before they even got close. The Pawnee camped there had warriors watching from the top of the bluff and from up there they could see any movement on the prairie for miles around their camp. Zach and Running Wolf were confronted by a dozen Pawnee while they were still over a mile away from the camp.

The only contact Zach had ever had with the Pawnee was when General Ashley had traded with them for horses and food during their trip west and they had been friendly enough then. Zach made the sign for peace and friend and a moment later the sign was returned.

Jimbo made a greater impact on the warriors than either Zach or Running Wolf. His size soon spread through the camp and soon many had come to see the big medicine dog.

The Pawnee did not recognize Running Wolf's Ute dress and were curious as to what tribe he was from. These Pawnee knew of the Utes but none of them had ever had contact with them.

After Zach was convinced the Pawnee were not a threat he asked them about the snake people, trying to find out if the Pawnee would be hostile to Sun Flower, Raven Wing, Red Hawk, and Buffalo Heart. It seems that several years ago while hunting buffalo, a band of Shoshone hunters had helped the Pawnee fight the Dakota who were the Pawnee's hated enemy and so they considered the Shoshone friends.

Running Wolf then left with two Pawnee Warriors to bring the others into the village. That evening the Pawnee held a celebration for their new friends. Chief Broken Knife told them that they had heard of Grizzly Killer and his big medicine dog. The Arapaho, their neighbors to the west whom they had a tentative peace with had told them of Grizzly Killer, their great enemy that lives far toward the setting sun and the great medicine that he possesses.

This was a temporary camp the Pawnee had set at the bluff for hunting buffalo, their main village was three days ride to the east. The buffalo had returned to the Platte River valley from wintering far to the south and with their meat supply short, this was the first major hunt of the year. Broken Knife told them that with the buffalo returning all of the plains tribes would be roaming the land hunting.

The Pawnee warriors were easy to identify as they wore the hair standing straight up in a ridge similar to the Mohawk people Zach's Pa had told him about. Their hair was caked with fat to make it stand up and some had colored their spiked hair with different paints. They were a proud people and Zach had no doubt they could be fierce enemies.

After seeing a few of the Pawnee had old trade rifles he made them a present of a pound of powder and one bar of lead for their hospitality and that night Zach and the rest of his group camped just outside the Pawnee village.

The next morning, Broken Knife and several of his warriors told them that the Arapaho were hunting just south of there and it may be a good idea to travel well north of the river for two days until they came to the main Pawnee village. Once there they should be safe from the Arapaho and they could trade for dried squash if they wished.

Zach had not realized when he had met the Pawnee with General Ashley that they were farmers as well. Unlike many of the Plains Indians, the Pawnee's villages were permanent, with log and mud structures so the area around the villages was farmed. They grew squash, pumpkins, beans, and corn, and dried it all to last through the winter.

Zach had been uneasy at first with the Pawnee, but the next morning as they loaded up to continue toward St. Louis he felt like they had made new friends. Jimbo had won the hearts of most of the children in the village, although some remained fearful of his size. Luna wasn't nearly as sociable as Jimbo, the white wolf stayed right by Running Wolf or Grey Wolf and shied away if anyone got near.

Taking Broken Knife's advice, they crossed the river and made their way nearly five miles north before turning and heading east again. They had left the Rockies well behind them and now faced hundreds of miles of windswept plains.

The buffalo had indeed returned to the Platte River Valley, there were buffalo wherever they looked. Zach thought back to that terrible cold, windy winter as he tried to find the game to feed the starving men, going day after day without seeing anything. Now every hill and swale was covered with the big humpback animals.

The horses were doing well, with plenty to eat of the nutritious grass of the prairie. There was no longer sage growing and there were no trees except the occasional cottonwoods along or on the islands of the river. The low rolling hills went on in every direction with nothing but grass to look at for as far as the eye could see and the feel of the wind as it blew across this flat terrain.

Zach figured they were making at least twenty-five miles each day now and with the possibility of the Indians hunting in the area, they continued to ride with points posted well out in the lead. So far all they had seen were buffalo, antelope, and a few deer in the thickets along the river. They were three days east of the Bluff's when they saw the Pawnee village and as they rode in there were many women working in the fields, planting this year's crops. They stopped only long enough for a friendly greeting for they had nothing to trade and at this time of the year as the Pawnee's supply of dried squash and beans were running low.

Zach figured it was about the first week of June or Daa'za-mea', the moon of summer starting, as the Shoshone called it. By now they were all getting weary of the trail. Every day was the same, get up, load the horses and follow the river downstream, stop at midday unload the horses and let them rest and feed while they ate. After an hour or two, depending on the stock, they loaded up again and moved on until two or three hours before dark when they would camp for the night. It had become a tedious routine and the worst of it was the land never changed. The same rolling hills covered with grass for as far as you could see in every direction. The only thing that seemed to change were the buffalo. There were great numbers of them in some areas and in other areas there were none at all, but their little group never went far before seeing more of the big shaggy animals. The buffalo were the lifeblood of the people that lived on the great prairie, without them the plains Indians could not survive.

They all enjoyed watching the buffalo calves as they would run and play. They all agreed it looked like the buffalo were dancing as the young bulls would lower their heads and push each other around and the little calves would run and jump. Zach smiled at that and said this truly is the land where the buffalo dance.

Along with the buffalo, there were the prairie wolves always watching for an opportunity for a quick kill. The young, old, weak or injured were all the targets of the hungry wolves. With so many buffalo covering the land,

Zach didn't think the wolves would ever go without. There were coyotes and foxes as well but it was the wolves that seemed to live off the buffalo.

It had been a month since they left the Sweet Water to follow the North Platte and it had been several days now since they reached the confluence of the North and South forks of the river. From Zach's position on the right point, he could see a heavy dust cloud in the air several miles in front of them. Fearing it may be an Indian village on the move he rode back and had the others stop as he and Benny went to investigate, leaving Running Wolf, Red Hawk, and Buffalo Heart to protect the women and children.

Staying behind the rolling hills, they rode nearly five miles before they figured they were close enough to see but still be out of danger. They dismounted and crawled to the top of a hill. Zach couldn't believe what he was seeing. There were wagons down there, ten of them all heading west, and along with them, there were two Dearborn carriages. Neither Zach nor Benny said a word for several minutes. Benny finally said, "Well, least we know is they are white men."

Zach smiled and answered, "You're right about that, let's go see what crazy fool is tryin' to take wagons west and how far they're plannin' on goin'."

They mounted up and rode slowly toward the oncoming wagons. Along with the wagons and drivers, there appeared to be nearly a hundred other mounted men and after Zach and Benny were seen a dozen or so rode forward to meet them.

They were still fifty yards away when Bill Sublette recognized Zach and busted out laughing. Only moments later Zach and Benny both saw it was Sublette. As Zach and Benny rode up to them Zach said, "what are you laughin' at Bill and what are you doin' with wagons and carriages this far from the settlements?"

Bill answered, "Grizzly Killer, you is not who I expected to see out here in the middle of nowhere and I am taking these here wagons all the way to the Rendezvous." Several of the men with Sublette didn't know Zach but they had all heard the many stories of Grizzly Killer. Young Joe Meek was one of them, he was nineteen years old, the same age Zach was when he first came west.

William Sublette had left St. Louis on April 10th and had been on the trail for nearly seven weeks by the time they met up with Zach and his party. He had eighty-one men with him all mounted and each one of the ten wagons was pulled with five mules. This was an impressive sized brigade and Zach didn't think any of the Indians along the way would bother a group that big.

They camped together that evening on the banks of the Platte near a large island in the river that the first French fur traders in the area called La Grande Ile. Zach figured they were about at the halfway point of their journey. They were now over a hundred miles downstream of where the North and South Platte joined and now at the peak of the runoff the river was nearly a half mile wide and was a rolling torrent of muddy water. Zach wasn't looking forward to crossing it but he knew sometime in the next couple of weeks they would have to do just that.

Once again, for anyone that had never seen Jimbo his size both impressed and scared many of the men. But it was the beauty of their women that attracted the most attention. Although Little Dove didn't have the natural beauty of the others, she was young and attractive and to men that had been out on the trail for weeks, it just had to cause problems.

Sublette asked how the trapping had been and wondered where all their plews were. He smiled learning that Grub and Ely had the plews and they would trade them for the needed supplies at Rendezvous. He warned Zach to be mighty careful, that two weeks ago they were followed for at least two days by what he thought were Rees and he figured the only reason that they didn't attack was the size of his party. Zach took the warning seriously he knew the stories of the Arikara attacking trappers and his small party would be attacked if they were seen.

While Zach and the men with him were all talking to Sublette two of Sublette's new men approached Sun Flower and Little Dove, as those two didn't have babies with them, and when they got turned down one of them made the mistake of grabbing Sun Flowers arm. He hadn't even got her turned around when Jimbo's jaws clamped down on his wrist and they all heard the bone snap as Jimbo bit down and tore his hand away from her.

His scream sent everyone running towards them. It was only seconds when Zach and the others arrived. He could see the dread in Sun Flower's eyes just as she could see the fury in his. She said, "Grizzly Killer no harm was done to me, Jimbo was right here, he knows now I am your wife and I heard a bone break in his hand." Zach stared at the two men and the fury they saw in his eyes frightened them both. Finally, he told all of them to stay away from his camp.

William Sublette remembered the last time a man approached and insulted Sun Flower at the Rendezvous on Sweet Lake and that man was buried right where he fell. He told that to his injured man as he was binding up his wrist. He also told them the story of the three French men that had raped another Shoshone woman, and after the big dog had seriously injured them the Shoshone finished them off. He made sure they all understood there were many willing Indian women, but never mess with another man's woman unless they are first invited too.

Zach understood what had happened but that didn't lessen his anger. The next morning he told Sublette he had better teach his new men proper manners or they wouldn't survive their first year. The injured man came to their camp as they were loading up to go and asked Sun Flower and Little Dove's forgiveness, telling them he did not know they were married. With Zach standing right there the two women accepted his apology and Zach stepped forward and told him that Raven Wing was a healer and if he would allow her to treat his arm it would help.

The broken bone in his wrist was not as bad as the jagged wound where Jimbo's teeth had ripped open the skin. Raven Wing told him it would take much time to heal. She mixed a poultice together of her healing plants and rebound the wound, then with Sun Flower's help they wrapped a piece of cottonwood bark from the back of his hand nearly to his elbow to keep his wrist from moving and told him he would need to keep it like that for the next moon. He thanked her then turned to Grizzly Killer and said, "I really didn't know, I had heard the stories about the Indian women and..." at that point, he stopped and put his head down looking at the ground. Zach told him he appreciated his honesty and that there would be many willing women at Rendezvous and in the villages but it was up to him to learn who was willing and who was not.

ZACH WATCHED THE WAGON AND CARRIAGES MOVE ON westbound as he and his party continued east. As the great grass prairie stretched out before them, Zach knew that it had been boredom that had caused what was normally courteous men to act the way they had with Sun Flower and Little Dove. He was tired of the trail as well and had decided the next likely spot they came to he would stop for a couple of days to rest and hunt to break up the monotony of their trek.

A day's travel further east they came to another river flowing into the Platte from the north. It was lined with cottonwoods, and Zach remembered passing it years ago and the men calling it Wood River because of the trees along its banks. It had left an impression on his memory for it had been the first time in weeks they'd had enough fuel for good fires to keep them warm. Besides wood to burn, the cottonwoods provided bark for their horses to eat and they had stopped there for a few days.

The Wood River wasn't nearly as large as the Platte but its waters were running clear. They all were glad for a break from the daily monotony of the endless prairie. They had been on the trail now for a little over a month but it had seemed much longer. The buffalo had been plentiful in most places along the Platte River and now the women were taking the time to work on several hides they hadn't had time for while traveling every day. Red Hawk, Buffalo Heart, and Benny scouted the area to the north the following day and watched from just below a rolling hilltop as ten Pawnee hunters surrounded a herd of buffalo. They then stampeded the herd straight into fifteen or twenty more hunters that were waiting.

As the hunters came out of the grass with their long stone tipped lances, a large bull charged right into one. He sailed through the air when the buffalo hit him, the hunters lance sticking from the bull's neck as he ran on out of sight. The small group of hunters all watched in silence as the Pawnee's limp body fell out of their sight in the prairie grass. Buffalo Heart was the first to speak when he said, "Hunting Buffalo should not be done on foot, a hunter needs a good horse under him to hunt something so large." Benny and Red Hawk nodded their agreement.

The Pawnee hunters that the boys had been watching were from a village on the Loup River that was fifteen or twenty miles to the north. The Pawnee had killed five buffalo from that herd and it wasn't long after the stampede that the women moved in to start skinning and butchering the meat. They stretched the skins over their travois' and piled the cut meat on the skins, then they led the burdened horses out of sight to the north. The hunt had been successful for the Pawnee, with over a ton of cut meat, but it had come at a cost. The hunter that had been hit by the charging buffalo appeared to be dead and they watched another man as he was helped onto a travois to be carried back to their village, unable to ride his horse.

That evening around a small fire that Benny had scooped-out back in the trees, the boys told of watching the Pawnee hunt the buffalo. They told them how the hunters stood there to bury their lances deep into the running buffalo's side. Buffalo Heart told of the buffalo hitting the hunter and throwing him into the air, then Benny added, "Even from as far away as we were you could hear the thud when the big bull hit him and again when he hit the ground." Although the Pawnee back at Scott's Bluff had been friendly enough and it had been the Loup Pawnee that General Ashley had traded with, they all knew times change and they didn't know if these Pawnee would be as friendly so they thought it best to keep their presence unknown if that was possible.

After they had eaten their fill, Zach took Sun Flower and Shining Star for a walk out onto the prairie. It was a warm June night and as the land cooled the winds had nearly stopped. The grasses were now green even though it had been several days since they had any rain, the prairie seemed alive with it gently waving in the breeze.

Zach laid down on his back pulling Sun Flower and Shining Star down with him and they watched the stars for the longest time. They could hear night birds along the river and coyotes yipping off to the north. Zach figured the coyotes may be fighting over the carcasses of the buffalo the Pawnee hunters had taken earlier today. A shooting star streaked across the sky and Sun Flower said, "Maybe that star is the hunter finding his way along the great milk river in the sky to his home on the other side." Zach smiled, although he believed like his mother and father had in the Christian after life he didn't dismiss his wives' beliefs and he too had wondered about it when he had watched shooting stars cross the night sky.

Sun Flower told them she had some things to do and left Shining Star and Zach lying there in the cool grass. The moon was a few days past being full so it was rising later each night. The two of them laid there until they could see the glow of the moon as though it was growing out of the prairie to the east, then Shining Star stood and pulled her doeskin dress over her head. Zach watched her beautiful body in the dim light of the stars, her breasts were large and full with the milk for their daughter as she dropped down to her knees and helped him out of his buckskins. They made love in the cool night air, then laid there holding each other until the moon was well above the horizon. It had been a long time since they had any time to be alone together and as Zach had thought, as he had many times in the past, that his two wives had this planned out. He just smiled thinking that he had to be the luckiest man in the mountains, then looked around and added to his thought, or on the prairie as well.

It was past midnight when Zach and Shining Star got back to camp and Sun Flower was asleep with Star in her arms. They barely disturbed her as they crawled under the soft buffalo robe of their bed.

JIMBO AND LUNA went out on their hunt the next morning and no one in camp even moved. Red Hawk had the last watch and he just smiled as the huge gray dog and white wolf left. Although they all had hunted buffalo on the plains along the Sweet Water River, Zach was the only one that had ever been to an area where you couldn't see a mountain in any direction.

Red Hawk stared out across the prairie as he was hidden in the thick cottonwoods where they were camped. This flat land they were crossing gave him an eerie feeling. There were no landmarks, only the river to follow. He wondered if all the land to the east was like this treeless windy prairie, if so it was no wonder Grizzly Killer said the white men would be coming west. He had decided he didn't like the prairie and he longed for the sight of the jagged mountain peaks of the Rockies.

Midday found them all out in the cold water of the river scrubbing the dust of hundreds of miles of trail from their bodies. Although Zach had become used to this by now Benny was having a hard time just stripping down in front of everyone to bathe, his eyes about popped out of their sockets as he watched all the women get completely naked and run out into the water. After everyone else was naked and in the river he forgot his bashfulness and joined them. Little Dove washed him all over and after that, he decided bathing together with her was just fine.

The rest and relaxation this day felt so good to them all they decided to stay for one more before continuing on to the east. Zach knew they still had nearly a month to go before reaching St. Louis.

Another day without travel did them all good. Wood River, with its tall trees was a pleasant place, the cotton-woods and willows were now all leafed out and even the prairie grass was green. Ol' Red and their horses had started to put on the weight they had lost over the winter but they were using up nearly all of the nutrition they were getting from the grass in walking twenty to twenty-five miles most days. Yes, a couple of days of rest was good for all of them.

Jimbo didn't understand the delay, as he had gotten used to running out in front scouting each day and he liked his job and wasn't understanding why they had stopped. But with a dog as active and intelligent as Jimbo, it didn't take long for him to be hunting the new area upstream along the Wood River.

Even days of rest were full of work for the women. The Indian woman normally worked during all daylight hours. Zach's wives, along with Raven Wing and Little Dove were no exception. As soon as their time of bathing and swimming in the river ended they all started right in working the buffalo hide they had just rolled up and brought with them. They found that two of the four hides they were carrying had already started to spoil in the heat of the June sun.

The buffalo, deer, and antelope had been so plentiful they were able to take what they needed whenever they needed, but Zach wondered if that would be the case once they reached the Missouri. After talking about that, they decided to take a young buffalo and dry the meat before moving on. Zach wasn't sure but he figured they were about a week from reaching the Missouri River.

They had stayed there where the Wood River ran into the Platte for five days and all felt refreshed from the rest, all except Sun Flower. She had not felt herself for several days now but she refused to say anything about it, figuring it was just the endless days of travel. Ol' Red and the horses seem ready to go again and they all were amazed how they had filled out in only five days, but Running Wolf said, "It might have only been five days but it was five days of none stop eatin', I don't think they even stopped to sleep." They all got a laugh out of that and it was easy to see everyone including the animals were all in much better spirits.

On the morning of the second day after leaving their Wood River camp, they spotted about a half dozen Indians following along with them about a half mile across the

Platte south of them. They were too far away to identify which tribe they might be, but then Zach figured that didn't matter because the only tribe any of them could identify were Pawnee because of the way they wore their hair. He didn't think he would be able to tell if they were Ree, Dakota, Kiowa, Kansa, or any of the other tribes that may be hunting these plains.

The unidentified Indians never came in any closer and after an hour they turned off heading back to the south. By late that afternoon, they reached where the Loup River entered the Platte and there they found another Pawnee village. This one was nearly as large as the last one they had been to, but once again only Zach and Running Wolf advanced as friends. Zach smiled as he saw the cultivated fields around the village. There were green sprouts growing from the planting mounds, squash and pumpkin and beans, they appeared to be.

After meeting with Long Lance, their chief, letting them know they were just passing through on the way to the white settlements, they asked if they had enough dried food to trade. Two of the tanned buffalo robes the women had just finished was traded for as much dried pumpkin and squash as they could carry.

That night they camped only a few miles down-river from the Pawnee village and just after dark two young Pawnee warriors approached their camp. Zach figured the one in the lead was about the age of Red Hawk, Buffalo Heart, and Benny. He was leading five beautiful horses. He stopped just on the outer edge of the light that their fire provided then signed to Zach that he wanted to trade these horses. He said, speaking Pawnee and using sign language as well, "I am Horse Talker and these are the best horses in the whole village." Looking at these five beautiful animals neither Zach nor Running Wolf doubted his word. They really were great looking animals.

Zach stepped forward and asked as he signed, "What do you wish to trade for these fine horses.

Horse Talker didn't hesitate as he pointed at Sun Flower then said, "I give you all five for that Squaw."

Sun Flower wasn't sure whether to be flattered or nervous. She knew very well Grizzly Killer would not trade her away, she could feel his love for her every day but she remembered being taken by the Cheyenne and how hard of an ordeal that had been on them all. When Grizzly Killer and Running Wolf finally caught up and rescued her it had required much killing and had been very dangerous for them all and she hoped nothing like that ever happened again.

Zach refused Horse Talker's offer telling him that Sun Flower was not for trade. The disappointment was evident on his face as he led the five horses away. Less than an hour later Horse Talker returned, this time he had two helpers and fifteen horses. He hadn't understood Zach completely and he figured the price just wasn't high enough for such a beautiful woman and he was sure no man would turn down fifteen fine horses for a squaw.

The disappointment on Horse Talker's face now turned to disbelief as Zach told him that Sun Flower was not for trade. He just stood there for the longest time staring back and forth between Zach and Sun Flower. He just couldn't believe that every horse he owned wasn't enough to buy one squaw, even if she was the most beautiful woman he had ever seen.

Horse Talker left so disappointed Zach wondered if he may try another way to get her. Not wanting to fight, if it came to that, they decided to load up and travel through the night. Zach knew that if Horse Talker could recruit enough help mounted on the fine horses he had, they would not be able to outrun him but the farther they moved away from the village the safer they would be.

Horse Talker wanted the pretty squaw and he had taken it as an insult that fifteen of the finest horses in all of the Pawnee nation would not buy her, so he would have to take her. He found recruiting help was much harder than he thought it would be. Even the Pawnee out here on the plains had heard the stories of Grizzly Killer and his big medicine dog. By giving a horse to each of six friends they finally agreed to ride with him.

It was past midnight when Horse Talker and his friends reached the place where Grizzly Killer had been camped. There was some argument over whether or not to go on. By now it was nearly the dark of the moon and they wouldn't be able to follow the tracks. Horse Talker wouldn't be discouraged though telling them that all they had to do was follow the river and they would find them.

As daylight flooded the prairie with light Zach knew the women and horses all needed to rest. He moved them off the river nearly a mile and set up a camp between two small rolling hills. They didn't build a fire, just ate jerky and water, then after leaving Red Hawk, Buffalo Heart and Benny to watch the horses and women, Zach and Running Wolf rode back toward the river.

They build a fire near the river and started a pot of coffee. Zach wasn't sure Horse Talker was coming but he figured he would and he was right.

Horse Taker saw the smoke from Zach's fire and thought to himself, *"This is just another dumb white man, making a fire for us to see."* Horse Talker and his friends all dismounted and tied their horses to trees nearly a quarter mile from where Zach was with his fire and started to sneak in to surround their camp.

What Horse Talker didn't know was they were being watched by Running Wolf and Jimbo. As soon as the Pawnee were halfway between their horses and Zach, Running Wolf snuck in and took all seven of their horses. Jimbo ran head to let Zach know they were coming and as soon as the dog got there Zack mounted up on Ol' Red and he and Jimbo loped away. When Horse Talker and the other Pawnee saw Grizzly Killer ride away they all ran back to their horses only to find they were all on foot and over twenty-five miles from their village. They all had a long walk to think about how Grizzly Killer had outsmarted them.

Horse Talker was the best man with horses in the entire village and had been ever since he was a small boy. He had a way with them that they responded to. As an early teenager, he had become an accomplished horse thief, stealing horses from many of the tribes of the plains. He thought if Grizzly Killer returned he would learn what it was like to feel being left afoot, he would steal every horse they had.

Sun Flower did not get feeling any better and now Raven Wing could tell something was wrong. That night after they made camp, Raven Wing asked her sister what was wrong but Sun Flower didn't know either and just shook her head saying nothing. Zach and Shining Star both had noticed Sun Flower seemed to tire much faster than she usually did.

Two days later, just after they started for the day, Sun Flower nearly fell off her horse. Zach was riding out in front and it was Shining Star and Raven Wing that helped her.

With her feet on the ground the world seemed to be spinning around her and she retched over and over again.

With the women now stopped, Red Hawk and Benny soon caught up to them and Red Hawk rode ahead to get Grizzly Killer. Little Dove and Benny each took a child as the two mothers helped their sister through this bout of sickness.

When Zach arrived, Sun Flower was pale and tried to smile at him but one glance and he could tell she was sick. Sitting there on the prairie, Raven Wing started asking her questions about how she felt trying to figure out how to treat her, but it was soon evident that none of them knew what was wrong.

Raven Wing opened her Medicine Pouch and carefully took out the crystal that the mountain had placed in her hand. She reverently unrolled it and placed it in Sun Flowers' and told her to hold the clear stone next to her heart. She then cut a piece of the soft leather she had the crystal wrapped in and while Sun Flower held the crystal Raven Wing tied the piece around its rough end. She then tied it around Sun Flowers neck so the crystal hung between her breasts next to her heart.

Within minutes this bout of sickness had passed and the color started to return to her pretty face and she tried to give the crystal back to her sister. Raven Wing made her keep it around her neck; she didn't know what was wrong with Sun Flower or just what the crystal's magic was doing, but it had made her feel better and for now that was enough.

Zach would have normally just turned the captured Pawnee horses loose, but these were exceptional mounts. Even better than what Benny and the women were riding. They all decided they would keep these seven horses. Zach didn't consider himself a horse thief but to Red Hawk, Buffalo Heart, and Running Wolf like so many other Indian tribes believed, stealing horses was a badge of honor.

The following day the Platte River made an abrupt turn to the south and Zach figured they would be to the Missouri River in less than a week. They were still on the north side of the Platte and Zach knew they must cross over to the other side before they reached the Missouri. The next day as they were following the river heading south, they came upon a prairie dog village and Jimbo and Luna started after the hundreds of them that were standing as still as statues atop their mounds of dirt. Zach smiled and Red Hawk burst out laughing as every one of the little statues disappeared into their burrows as soon as one of them barked a warning as the big dog and wolf approached.

Jimbo and Luna started digging at the burrow's

entrance only to see a prairie dog run out of that tunnel many feet away and into a different one. Zach and the rest of them enjoyed watching Jimbo and Luna running from one hole to the next, digging unsuccessfully as the little prairie dogs stayed well away from the dog's deadly jaws.

As they started again Zach watched a ferret carrying one of the unlucky rodents toward the river. He figured it probably had a den with young, being the time of year it was.

The following day they came to a place where the river widened even more. It was still running nearly full but not nearly as high and wild as it had been over the last couple of weeks. They all thought that this would be a relatively safe place to cross.

They pushed the herd of seven Pawnee horses ahead of them as they forged across the wide river. There were several channels they had to cross with sand bars in between each of them. They were down to just a couple channels left to cross, less than 75 yards to go when the lead horse bogged down in quicksand. As the horse started to panic, trying to fight his way out of the muddy sucking sand, the mare directly behind him got stuck as well.

Red Hawk and Buffalo Heart advanced and stopped the other horses from following as Zach, Running Wolf and Benny carefully approached the two panicking horses. Running Wolf tried to calm them down by softly talking to them, for the more they thrashed about trying to escape the deeper they were pulled into the mire of sand, mud, and water.

Shining Star led Sun Flower, Raven Wing and Little Dove and the pack horses upstream from the men and the floundering horses. Red Hawk and Buffalo Heart watched the women successfully reach the other side then they pushed the six remaining horses to follow the path the women had taken. Once they had the horses and women safe and secure, they followed the same path back out into the river to help try and free the two horses.

Running Wolf and Benny both had ropes on the rear horse and Zach was trying to get a third on her when Red Hawk and Buffalo Heart reached them. They tried to get their ropes on the lead stallion but the bottom proved to be too soft for them to get close enough. By now the stallion had sunk into the quicksand nearly to the top of his back and they could see the fear and panic in his eyes. With no hope of freeing him, Buffalo Heart got his rifle and shot the panicked horse, ending his fear quickly, rather than watching the scared animal drown.

Running Wolf and Benny couldn't pull the mare free and had stopped trying when Zach finally got in position to get his rope on the beautiful young horse. Once he did, with Ol' Red's hooves digging into the sand behind her she started to pull free of the mire. Once free she just stood there shaking and exhausted as Running Wolf tried to calm her. With his soothing voice and Ol' Reds calm demeanor her breathing started to slow and within a few minutes, they led her calmly around the deadly quicksand and to the other side of the river.

Buffalo Heart felt bad about killing such a fine horse, for the stallion could have bred many fine colts, but they all assured him he had done the right thing. It would have been cruel to let the panicked horse slowly drown.

The quicksand was just one more danger they had to be aware of and it had set a solemn mood for the rest of that day. Now being on the south side of the river it meant they didn't need to cross another all the way to St. Louis.

The water in the Platte was dropping each day as they

traveled and on the morning of the third day after crossing they came to where it emptied into the Missouri and stopped for the day just downstream. None of them but Zach and Benny had ever seen a river as big as the Missouri was and then Zach told them about the Mississippi being even bigger.

Red Hawk asked him, "Where does all this water come from and where does it go?"

Zach thought for the minute before saying, "Think about all the streams and rivers that flow from the Wind River Mountains. There is the Sweet Water, and the Popo Agie, the Sweet Water runs into the North Platte, the North Platte and South Platte join and then they run into the Missouri. Then it runs into the Mississippi and the Mississippi runs into the Ocean. The Popo Agie runs into the Wind River, the Wind River runs into the Yellowstone and then the Yellowstone runs into the Missouri and so on."

After Red Hawk thought about it a minute he said, "But if all that water keeps running into the ocean why doesn't it fill up?" Zach wasn't sure how to answer him in a way he could understand.

Zach thought about the question while they set up camp. So far they hadn't seen any buffalo since they had crossed the river so the women filled their black iron pot with water to start some jerky boiling then added dried squash to the water as well, and they all enjoyed the change from the all meat diet they had been used to.

After they ate, Zach tried telling them about the ocean. It was difficult for him to describe something he had never seen. His father and mother had tried their best to educate Zach as he grew and with Zach's natural curiosity he was always asking questions. He had been told the stories of the first settlers coming to America from across the ocean and the dangers and hardships they went through before ever reaching this land.

He told Red Hawk and the others that the ocean was bigger than all the land in the world, that for over a moon now they had been crossing the prairie but it took many moons to cross the ocean. Then he went on to explain that the water that runs into the ocean dries up in the sun like the water in a buffalo wallow dries up in the summer. So all of the rivers in the world running into the ocean just replace the water as it dries up.

Red Hawk and the rest understood that water dried up in the heat of the summer sun. As they looked out across the Missouri, Buffalo Heart said, "With all that water running in it must be a mighty big buffalo wallow."

Zach went on to tell them about the great beasts that live in the ocean, whales that are bigger than ten buffalo all put together, but none of them knew what a whale was. It was Shining Star that asked, "What is a whale, my husband?"

Zach told them a whale was like a fish that breathed air. They all laughed at that thinking Grizzly Killer was joking with them for they knew fish couldn't breathe air. Zach explained that is why they are whales and not fish but they live in the water of the ocean like the fish do.

Then Running Wolf asked, "Grizzly Killer, have you seen these great beasts?"

Zach shook his head and said, "No I have never been to the ocean, but my Ma and Pa lived by it in a land far to the east called Virginia before they moved to Kentucky."

Zach realized how little of the world he had seen and he knew he had seen much more than any of the others. Benny had been silent up until now and he started to realize how big of a shock St. Louis was going to be to them. The biggest villages they had ever seen were a couple of hundred teepees and St. Louis had nearly 15,000 people living there. Benny said, "Everything Grizzly Killer said is true, although I too have never seen the ocean I have been on the Mississippi River. The big river is nearly a mile across and there are boats like big canoes on the river that will hold over a hundred men and their supplies."

Benny never really saw the good side of St. Louis, during the times he'd been there after leaving the family farm. He had worked on the river with the hard-drinking, hard-fighting men that were drawn to that type of life. He had been into the city bars and a mercantile, and had seen nice people but most the men he had been around was the type you wouldn't want to turn your back too. He was trying to figure out a way to explain not just the city but the rough men that lived there. Zach could see he was struggling to explain and said, "I think what Benny is tryin' to tell you is your goin' to see many different kinds of people there. There are more people livin' in St. Louis than in all of the Shoshone villages combined. Some people are good and honest but others are mean and dishonest. Some will welcome us but others will want nothing to do with us because we are different from them."

It was Running Wolf that said, "Because we are Indian."

Zach nodded and said, "Yes because you are Indian and because me and Benny choose to be with you. It will not be easy for any of you in St. Louis but that is the reason we needed to make this long hard trip. You need to learn and understand the type of people that will be moving west into the land of the Shoshone and the Ute."

Red Hawk then spoke up, "If they try to move into our lands we will drive them away."

Zach remembered his Pa telling him of the great Shawnee Chief Black Fish and his son Tecumseh, and how they had tried to keep the whites from moving west into Tennessee, Kentucky, and Ohio. But, the number of whites and their ability to manufacture weapons and equipment overpowered the Shawnee and every other Indian tribe to the east. Zach himself had seen the Cherokee being slowly pushed from their lands. Although the Cherokee were much more willing to accept the whites and trade with them they were still being pushed off the land.

Most whites didn't understand the Indian culture, it being so different from their own. They thought of them as ignorant savages to be exterminated not as people loving their families and struggling to survive in a changing world. Zach looked at Red Hawk and said, "Red Hawk so many before you have thought the same thing and for a short time that may work, but in the end, all of the Indian peoples have had to accept the coming of the white man or die." Zach told them of the great battle of Boonesborough when Daniel Boone and a much smaller number of settlers defended their settlement against the Shawnee. For nearly two weeks Black Fish and an overpowering number of Shawnee tried to take Boonesborough only to be defeated because of the weapons and defenses the settlers had built.

Zach could see the defiance in the young warrior's eyes and continued saying, "Red Hawk I have known you since you were young and I know how good warriors you, Buffalo Heart, Spotted Elk, and the other Shoshone are, but what you don't realize is how many white men there are, and that is why I wanted you to see for yourselves. St. Louis is only one city and there are many, many cities further east that are even bigger."

Red Hawk still had a look of defiance but Zach could

also see a questioning look on their faces, except Benny's, he understood. Running Wolf asked, "Where do all these people come from and why do they not stay in their own lands?" Zach once again didn't know how to answer him. He himself had never been east of Kentucky, but all the time he was growing up he'd loved listening to his Pa tell stories of the east and the great cities back there. Captain Jack, as his Pa was called, had told young Zach of the ocean and the people coming from England, France, Ireland, and the rest of Europe on the big ships. It saddened Zach to know it was explorers like his Pa, Daniel Boone before him and now he himself and the other trappers and mountain men that were opening this vast wilderness for others to soon follow.

Zach explained to them that there had been powerful Chiefs called Kings across the ocean that claimed all of the lands for themselves and in order to have a place to farm without the Kings taking it they sailed across the ocean where they could live and be free. So many of them came and are still coming so they have to keep moving toward the setting sun in order to find more land. Buffalo Heart spoke up, "But it is our land, the Shoshone have lived here since before the time of our grandfather's grandfathers."

Once again Zach didn't know what to say. He knew Buffalo Heart was right, the land he himself grew up on had once belonged to the Cherokee, and he had lived as friends not far from their village. Zach knew it was possible for the Indians and whites to live in peace together but it would take much patience and understanding on both sides. He knew that most whites, as well as most Indians, weren't interested in living side by side. He himself loved the Indian people and their way of life. Men like Grub and Ely and many of the other trappers loved the Indian way of life and the freedom it provided. Farming however, for the most part, interfered with the free-roaming lifestyle of most Indian tribes and Zach knew eventually that would cause conflicts that would lead to war in the west just as it had with the Shawnee in Kentucky and other tribes further east.

Zach continued the conversation with Buffalo Heart and said, "Yes you are right about your land, but what would you do if there were no more buffalo or antelope on the prairie or deer or elk in the mountains around your home?" Buffalo Heart looked puzzled, that was something he had never considered before. Zach pushed him for an answer asking again, "If you hunted for a month without finding enough food to feed your village what would you do? What if you saw people starving and babies dying because they didn't have enough to eat and then someone came to your village and told you there were plenty of buffalo in the land of the Blackfeet, what would you do?"

Buffalo Heart then answered, "I would go to where the buffalo were."

Zach nodded and then asked, "What if the Blackfeet said, they are our buffalo and you can't have any of them what would you do?" They started to understand then what Zach was trying to tell them, for they all knew they would fight the Blackfeet and drive them away and take the buffalo they needed.

Zach could see the understanding start to show on their faces, then asked, "Would it be right for you to go to the land of the Blackfeet and take their buffalo?" He then answered his own question saying, "The Blackfeet have lived on their land and hunted their buffalo since the time of their grandfather's grandfathers, but the Shoshone would have no choice but to go there and hunt their buffalo." They would push the Blackfeet from their land if that was the only way the Shoshone could survive. "The white people are no different they are moving west in order to provide for their families because there are too many of them for the land to support across the ocean and in the east."

There was silence around their camp after that, each one of them deep in their own thoughts. For the first time they were starting to understand what Grizzly Killer was telling them but they still could not imagine as many people living anywhere in the world as he was describing. Finally, Red Hawk said, "It will take a long time for enough people to come and fill up this great prairie we are crossing before they get to the land of the Shoshone and the Ute."

Zach nodded knowing he was right then said, "Yes it will, it may not be before you and I no longer walk on this land, maybe not even in the lifetime of our children, but it is up to us to teach our children and grandchildren to live with the whites so they are not pushed from their land completely, just like it would be up to the Shoshone and Blackfeet to learn to live together and hunt the buffalo if both were to survive."

Red Hawk made one last remark, "Who would want the Blackfeet to survive." Zach knew that simple sarcastic remark marked the deep seeded hatred the different peoples felt toward one another, that was the main cause of conflicts between the Indians and whites just as it was between the Blackfeet and Shoshone.

THE NEXT MORNING THEY MOVED ON, FOLLOWING THE Missouri. The river was flowing south and Zach figured they had traveled twenty to twenty five miles each of the last few days without incident. As they started out on the fifth morning of following the big river, Jimbo took the lead running out just as far in front as he usually did. There was a breeze starting up, blowing from the south and soon Zach could tell something was bothering his big dog. After being on the trail for a couple of hours Jimbo came back to him with his hair standing on end down the center of his back and growling his soft low growl that came from deep in his throat.

They stopped and while Running Wolf, Benny, and Buffalo Heart stayed with the women Zach and Red Hawk followed Jimbo downstream. No more than a half mile ahead they found where several men had camped. The coals of their fire were still warm to the touch. Red Hawk started looking for horse tracks and found none, but Zach found where there had been two canoes pulled up onto the bank. Whoever had camped there were all wearing moccasins but Zach couldn't tell if they were white men or Indians for they had left nothing behind. Zach then sent Jimbo back to bring the rest of them up to where he and Red Hawk where waiting.

He had an uneasy feeling he didn't understand. Whoever had camped there had left on the river and if they were going downstream they would be far ahead of him and his party, so they would not be a threat. If they were going upstream he believed he would have seen them, but he hadn't. His uneasiness came from not knowing where or who they were.

There was a small knoll rising from the prairie not far ahead and just a few hundred yards from the river. Zach sent Red Hawk out to see what he could from that vantage point while they waited for the others to catch up. Red Hawk had been taught well, he crawled to the top of the little knoll and carefully parted the grass to study the other side. What he saw surprised him; once again there were buffalo stretching out away from the river for as far as he could see. There were thousands of them and as he raised his head a little higher he saw six hunters waiting near the bottom of the opposite side of the knoll. Red Hawk had no idea what tribe these hunters were from and not knowing whether or not they would be friendly he carefully moved out of site then hurried to his horse and back to Zach to report on what he had found.

The others had reached Zach by the time Red Hawk rejoined them and Zach was worried when he heard the hunters were less than a mile away but if they were occupied with hunting he hoped they might be able to sneak past them. He told Red Hawk that in this area there could be more Pawnee, or Kansa, Omaha, or maybe even Missouri. He hoped his group was a little too far south for them to be Rees or Lakota but he knew any of the tribes could and would travel great distances to find the buffalo.

Red Hawk had never heard of Kansa or Missouri or Omaha Indians before and he was just starting to realize how big the world really was. He thought back to many of the other Indian tribes that Grizzly Killer had told them about; the Cherokee, Shawnee, Mohawk, and Delaware and he finally asked, "How many different Indian tribes are there Grizzly Killer?"

Zach had never thought about that before and said, "I do not know, Red Hawk, I can think of dozens and there must be many more that I do not know about." So far this trip had been an eye-opening experience for all of them for none realized how big the world really was outside of their mountain villages.

Just as Zach was ready to lead them along the river bank and out of sight of any hunters Red Hawk had seen, they all heard rumbling and could feel the ground faintly shaking. Zach looked across the seemingly flat prairie toward the small knoll just as hundreds of buffalo came charging around it. The rumble increased to a steady roar as hundreds more of the panicked animals stampeded northward less than a quarter mile from where they were watching from along the river bank.

The buffalo kept coming and as the dust kicked up by the many thousands of hooves blocked their view. The roar of the pounding hooves was sounding closer but the dust became so thick they couldn't see the stampeding animals. The wild panicked beast kept coming, there were now thousands of them all running to the north. They were now coming not only around the little knoll but over the top of it as well. Zach couldn't really see them but he could tell through the dust the buffalo were getting closer to them.

Zach yelled over the roar of the stampede to ride hard and he kicked Ol' Red into a full run. He knew it was a risk but with the thousands of stampeding buffalo and all of the thick dust, he thought now was the best time. They all kicked their mounts into hard run. Staying as close to the river as possible, they ran full out for nearly two full miles, then slowed to a gentle lope for another two. The great stampede was behind them now but the dust cloud was still billowing into the air hundreds of feet above the prairie. Zach figured it was the hunters that had started the stampede and wondered briefly if any of them were hurt or killed for their efforts.

Two days after the mighty buffalo stampede they reached the place where the Missouri turned once again back toward the east. Zach tried hard to remember how long it took them to reach this place when coming west with General Ashley all those years ago, best he could figure they were about two weeks from St. Louis.

They moved ever eastward now, following the river for the next few days and stopped to make camp at a place that was plain to see had been used by travelers many times before. They had their horses taken care of and hobbled on the lush prairie grass when Benny spotted two keelboats coming up the river. Both boats had their sails down and were being poled along by men using long poles. They were out in the center of the river and nearly even with the camp when the boats abruptly turned and headed right for their camp.

With the women staying back around the fire, Zach met the first boat and helped it dock as men jumped into the water with ropes, securing it to the river's bank. Soon both boats were docked and as the leader of the group approached Zach he held out his hand introducing himself.

Their leader was James Kipp an employee of the American Fur Company. He was leading this expedition to build a fort for trading with the Mandan's and other tribes along the upper Missouri.

Kipp had his men set up their camp less than a hundred yards from where Zach and the others were. Jimbo and Luna watched the men carefully as they carried the supplies they would need from the boats. Jimbo's size was once again of great interest to the men with most of them walking way out around the huge dog. Running Wolf smiled at the nervous looks on the men's faces as Jimbo and Luna watched every move they were making.

Kipp was carrying tools for building and goods for trading in his fifty-foot long keel boats, and Zach's impression of the man was good. He wasn't so sure about all of the thirty-four men that were with him. As part of the supplies they were carrying to trade with the Indians, were 30 barrels of rum that had been brought up the Mississippi from New Orleans. Once the men all had their chores completed Kipp let them tap a barrel and have a drink. He was careful with the liquor, warning the men only one drink each. He offered the rum to Zach and was surprised when he and the others all turned it down. Kipp said, "This ain't that local stuff, this is real rum from New Orleans." Zach shook his head, telling him he didn't drink.

Sun Flower approached and said, "Grizzly Killer, the buffalo and squash are ready." James Kipp just stared at Sun Flower's pretty face and she smiled back at him and asked Zach if his friend would be eating with them.

Zach looked at Kipp and said, "Mr. Kipp this is my first wife Sun Flower Woman, Sun Flower this is Mr. Kipp." Then looking at Mr. Kipp he asked, "Would you care to join us for supper Mr. Kipp, it's just simple trail fare, roast

buffalo and boiled squash we traded for with the Pawnee."
James Kipp looked up at Zach's suntanned face and asked,
"Did she call you Grizzly Killer Mr. Connors?" Zach
nodded and said, "That is my Indian name, the Shoshone
first started calling me that years ago."

Mr. Kipp then answered, "Why yes, I would be pleased
to join you for supper."

Although Sun Flower still felt queasy and not herself,
she was able to hide it from everyone except her sister.
Raven Wing insisted she continue to wear the crystal
around her neck. To everyone the crystal had become "The
Healing Stone" and even Zach had started to wonder if it
really held the power all the others believed it did.

As they all set around the fire, James Kipp told Zach
that he had become quite a legend in St. Louis. That there
were all kinds of stories told about how he had fought Blackfeet, Grizzly Bears, and murderin' white men and had killed
them all bare handed. Zach turned red and said, "Don't
believe everything ya hear Mr. Kipp no man can kill a
Grizzly with only his hands."

But Kipp continued "They say you are the deadliest
man in the Rocky Mountains, that even most Indians are
afraid of you."

Running Wolf then spoke, "Mr. Kipp, Grizzly Killer is
the greatest warrior I have ever seen, but only those that
would do us harm has anything to fear from him." Red
Hawk and Buffalo Heart both nodded their agreement and
Mr. Kipp asked them how they came to speak English so
well and they all pointed to Zach, then Running Wolf
continued, "Me and my sister are Ute while my wife, and
Sun Flower, Red Hawk and Buffalo Heart are Shoshone.
Since before any of us can remember the Ute and Shoshone
were enemies but Grizzly Killer has changed that. We now

ride side by side as brothers and all of our people honor Grizzly Killer and his powerful medicine for his friendship."

Jimbo being next to Zach started his soft low growl, one of Mr. Kipp's men was approaching. Zach and Mr. Kipp stood and stepped away from the fire. It was obvious the big burly man had much more than one drink. His name was Homer Gooding, and he had been trouble since they left St. Louis. He was a bully pushing the other men around and James Kipp realized instantly he had made a serious mistake letting the men have rum at all. Kipp ordered him back to camp to sleep it off but the big man just stared, then said, "Get the out of my way little man, I's is gonna dance with one a them purty Injun squaws."

Kipp was turning red with anger and said as he stepped forward, "Homer I'll have you flogged for this, now get back to camp."

Suddenly the much bigger man backhanded Kipp, sending him to the ground then he looked at Zach and said, "Get outta my way squaw man or you is gonna get the same. "Homer stepped forward to push Zach out of his way but he never got to touch him. Zach's fists were so fast the drunken man never saw them coming. Zach's right fist hit Homer right below his rib cage completely knocking the wind out of him, and before Homer had even doubled over he caught Zach's left fist right in the center of his face.

Mr. Kipp was just standing up when the big man landed flat on his back, out cold. A cheer went up from the rest of the men as James Kipp looked at Zach in disbelief and said, "I am so sorry Mr. Connors, I hired Homer because of his size and strength, I felt like he would be a great asset in building a fort, but as you can see he has been nothing but trouble and none of the other men dared fight him." He then told some of his other men to drag Homer back to camp and hogtie him. They would deal with him when he was sober the next day. As several of the others were walking toward the big man, Jimbo walked and sniffed at him then lifted his leg and peed right on Homer's head. A roar of laughter went up from everyone, even the women all laughed. Sun Flower called Jimbo to her so he was out of the way.

The next morning before Zach left, he walked over to say goodbye to James Kipp and to wish him luck with his trading post. Homer was still tied but awake, both eyes were black and blue and his nose and upper lip were swollen nearly beyond recognition. He stared at Zach as he shook hands with Mr. Kipp, with a hatred that Zach had seen before. He was glad they were going in different directions for he didn't want to have to kill that man but if they stayed together he figured he may have to.

As they rode out of sight, James Kipp told Homer Gooding he had two choices. He could receive 10 lashes or he could be left where he was. They would not put up with more of his troublemaking. Homer looked at him and said through loose front teeth and his swollen and split lip, "I will kill any man that touches me with a whip."

Mr. Kipp told one man to get him his rifle and possibles bag but to make sure the rifle was empty. As the man approached he fired the rifle into the air, then Mr. Kipp told him while the others finished loading the keelboats to run downstream a half mile and leave the rifle in the bushes there. He then looked at Homer and said "If you walk every day from sunup till dark you should make St. Louis in two or maybe three weeks." When the boats were ready to push off James Kipp cut the rope binding Homers hands but left his feet bound and went to the boats and pushed off. Homer had his feet free and was just standing up when the two keelboats reached the center of the river, and the men manned the oars to slowly move the boats upstream.

LIKE ANY OTHER normal day of travel, Zach was in the lead with Jimbo scouting ahead. Today it was Running Wolf riding point on the right and there was no need on the left because the big muddy river was there.

The day, like the vast majority of days since they had left home, passed quiet and uneventful. They stopped and camped under an ancient oak tree standing by itself as a lone sentinel along the river. Just as they normally did, they stopped and made camp about two hours before dark and the women had supper nearly ready when Jimbo started to growl. Zach, with a silent hand signal, told Jimbo to go and the big dog disappeared down the river bank.

They were all armed as they saw two Indians approaching carrying some furs. They raised the arm in the sign of peace and Zach waved them in. The two Osage Indians wanted to trade some furs for whiskey and were disappointed when Zach let them know they did not have any. Zach asked them if they wanted a meal but they declined, then asked who the white wolf belonged to.

Running Wolf stepped forward and signed to them, *"The wolf belongs to no man, she is free, she chooses to stay with me, I am Running Wolf of the Ute nation and she is my spirit helper."* The two Osage men nodded and left, disappearing just as they had appeared from the prairie.

The next couple of days saw the grass-covered prairie give way to large patches of trees and they all could feel heavy moisture in the air. It felt muggy all of the time now with the full heat of summer. It was now July, Daza-mea`, the summer moon for the Shoshone and the days were long and hot.

Two more days and the prairie was gone, now they were following rough trails and wagon roads through the woodlands. That night Benny told them all they would reach the city the day after tomorrow. Once there he would take a ferry across the river, for his family's farm was nearly a day's ride north-west of there. Zach told him to come to the city first and get new clothes for himself and Little Dove and show what a successful man he had become.

Benny told him he didn't bring any furs to trade then Zach pulled the pouch of gold nuggets and put a half dozen in his hand, again he looked at Zach said, "I can't take your gold it is yours and Running Wolf's."

Running Wolf stepped forward saying, "Take it Benny, the gold does us no good in the mountains and we will not come here again."

Benny smiled as he took the nuggets thanking them then said, "We will need to find a bank first and change these nuggets for coins. We do not want anyone to see we have gold."

Zach nodded his agreement and Running Wolf asked, "What is a bank?"

Zach smiled and said, "You will see."

They started passing farms where the fields were cut out of the thick woodlands and then on the second day about mid-morning just as Benny had told them, St. Louis was spread out before them.

THE AIR WAS CALM TODAY AND A HEAVY SMOKE-HAZE hung low over the city like that of an Indian village only much, much thicker. Of the group only Benny had seen the city like this. It had nearly doubled in size since Zach was last here and as he looked at the mass of buildings, he wasn't even sure he would be able to find William Ashley's warehouse.

Shining Star with disbelief in her eyes looked up at Zach and asked, "Does the village you come from look like this?"

Zach smiled as he shook his head and said, "Pottersville only had a few buildings when I was there last. It was mostly just a few scattered homesteads where we farmed."

Running Wolf, still staring at the mass of buildings all jammed so close together said, "I can see why you never came back here to live Grizzly Killer, the people here don't have room to ride, and what do they eat? We have not seen any game for the last three days."

Zach called Jimbo in close and told him to stay as he followed Benny toward the city. Benny knew the areas around the docks and waterfront where he had worked, much better than the more affluent side of town, so that is where he led them. They circled around the northern edge of the city and it wasn't long before the Mississippi came into view. Once again those that had never seen the big river were amazed at its size. They couldn't believe there was that much water anywhere and they wondered how big the ocean must be to be able to hold all this water.

They passed a small farm just before entering the city, and Zach watched a boy he thought was about twelve or thirteen chopping firewood. Another child with bright red hair and maybe three was playing in the dirt not far away and it brought back pleasant memories of Zach's own youth. There was a very large vegetable garden and a pair of mules grazing in a large pasture. A hog pen set in the corner of the pasture had a sow and ten little weaner pigs, and one milk cow was in a small corral behind the cabin. None of the Indians had even seen a hog or a cow before and Red Hawk and Buffalo Heart were pointing asking what the strange animals were.

A barn that had been started but not finished was on the side of a large pasture. Zach stopped and climbed off of Ol' Red and approached the young man. Jimbo was right next to him and the boy looked afraid being approached by this very large man that looked more Indian than white and this huge mean looking dog. As Zach got closer he said, "Hi, my name is Zach Connors what's yours?" The boy was just staring at Jimbo almost too afraid to speak. Zach could see the fear in his eyes and told Jimbo to sit. As the big dog sat on his haunches Zach rubbed his ears and said, "He's friendly enough son, he won't hurt ya."

The boy's lips turned up into half a smile and said, "I'm Henry Dodds."

Zach replied, "Well it's very nice to meet ya Henry, is this your family farm?" Henry looked suspicious as he nodded his head.

Zach asked if his Pa was home and the boy then said, "No, Pa and me works down on the docks when there is steamers to load or unload but today they only had work fer Pa not me, so I'm doin' chores fer Ma."

Zach then said, "Well then son how about gettin' your Ma so I can meet her too."

Just before Henry turned to the house he looked back at the others and asked, "They look like wild Injuns with ya, is they?"

Zach smiled and winked at him as he said, "Just as wild as they come, but any friend of mine is a friend of theirs too." Henry smiled a big genuine smile then turned to go inside.

While Henry ran into their small log cabin telling his Ma there was a bunch of wild Injuns that wanted to talk to her the others all got off their horses to stretch their legs. A moment later Henry burst through the door and to Zach's surprise a beautiful auburn haired woman stepped through right behind the now excited young man. Her apron was covered with flour from the bread she had been making and her sparkling green eyes stared at Zach as she recognized the familiar form standing there staring at her. A moment later tears burst from her eyes and she yelled, "Zach" and ran to him, throwing her arms around him.

Zach was stunned speechless, he had never expected to see Emma Potter again. They had grown up together in Pottersville, Kentucky. It was her grandfather the town had been named after. She was his first love and he hers, it was her he had promised to return to. He had never expected she would be the first person he would see in St. Louis.

Sun Flower and Shining Star along with the rest of them had turned and looked as Emma shouted Zach and they were all stunned as this woman with long red hair ran to him. Young Henry's mouth was agape as he stared at her with her arms around this strange man dressed as an Indian right in front of him. She finally released her arms from around his neck and softly said, "I thought you were dead."

Zach still couldn't speak he just stared into her emerald green eyes for the longest time. In a weak voice he finally said, "Emma after Pa was killed I just couldn't come back."

She smiled, looking up at him as the shock of seeing him again was finally wearing off. She stepped back and looked up and down his tall muscular frame and said, "Zach what has happened to you? You look like an Indian."

Zach looked back at his wives and the others. It was obvious to them all Zach and this woman knew each other. Although he had told Sun Flower and Shining Star about the promise he had made to return to Kentucky and that he felt bad about breaking that promise, he had never really told them about Emma. He motioned them all forward and for the first time Emma saw they were all Indians but one.

Zach now said, "Emma I would like you to meet my wives." The look on her face was one of shock and disbelief as she looked at these two beautiful women with their long black hair and dark brown eyes. She looked back at Zach and stated, but it came out more like a question, "You married an Indian?"

Zach smiled reaching out to Sun Flower and said, "Emma this is my wife Sun Flower Woman" Emma was speechless as she tried to smile. Zach continued and said, "And this is my wife Shining Star and our daughter Star." He then turned to his wives and said, "This is my good friend Emma Potter or is it, Emma Dodds?"

Emma nodded as he looked back at her.

Henry ran to his mother's side and said, "Ma your friends with Injuns, wait 'til I tell James and Willy." She was still shocked as she stared at Zach in disbelief. The look in her eyes told both Sun Flower and Shining Star that their husband and this pretty red-haired woman had been much more than just friends.

Emma finally turned and picked up the little red-haired toddler and held her up to Zach and said, "This is my dirty little girl Charlotte," as she tried to brush some of the mud off of her clothes and hands.

Zach finished the introductions and then Henry asked, "Is that white dog a wolf?"

It was Running Wolf that said, "She sure is, she is a pure wolf and my spirit helper."

Henry looked puzzled and asked, "What is a spirit helper?"

Running Wolf wasn't sure how to answer him as he couldn't believe any young man didn't know of spirit helpers.

Emma looked back at Zach and asked, "How did you find me?"

Zach shook his head and said, "I didn't, I just stopped here to see if I could rent part of your pasture for our horses while we are here for the next few weeks. I had no idea it was yours or that you were even in St. Louis."

Emma looked at Henry and told him to go open the gate, then said, "I'm sure Charles won't mind. Our two mules and the milk cow sure can't eat that much grass." Then she said, "Charley will be home in a few more hours you must meet him." Zach smiled and told her he would but right now they needed to find William Ashley and a bank and a place to stay while they are here.

They left all the horses except the ones they were riding at the Dodds farm, along with most all of their packs of supplies and equipment. They had covered it all with buffalo hides and Zach had told Emma they would be back in the next day or two.

It was only about a mile or a little more into the city they entered St. Louis on Front Street, which ran along the Mississippi. Dozens of businesses and large warehouses were built on the city side of Front Street down the full length of the riverfront. Docks and levees had been built along the river side of the street and the mighty steamboats, that brought in supplies from New Orleans and from the cities along the Ohio River then loaded up goods in St. Louis to take back, were docked there.

At first, buckskin-clad mountain men riding down the middle of Front Street with Indian squaws didn't draw much attention, it was a site most had seen before. The street was crowded with people going in every direction and Sun Flower wondered where they all could be going in what seemed like such a hurry. Someone then noticed Jimbo and Luna, and he pointed, telling his friend to look at the big dog and wolf. As they looked the beauty of Sun Flower and the other Indian women was noticed. Soon everyone on the street was watching and pointing as they rode by.

They were approaching the first of four steamboats that were docked when it blew its steam-powered whistle. They all jumped, including the horses, at the sound then they watched as the side-wheeler cast off and started its large wooden paddles turning. Only Benny had been around the large steamboats before and even Zach was amazed at the power of the big paddles as they churned the water, carrying the one hundred and twenty-foot boat out into the current of the mighty Mississippi.

As they rode by where the boat had been tied they saw several slaves. It was the first time any of them but Zach and Benny had seen a Negro before and Little Dove asked, "What is wrong with those men? Why is their skin so dark?" Before Benny could answer her their master cracked a whip and they all jumped up and headed for the wagon.

All of them listened as Benny explained they were slaves and came from a land far across the ocean. They all understood slaves, for most of the Indian tribes made slaves out of their captives. It was Red Hawk that asked, "But Grizzly Killer says the people across the ocean are white men."

Benny nodded his agreement and said, "There are many different lands across the ocean. White people like me and Zach, our grandfathers came from a land called Europe, but the slaves come from a land called Africa."

Buffalo Heart said what they all were thinking, "The Earth must be bigger than I can imagine." Zach now believed they were starting, at least in the small way, to understand why he had brought them here. To see for themselves some of the things he had been telling them.

They passed the old stone building that had once been Manual Lisa's fur trading post, but now had been turned into a tavern, and a few minutes later they came to Ashley's Trading Post. It had been six years since Zach had been in St. Louis and it had only been for three or four weeks. He had only known General William Ashley as a fur trader and leader of expeditions into the vast wilderness of the Rocky Mountains.

Ashley was a well-known and important man in St. Louis. He had been Lieutenant Governor of Missouri and had run but narrowly lost the election for Governor in 1824. Ashley was a natural leader and had interests in banking, mining, and politics, but it was the fur trade that had made him a very wealthy man.

William Ashley was surprised when one of his clerks told him there were a bunch of Indians asking for him. William Ashley was a man that Zach trusted, he had always been fair and honest with Zach and his pa when they worked for him, and Zach would always be grateful to him. If General Ashley wouldn't have hired him and his pa, Zach may have never found this life he loved so much.

It was a happy reunion for Zach as William Ashley came forward recognizing him immediately. Ashley acted a little disappointed when he learned Zach had left all of his furs in the mountains with Grub and Ely to be traded at Rendezvous, but seemed happy enough to take Zach to his bank for his gold exchange. Ashley also gave Zach and small bank book with one deposit that had been made four years ago. It was money that Ashley owed Zach from the Rendezvous in Willow Valley, back in 1826.

Running Wolf and the Indians made quite a spectacle as they waited on the street for Zach and Benny to exchange the gold for coins that could easily be spent. The few nuggets Zach had given Benny weighed 8.1 ounces and he received just over one hundred and fifty dollars for them. The bag of nuggets that Zach had weighed in at 128 ounces, eight pounds of gold, giving Zach over twenty-four hundred dollars. Zach took the money along with the other six hundred the bank was holding, giving him a little over three thousand dollars in gold and silver coins. That was more money than Zach had ever seen.

After thanking Ashley and the banker, Zach asked them if there was a boarding house or someplace they could stay where they could bath and get new clothes. The banker's name was Maurice Chouteau and he had a boarding house that would be glad to take care of him and his party. Mr. Chouteau was the grandson of one of the original founders of the city. He walked them to the door to say good day but when he saw the Indians just outside and the group of people watching them, he decided he better take them to the boarding house to make sure Mrs. Bossard would indeed take them in and give them everything they needed.

The boarding house was on Market Street, just above Broadway, only a few blocks from the river. It had a very well kept stable behind the house and the slave that took Ol' Red and their horses assured them they would be taken care of in the very best way. He said, "My name is Jacob, sir, but most just calls me Old Jake." Zach watched him smile as he took the big red mule by the lead and Zach figured the old black gentlemen had been a field hand when he was younger and had worked a lot with mules. Ol' Red went with him without hesitation and Zach knew then he didn't need to worry, about Ol' Red and the horses for they were in good hands. Mrs. Bossard wasn't sure she wanted the huge dog and wolf in the house, but when Zach offered to pay for an extra room for them she relented.

Mrs. Ruth Bossard was a middle-aged woman whose husband had died in a duel several years before and she had been forced to go to work to survive. She had worked for the Chouteau family in her youth and Maurice had let her run his boarding house ever since her husband was killed. He had furnished her with old Jake to run the stable and three more slaves for the inside. She ran a clean and efficient house and, although skeptical when she saw the Indians, she was kind and gracious to them all. It surprised her they all could speak English and surprised her even more that they spoke it better than many of the slaves and men that worked on the river.

Zach paid for a week in advance in gold coin then offered Mrs. Bossard two ten dollar gold pieces if she would help the women shop for clothing, for neither he nor Benny felt they could do it. She smiled at the fear she saw the two big rugged men had about taking their Indian wives to a dress shop.

The only places any of the Indians had ever bathed had been in streams or lakes, they laughed thinking it was a joke as the black women filled small round tubs with warm water. They were each handed a cake of lye soap and a large piece of thick rough cloth for a towel. They didn't know what the soap was or what to do with it but after Zach showed them they used it with delight. Being clean was a good feeling for all of them, Zach had asked for a razor and when he was finished bathing he tried to shave off his thick sandy-colored beard, but he had never shaved before and finally gave up.

It was late afternoon when they all left, Mrs. Bossard leading them to the shops along Main Street. Zach gave Mrs. Bossard the money she thought she would need and took the four women into a dress shop. They were all nervous and when asked which of the colors they liked best it was Sun Flower, always the bold one that spoke up.

Just a few doors down the street Zach found a barber shop and both he and Benny went in to get a shave. Running Wolf, Red Hawk, and Buffalo Heart watched nearly in shock as the barber cut off the long hair of his beard and then after working soap into a lather he covered Zach's face and started to shave him. Running Wolf stood up and got close to see what was happening for it looked to him like Grizzly Killer was getting skinned.

When the barber was done, Running Wolf, Red Hawk, and Buffalo Heart just stared at him; they were all speechless. They had never seen him without a beard and to them, it looked like half his face was missing. Zach even wondered what he had done. His face felt so different, the barber kept asking if he wanted his hair cut but he wouldn't let him touch it. Although Benny's beard wasn't as thick and long as Zach's the results were the same, they didn't look like the same men without them.

Just a few doors down from the barber shop was a mercantile that sold men's ready to wear clothing. Zach and Benny picked out three each of trousers, shirts, long johns, socks, and mackinaw coats, for them all including the women. He tried on boots but after six years of wearing moccasins, they just didn't fit his feet. When they were satisfied with what they had he paid for it all, not letting Benny pay for his own things. He told Benny he may need the money when he left them to go see his family.

The women spent much of the afternoon in the dress shop, their laughter and giggling could be heard well out into the street. Mrs. Bossard and even the lady helping them in the store was having fun showing these four lovely Indian women everything that white women wore and then they would laugh at the reactions.

In the end, they each bought two modest dresses, undergarments, and some jewelry. They called the jewelry foofaraw, for that was all they had ever heard it called by the only white men they had ever known, the mountain men and trappers at Rendezvous that wintered in their villages. The perfume was another first for the all, including Zach. Sun Flower again was the bold one that was first to put a few drops of the water that smelled like wildflowers on her neck like the lady in the store showed her. Then Raven

Wing and Little Dove, and finally Shining Star put on just a little of the smelly water.

Zach and the others were sitting on the hitching rail just down from the dress shop when they came out of the store. Several men were walking down the street and they just stared at the four beautiful women. Right now no one could tell they were Indian, maybe Spanish or Creole but no one would have guessed Indian.

Zach started toward his wives, but when Sun Flower and Shining Star saw him they stopped. Sun Flower just starred as did all the others. Then he saw the horror in the eyes of Shining Star and tears start down her cheeks as she said, "What have you done, your face is gone." Even though his beard had thickened and grown longer with age none of them had ever seen him without a full beard.

THE WOMEN, ALTHOUGH NOT FEELING PARTICULARLY comfortable in their new dresses, were pleased with the smiles on their husband's faces. Mrs. Bossard laughed right out loud as she saw the reaction not only from Zach, Benny, and Running Wolf, but at the looks these lovely Indian women were getting from others on the street as well. She had truly enjoyed herself today and had been paid extremely well in doing so.

When they got back to the boarding house it was late in the day and when they entered to the smell of the cooking dinner, all of their mouths watered. None of them had eaten since early morning. Not long after they arrived dinner was served. Zach and Benny were the only ones that had ever sat at a table to eat, and the women had never eaten anything that hadn't been prepared by themselves or their mothers.

Mrs. Bossard had not only been surprised at the English these Indians spoke but at their manners as well. It had never before occurred to her that the wild savages she had heard so much about were just people like anyone else. She knew nothing of the gold or how much money Zach had, but for Mr. Chouteau to personally escort them to the boarding house she figured he must be rich.

A dinner of pork chops fried in lard, greens, boiled potatoes with gravy, and freshly baked bread was served. Mrs. Bossard had given instructions to the cook before they had left that she wanted a special meal prepared for this evening.

Zach had been surprised and extremely pleased so far, other than staring and pointing, the people they had met had treated them with respect.

None of the Indians had ever tasted pork, greens, potatoes, or bread and dinner turned out to be quite a treat for them all. When Zach told them what they were eating was hog, like the one they had seen at the Dodds farm, they nodded and understood why these people kept the strange animal. After dinner, a dried apple cobbler was served with a glass of fresh milk and they were all delighted. Zach thanked Mrs. Bossard and the Negroes that had prepared the meal for their hard work. The slaves were surprised and pleased with the compliments, the only time most whites said anything to them was to give them an order.

So far this day had been a novelty to them all, seeing so many strange and wonderful things. They had all been treated with the hospitality fit for dignitaries but Zach and Benny both understood why, it was the money they were spending.

At dinner that all changed, they had met four other gentlemen and one of them kept looking at Running Wolf, Red Hawk, and Buffalo Heart. After dinner, that man asked Mrs. Bossard if the Indians were going to stay the night and when she told him they were he asked, "You expect the rest of us to stay under the same roof with those murdering savages." Mrs. Bossard tried to assure him that they were not murdering savages but he continued getting louder and more animated, "We might as well cut our own throats right now as stay here, we won't be alive in the morning anyway."

That last part Zach overheard and he walked over to the much smaller man and looked him square in the eyes and said, "Mister, none of my friends have ever killed a white man, but I have." He reached into his pocket for a coin and gave the man five dollars and told him to go find another place to stay. The man swallowed hard and turned to go back to his room. A moment later he left with his bag under his arm. Zach then apologized to Mrs. Bossard and said, "Hope we don't cause ya more trouble."

She smiled at him and nodded wondering if what he had told the man was true.

After checking with the cook about any leftovers to feed Jimbo and Luna, they all went out to the stable and checked on Ol' Red and the horses. Old Jake had just left and the stalls were clean with fresh grass hay in each one. Jimbo and Ol' Red touched noses, letting each other know they were okay.

The evening was hot and muggy, the air felt almost hard to breathe to those used to the cool thin air of the Rockies. They were all sweating some and Sun Flower commented that her skin felt wet all over, Zach smiled for his did too and it brought back memories of the hot muggy days in Kentucky when he was young. The new clothes they were all wearing made them fit in better, but none of them liked wearing them much, their buckskins were much more comfortable. The underclothes they wore were now sticking to their skin, adding to their discomfort.

Sun Flower was feeling much better but she could tell something was still wrong and she figured it was just the muggy air and city that had her feeling this way. She reached up and held the crystal that still hung around her neck under the store bought dress as she said, "This is sure different than in the mountains." Shining Star and Zach both nodded.

The next morning found Zach, Sun Flower, and Shining Star sleeping on the floor with little Star being the only one on the soft bed. Zach hadn't slept much at all, he didn't like being in a building. The room creaked and there were other unfamiliar sounds, he could hear Jimbo panting and pacing the room most of the night. Zach was up at the first hint of light and it was obvious none of them had got much sleep.

It was barely light enough to see when he took Jimbo out to check on Ol' Red and the horses when he found Red Hawk and Buffalo Heart both asleep, laying on the hay at the end of the stable and he smiled, wishing he would have thought of that.

Breakfast was another delight for them all, none of the Indians had ever had chicken eggs or cured ham before. A big platter of fried eggs and thick slices of smoked ham along with biscuits and plenty of hot coffee was set on the table in front of them. This was the first fried egg Zach had had since he and his pa left home and he ate a half dozen of them. In fact, the cook had to fry another platter full they were such a hit.

After breakfast they went out and saddled up; Zach wanted to ride all around the city. He hadn't lost sight of the purpose of this trip, but he felt he needed to make his family and friends realize no one could possibly stop the numbers of whites that were rapidly moving ever westward.

As they rode down Market Street toward the river, Zach could see clouds of smoke coming from the stacks of one of the steamboats. As they got closer, there was a line of at least fifty men loading heavy crates onto the decks and still others securing loads. Zach stopped and they watched as the black smoke billowed from the stack with the boilers building steam. The smoke added to the thick haze that seemed to perpetually rest over the city.

As the men finished up, Zach heard his name called and stopped to look as young Henry Dodds came running toward him and just behind him was a man that Zach could tell was his father. Zach stepped out of the saddle and he reached out to shake the young man's hand. Henry stopped and stared at Zach and said, "You shaved off your beard."

Zach smiled and nodded and asked, "What do you think?" as he rubbed his chin.

Young Henry turned up his nose and said, "I liked the beard."

Zach looked back at his wives and they were both nodding in agreement.

Charles Dodds introduced himself and as they shook hands it was obvious that they were sizing one another up. Charles was a stout, strong man, though not as tall as Zach he had a heavy mustache but clean-shaven chin. After they had introduced themselves Zach introduced the others.

Charles Dodds then stood back looking Zach directly in the eyes and said, "So you're the man that made me wait over a year to marry Emma." Zach looked puzzled and Charles continued, "I asked Emma to marry me every week for over a year but she wouldn't do it 'til she was convinced you weren't comin' back. I always wondered who I was playin' second fiddle to."

Zach looked down and said, "She made the right choice, I would never have made her or myself happy being a farmer, I knew that and that was one of the reasons I never came back and I ain't gonna be here for long. A month or less and were headin' back to the Rockies."

Charles nodded as he watched his son kneeling down gently petting the white wolf.

Zach asked, "I really appreciate bein' able to leave our stock in your pasture, how much rent do I owe ya?"

Charles shook his head and said, "Nothin' at all, if I took yer money Emma would have my hide." Zach smiled and nodded, he felt good now knowing she had found a good man and the happiness that he had found.

Before they left the boarding house that morning Benny had given Zach directions to find his family's farm. He said goodbye to everyone as they reached Front Street and headed north out of the city.

Zach and the rest spent all of the morning and into the afternoon surveying the size of St. Louis. There seemed to be people everywhere they went. Not much was said as they rode around that day, they were all in deep thought. Several times they heard the loud steam whistles coming from the boats on the river as they left or as they arrived. There were nearly fifteen thousand people living in St. Louis that summer of 1830 and the city was definitely a busy place.

On the southern edge of the city they came to a road-house and stopped to eat lunch. As they walked in they found six of the eight tables were already filled. Zach pulled the two remaining tables together and they all sat down around them. No one had paid much attention to them as they came in and sat down. Jimbo and Luna stayed outside and laid under the hitching rail. The proprietor came to the table to see what they wanted, although on the board above the bar it had simply said, "Today's Lunch-Stew."

The proprietor was a heavyset bald man with a large

belly and dirty apron. Zach looked up as he asked, "What'll ya." He stopped before he even finished asking and the look in his eyes turned to a venomous stare. As he looked all around the table Zach could tell there was going to be trouble. His eyes stopped as they got to Zach, and who smiled and said, "I think we will all have the stew."

The top of the man's bald head started to turn red as he said, "I ain't servin' no stinkin' Injuns squaw-man now get out of my place."

Zach and the rest weren't looking for any trouble and he would have left peaceably but the man made a grave mistake. He grabbed Running Wolf by the collar to physically throw him out. Running Wolf wasn't nearly as big and powerful as the proprietor was but his speed was surprising. He spun around, hitting the bigger man in the throat. As the proprietor went to the floor, trying to breathe with a very nearly crushed Adam's apple, three other men jumped up to rush toward Running Wolf. Zach whistled as he stepped forward swinging a rock hard fist into the first man's belly, doubling him over and sending him to the floor next to the proprietor. Three other men were getting up as Zach looked at Buffalo Heart saying, "Get the women to safety." As he had turned his head to Buffalo Heart a hard fist connected with his chin nearly making him lose his balance.

Three other men were just getting to their feet as Jimbo burst through the door. The huge dog jumped up on their table knocking the bowls of stew everywhere. His lips were curled up into a vicious snarl and the growl was so frightening all three of them froze.

When the man that had hit Zach tried a follow-up punch, his face was flattened by a fist that he never even saw coming. The last of the three of them came at Running Wolf but stopped dead in his tracks as the jaws of Luna clamped down on his leg, tearing through his heavy canvas trousers and into the soft flesh of his thigh. He let out a scream and grabbed for his knife only to find Running Wolf's already at his throat.

Running Wolf told Luna to stop and she released the man's leg. There was just a small trickle of blood at the tip of his knife, still resting against the man's throat as the scared man released his grip on the weapon he hadn't even got out of its sheath. Zach looked around the room and in a determined voice asked, "Is this finished now?" He was looking at the three men staring at Jimbo's bared teeth but none of them dared move or speak.

In a soft voice, Zach said, "Jimbo back." The big dog jumped off the table and stood at Zach's side. The relief was evident and all three of the men breathed out sighs of relief.

Running Wolf pulled his knife back and told the man to sit back down, which he did. The proprietor was still on the floor holding his throat but was now breathing normally and Zach knelt down by him and said, "All we wanted was a peaceful lunch and we were leavin' when you asked us to go. I don't know and I don't care why you hate the way you do, but you had better be careful who you lay your hands on, 'cause next time you might not live through it."

The room was completely silent as Zach, Running Wolf, and Red Hawk backed their way to the door. Then Zach said, "There will be two rifles aimed at this door for the next ten minutes. If anyone steps out they will die."

There wasn't a soul in the room that doubted anything Zach had said and after he stepped out and closed the door, a couple of men got up and helped the proprietor and the other man to their feet. The proprietor tried to say thank you but his voice sounded like a frog trying to croak.

In the back corner of the room sitting by himself in the

shadows was a huge man. As the proprietor slowly headed back toward the bar, this big man chuckled and as everyone turned their heads to look at him he said, "You dumb bastards don't know how lucky you is to still be breathin'." Ben Beaumont stood up and looking right at the man that had tried to throw Running Wolf out he continued, "Most of ya in here knew my brother Cal, some maybe even knew my other brother Bull. Well, that squaw man as you called him killed both of them in fair fights. That is the man theys call Grizzly Killer."

Someone said, "That guy killed both Cal and Bull in fair fights? I don't believe it."

Another said, "If he killed both yer brothers, hows come you don't want revenge?"

Ben looked at the man and said, "He coulda killed me just that easy but I wasn't dumb enough to try to fight 'em like Cal did. He outfitted me and give me directions to get back here. No, if it weren't fer that man I never woulda made it back and sure won't be dumb enough to ever cross 'em."

Zach and Buffalo Heart had stayed behind watching the door, he wanted to make sure the women were far enough away to be safe. He didn't know if someone inside might try and take a shot at them. Even after Zach and Buffalo Heart left it was over a half hour before anyone left the Road House.

They all met up again at Front and Market Streets then rode up Market Street to the boarding house. Their spirits were all down after what had happened and they were still hungry. When Mrs. Bossard heard what had happened she had the cook bring out ham and bread and the leftover biscuits from breakfast.

After their hunger was satisfied, they all sat in the

sitting room and at first no one said a word until Red Hawk said, "I sure don't like it in the city, and I don't think they like us being here." Zach had the same feeling and he knew his wives well enough to know they did as well. He didn't want to spend another sleepless night in the boarding house.

Shining Star then asked, "Grizzly Killer do you think your friend would let us stay on her farm?"

Zach wasn't sure how that would work out, but none of them wanted to stay in the city another night so he said, "Well let's ride out there and ask."

THE DODDS FARM WASN'T THAT FAR OUT OF THE CITY but it felt like a completely different world. They couldn't hear the whistles from the steamboats and there weren't people moving about everywhere all of the time. When they rode up to the farm, Charles and Henry were struggling with a timber for the barn that they had been trying to build for over a year now, and the four of them hurried out to help. With six of them on it, they had the timber set in place in no time.

Emma came out and Zach asked Charles if he would rent them a place they could stay, explaining that none of them liked the city. Zach pointed to the far side of the pasture under some oaks and said if they didn't mind, that spot would be great. Emma spoke up and said, "Wouldn't you be more comfortable in the barn? Even though it's not finished it will give you some protection." Zach and the rest of them were used to the wide open spaces of the mountains and they declined, saying the oak trees were enough protection. Zach offered to pay for the use of the pasture but again both Charles and Emma shook their heads, refusing.

It didn't take long to get all of their supplies to the far side of the pasture where the trees were standing and to Zach's surprise there was a small creek marking the end of the pasture. Within an hour they had a camp set up that they all were more comfortable in. The woods behind the pasture provided plenty of firewood and branches for setting up their lean-tos. Once they had a fire burning they all sat around it just watching the flickering flames. Watching the dancing flames of a camp fire burn is soothing and was like therapy to them all. This was the first time since arriving in St. Louis that any of them had felt at home and without much sleep the night before they were out in just a few minutes.

Zach didn't know how long he had been asleep when a gunshot awakened him. It came from the woods and both he and Running Wolf instinctively picked up their rifles and were ready to shoot. He then saw Red Hawk and Buffalo Heart were not there, and just a little panic shot through him. He jumped to his feet followed by Running Wolf only a spit second later, both stood with concern on their faces. Jimbo and Luna were both standing at the edge of the woods staring out at the unseen. Jimbo was shaking and Zach could tell he wanted to go but it was obvious Red Hawk and Buffalo Heart had told him to stay. Zach simply said, "Go boy" and Jimbo bounded out of sight into the thick woods.

Zach and Running Wolf separated, on each edge of their little camp standing as guards until they found out what had happened. It was just a few minutes when Jimbo came back, wagging his tail, letting them know there wasn't any trouble. A few minutes after that Red Hawk and Buffalo Heart could be seen coming through the woods dragging a deer. The whitetail buck was smaller than the mule deer of the western mountains but the meat was just as pleasing and they enjoyed their evening meal.

Just before the sun set, Charles along with Emma, Henry, and Charlotte came walking across the pasture. Emma was carrying a basket of fresh cinnamon rolls she had made. Spices of any kind were scarce on the frontier but Charles and Henry had unloaded a boat that had carried several boxes that had come from a ship in New Orleans. Although they were expensive, Charles had bought cinnamon and black pepper.

Shining Star made another pot of coffee and they all sat around the fire enjoying the sweet tasty treat. None of them, including Zach, had ever tasted cinnamon before and it was just one more marvel from the white man.

Zach asked about Pottersville and why they had left there, and Charles explained the town had not grown since he had first arrived. The people living there were surviving alright but not thriving, and he wanted to give Emma more of a life than just surviving. He went on, saying that St. Louis was the trade center of the Mississippi and the western frontier, so he figured the opportunity would be much greater here for a man not afraid to work and earn it. Zach smiled, he understood exactly what Charles Dodds meant and he was relieved Emma had found a man who truly cared for her.

Zach told them they had a beautiful farm here, and Charles continued telling them he knew it would be, some-day. It was taking longer than he hoped it would, he had spent every dollar they had buying the land and now he had to work on the docks just to live. That was why the barn wasn't finished or more crops planted. He had to sell his two horses for a plow and harnesses for the mules. When he had time, Henry and himself cut the timbers for the barn from the woods but the lumber they could only buy when there was enough work on the docks for Henry too. It was with that little extra they were able to build up the farm, but one day in the near future he hoped to have even this pasture all planted and would like to expand even beyond the eighty acres he now owned.

Sun Flower watched Emma's eyes as Zach and Charles talked, she could see both love and hurt in them. It was easy for her and Shining Star to see that Emma and their husband had once been in love. She understood that, for she could not see how any woman would not love Grizzly Killer and it made her feel good inside knowing he had chosen her rather than coming back here to this pretty red-haired woman.

The sun set and as the light started to fade bullfrogs croaked along the creek and tiny specks of light would appear and then disappear all along the edge of the woods. Zach watched the look on all of their faces and Red Hawk pointed and said, "There it is again." Zach turned to see what they were looking at and as he watched the fireflies light up and then disappear, he realized none of his family or friends had ever seen them before. Raven Wing wondered what form of magic this was.

Young Henry answered by saying, "Ain't ya ever seen fireflies before?"

Raven Wing looked at him and shook her head then asked, "What is a firefly?" Henry laughed and jumped up to catch one and in just a few minutes both Red Hawk and Buffalo Heart was with him trying to catch them. They all laughed at these two Shoshone warriors trying to catch the fireflies as they would glow and then disappear into the darkness. Charles and Emma couldn't believe these people had never seen fireflies before and then Zach told them that fireflies didn't live in the cold thin air of the Rocky Mountains.

Emma asked Zach how his pa died and if he got to see the Rocky Mountains. She could tell it still saddened him as he told of the grizzly bear attack. He told her that yes, he got to see the towering peaks as they reached for the sky and the animals that lived there. Henry's eyes were as big as dollars as Zach told them the bear that killed his pa was as big as their milk cow. He told them of the pure white mountain goats that live high among the peaks where some of the snow never melted, even under the summer's sun. He told of the bighorn sheep, and little antelope of the prairies that can outrun even the fastest horse, and of the land that is so big you can ride for weeks in any direction without seeing another soul.

As he talked Emma could tell the deep love he felt for the land he left her for, and as he went on telling them more of the wonders of the towering mountains and the western frontier she realized no woman would ever be able to compete with that. She could see the love both Sun Flower and Shining Star had for the man that she too once loved. She realized now how much he had changed, he truly was more Indian now than white man. She reached out and took her husband's hand, reassuring him as well as herself that she had made the right decision.

The next morning after saddling up, Zach and Running Wolf rode back into the city. Red Hawk and Buffalo Heart wanted to explore the woods that were so different than the forests of the mountains above their home and the women just wanted a day or two to relax and let the babies play.

Zach once again rode down Front Street to a large

stable and blacksmith shop he had passed the day before. There he rented two large freight wagons with teams of draft horses and after getting directions and taking some time showing Running Wolf how to drive a wagon they headed to the lumber and boat building yard.

Zach purchased enough sawn lumber to completely fill both wagons then took it all back to the Dodds farm. Zach nor any of the Indian people had any use for gold in the wilderness. There was nothing there to buy with gold, what commerce was done was through bartering. The wilderness itself provided everything they needed to live and the beaver provided a way to get supplies the wilderness didn't provide. Zach had talked it over with the others and they had all agreed if they ever needed more gold they would go back to the creek and find it.

The average man made about two hundred dollars for a full year of hard work and buying the lumber had hardly made a dent in the amount of coin Zach was carrying. He made a mistake when paying for the lumber, he wasn't used to having to be secretive. He had let others see the weight of coins he was carrying in his pouch and with all of the people in the city, he wasn't aware that he was being followed as they took the lumber back to the Dodds farm.

Charles wasn't there when they got to the farm, only Emma, Henry, and little Charlotte. Emma couldn't believe what she was seeing as Zach and Running Wolf started to unload the wagons. Emma protested but Henry jumped right in to help. Zach ignored Emma's protest until they had the wagons unloaded then finally said, "This is something we all want to do, and besides there is no use for money in the wilderness."

Emma looked a little suspicious at him and asked, "How did you get so much money?

Zach smiled and said, "Fur trappin' can be mighty profitable."

Emma looked even more suspicious as she said, "But you didn't have any furs with you when you got here." Zach wasn't surprised she had noticed, she was very observant even when they were teenagers.

The men that had followed them from the city watched from a distance as they unloaded the wagons and kept watching as Zach and Running Wolf walked out to the end of the pasture where their wives were drying the rest of the deer Red Hawk had shot. In the heat of the July sun, the meat would have been spoiled by the end of the day. As Zach approached their camp he smiled seeing all three of them were wearing their doeskin dresses. The store-bought ones were carefully folded and put away.

After checking in with the women they headed back to town with the wagons, but the men following them stayed there studying the lay of the land. They planned on waiting until after dark, then sneaking in on them. They figured there were only two men and one quick volley from their rifles would take care of them and the women wouldn't be a problem. They could attack and be gone with the heavy money pouch in just a couple of minutes.

At the livery, Running Wolf watched as the blacksmith was shoeing a horse. Having never seen this before he was amazed as nails were pounded through the hooves then twisted off and flattened out. He watched with interest as the blacksmith, after putting several metal rods in the forge, worked the bellows. As the air was forced through the burning coal he could feel the heat and watched until the rods glowed bright red, then how easy the metal was shaped with the pounding of the big hammer around the anvil that was set on a large oak stump.

After they had returned the wagons and left the livery Running Wolf asked, "Why did that man put the iron on that horse's hooves?"

Zach looked at his partner and said, "It makes their hooves stronger so the horse can do more without going lame."

Running Wolf looked puzzled as he said, "Our horses don't go lame." Zach nodded his agreement but he also knew if they did, another horse was chosen to ride from their herd. Where most white men didn't have a herd of horses to choose from. After explaining that, Running Wolf nodded but in his mind he thought the white men's horses must have weak hooves.

Ol' Red was much happier carrying Zach than he had been tied to the back of the wagon where he had been most of the day. Zach had another stop to make and headed back to Orlando's Mercantile where they had bought their shirts and trousers. There Zach bought a sack full of large nails and four hickory handled hatchets with flats on the back side for pounding. He then bought a side of bacon, ten pounds of coffee beans, enough sugar, flour, and cornmeal to last them through their return trip to the mountains. He saw there were several bottles of canned peaches on a shelf behind the counter and had the clerk add them as well. Fruit in tin cans were rare, in fact this was the first time Zach had ever seen it and he figured it would be a treat for them all. The proprietor just had a local farmer bring in some potatoes, carrots, and turnips so Zach smiled, adding some of each. He knew the vegetables and that the stew they would make would be a delight.

He had bought more than he had intended to when he came into the mercantile and ended up having to buy two large pairs of saddlebags to carry it all. Jimbo was lying on the boardwalk in front when Zach and Running Wolf came out, both he and Ol' Red tied to the hitch rail acted like they had been gone for days. It was obvious neither of them appreciated the crowded streets of St. Louis.

Riding out of the city a hunter was coming in; he had five large hounds in the back of his wagon along with a bear carcass they had taken. The dogs saw Jimbo and three of them jumped out right for him. Their hair was standing up down the center of their backs and they were baying, expecting him to run. Zach told his big dog to stay as the three dogs slowed their approach spreading out to attack from different sides. Zach yelled at the owner to call off his dogs or they would get killed. The owner laughed saying let them fight then they will be friends. Zach yelled again at the owner, "My dog will kill 'em, call 'em off." It was then too late and a big muscular brown dog with a dark stripe running down the center of his back attacked. As soon as he lunged forward the other two attacked as well. As the large ridge-backed dog hit Jimbo, the size and power of Zach's dog was evident and in less than a blink of an eye, Jimbo had the attacking dog by the throat and on the ground biting down hard enough to hurt but not kill, by then the other two were on him from behind.

Zach jumped off Ol' Red to try and stop the fight but it was too late, as the first hound bit into the back of Jimbo's neck he spun around, knocking the dog loose and biting into the side of his neck and tearing out a large piece of it of it. In the process of swinging that dog around, he knocked the third one off his feet. He rolled once, then came to his feet and he and Jimbo met head-on. The hound was no match for Jimbo just like the other two he was on the ground in seconds. Zach was there calling Jimbo off and only a moment later the owner of the hounds came to get his dogs.

Jimbo was bloody from the bite marks on the back of his neck and one gash just under his eye. The hound with the ripped out neck had already bled out, the other two though still alive were hurt and would take some time to heal. Their owner stared at Jimbo, not believing any dog could have done that to his three best hounds. The fight had lasted only seconds and Zach was upset and looked at the man saying with obvious anger in his voice, "I told you to call them off, I didn't want to see good dogs hurt and killed."

The man was speechless, he had made one serious mistake with his dogs and he wasn't going to make another with this big man standing in front of him.

Running Wolf helped the stranger get his dogs back in his wagon, including the dead one. Zach checked over the wounds on Jimbo, telling his faithful companion that Raven Wing would fix him up when they got to camp.

RAVEN WING CLEANED the wounds and worked a poultice of her healing plants into them just as soon they reached camp. Red Hawk and Buffalo Heart had made it back and had taken a couple of more animals. Red Hawk lifted up an opossum and Buffalo Heart a raccoon, none of them but Zach had ever seen these animals before and had no idea what they were. They skinned both and Sun Flower started scraping the hide of the raccoon to tan. They all thought the rings around its tail were unique. Both Running Wolf and Shining Star had seen the elusive Ring Tailed cats that lived in the dry arid country south of the Uintah Mountains, but none of the Shoshone and ever seen anything like them.

Zach was completely unaware, but the two men that were after his money bag were patiently waiting for the sun to set and full darkness to arrive. They were far enough away they couldn't see the camp and still had no idea there were more than just the two men they would have to kill.

Benny and Little Dove had ridden out of the city and followed the road along the Mississippi River. A few miles out of the city the road turned northwest toward St. Charles and the Missouri. They had stopped at the Dodds farm and picked up a pack horse, their bedrolls, and what personal supplies they needed. Along with a few day's supply of buffalo jerky, which there was still plenty of, and headed for the place where he had spent most of his life. Benny was nervous about going home but he really didn't understand why. Little Dove could sense it and that made her uncomfortable as well.

They rode a ferry across the wide Missouri into St. Charles and Benny was amazed at how much it had grown in the three years since he had last been there. They were dressed in their store-bought clothes and although Little Dove wasn't really comfortable in the dress she felt like she fit in and wasn't nearly as self-conscious as she would have been dressed in her doeskin dress. She was starting to get used to the underclothes but didn't really understand their purpose.

It was just a few miles from St. Charles, nearly straight west to Dardenne Creek, where the Lambert homestead sat and Benny slowed the horses down to an easy walk. Little Dove could tell he was in deep thought and she stayed silent, knowing he would speak when he was ready. A few minutes later he started telling her stories of the area he remembered from his youth, like the trouble he and his brothers would get into when they would sneak out of the field and go skinny dipping in the creek. He told her of a time they were hunting squirrels with their homemade bows and arrows and the family dog treed a bear, they had run all the way back to the cabin without stopping. He told her about fishing for catfish in the creek by the house and Little Dove asked him what a catfish was.

She could tell he was now enjoying the memories and some of the anxiety was leaving the closer they got. The road climbed up over a hill that was just high enough they couldn't see over it and from the top they were looking down at Dardenne Creek and the cabin where he had grown up. He took a deep breath and smiled as he saw smoke coming from the chimney.

He could see more land had been cleared and another cabin had been built to the northeast on the far side of the fields. They were all green with this year's crop that from their vantage point looked to be half corn and half cotton. The barn had been added on to as well and in the pasture behind the barn there looked be two or three dozen mules. In a corral right on the side of the barn there were six big Shire Horses and a couple of Mammoth Jack Donkey studs. His mother's vegetable garden had been enlarged as well, with a small patch of tobacco growing on the far side of several rows of green beans. The hog pen down by the creek was much bigger as well and there looked to be a dozen hogs in it.

The well in the front of the cabin was just as it had always been and he smiled as he told Little Dove of drawing water for his mother. As they approached, it was obvious to him his family had prospered since he had left home.

They stopped in the yard and dismounted just as two men came out of the barn to see who the strangers were. Benny recognized his younger brothers immediately; it was Jacob who was just a year younger than he was and Albert who was a year younger than Jacob. They both stared at Benny as if they were looking at a ghost, then Benny simply said, "Hi boys."

They both ran to him with smiles and hugs then Jacob stepped back and looking at Little Dove with her nervous smile asked, "And who is the lovely lady?"

Benny held out his hand to her and as she took it, said, "Boys this is my wife Little Dove."

Jacob smiled from ear to ear but Albert's jaw dropped open as he said, "You're married, wait 'til Ma finds out."

Just then the cabin door opened and their mother stepped out. She had tears in her eyes and her lower lip was quivering as Benny left his brothers and ran to her. She hugged him so tight he was having a hard time breathing then she stepped back and said, "Let me look at you son." The joy in her eyes at that moment alone had made the long arduous trip worth it. Even with the dangers and hardships, Benny knew right then that Little Dove had been right when she told him if her mother was alive that no trip would be too hard or too far to go see her.

Benny asked, "Where's Pa and Rachael, and Fae, and Ilene?"

He saw a sadness enter her pale gray eyes as she said,

"Little Ilene left us two winters ago with the fever. Rachael and Fae have gone over to the Trumbolt farm for the day and your pa took a pair of mules out to the Hardy place, I don't expect him back until supper time." The news that his baby sister had passed away hit him hard, and as he stood there stunned his mother nodded and said, "It was a terrible shock to all of us and it has left a big empty spot in our lives." She then asked, "And who is this with you."

Benny smiled and she could see the joy in his smile and he turned to Little Dove motioning her to come forward then said, "Ma I want you to meet my wife Little Dove" Although Little Dove didn't know what to expect, she knew if she was the one that had raised her husband she had to be a good women.

She held her arms out to Little Dove and Little Dove came forward and they hugged. She then looked at Benny and asked if they were married in a church. Benny looked down and shook his head saying, "Ma there ain't any churches where we live."

Little Dove then asked, "What is a church?" Benny looked at her and then at his mother trying to figure out how to explain to a person that had never heard of a church before what one was.

Although Little Dove was wearing one of her new store-bought dresses, with her darker reddish skin and accent as she spoke they all knew she was Indian, but just as Benny had been raised without prejudices, the rest of his family didn't have them either. Mrs. Lambert looked at her and smiled, telling her that a church was a place we gather to worship God. Little Dove still wasn't sure she understood so Benny then said, "It is where we go to learn about and pray to the One Above, the creator of all things."

Little Dove nodded and smiled, she understood but she

still had questions about it. Looking at Benny and then his mother, she said, "The Shoshone pray to the One Above, but we pray from a hilltop alone not with a group of people, the One Above can hear us better that way."

Mrs. Lambert smiled and nodded and said, "I can understand that but here we build a sacred building and we believe that God or the One Above hears us better from when we are in the church." Little Dove smiled at that, she understood what a sacred place was.

There were few preachers on the frontier and even fewer churches and Margaret Lambert was well aware of that and she said, "Well, now in just two weeks Jacob is gettin' married to Bess Applegate, maybe we can have a double wedding and make it all legal in the eyes of God." Then without waiting for a response she looked at the two of them and said, "You are going to be here that long aren't you?" Benny looked at Little Dove and could see the confusion on her face, she had no idea what they were talking about but somehow she knew it involved her.

Benny turned back to his mother and said, "I think so Ma, but I ain't positive. I give Grizzly Killer the directions to get here and when he does we will have to go with him. It is too dangerous to travel across all that wilderness alone." Then he looked at Little Dove and said, "A wedding is a ceremony and celebration for two people getting married. We believe when they get married and a Holy Man who we call a preacher performs the ceremony, then the One Above is pleased with them being husband and wife." Little Dove smiled, she understood that and if being part of the wedding ceremony pleased the One Above she wanted to take part in it.

Benny couldn't believe his little brother was old enough now and was really getting married and although he didn't really feel it was necessary for a preacher to say a few words to marry him and Little Dove, he knew it would make his mother feel better.

There wasn't any work done on the Lambert place for what little of the day was left. They all sat around a table of rough sawn planks setting on two barrels under an ancient oak tree by the creek and talked.

Benny told them all he hadn't liked working on the river even as much as he didn't like farming, so when the chance to go west came up he went. He told about the weeks and weeks of endless travel crossing the great prairie and of the first glimpse of the Rocky Mountains and how even after they could see Laramie Peak, it took over a week of hard travel to get there. He told them of the Wind River Mountains and the Tetons with their rugged rocky peaks reaching for the sky and of the brutally cold winters. He told them of his partner's Grub and Ely and of his good friends whom he came back home with. He told them about fur trapping and the Rendezvous. Jacob and Albert were spellbound by his stories then his mother asked him how he and Little Dove met.

Benny looked at her and smiled saying, "Ma I believe I was meant to be with her. There just ain't no other reason for the way we met." He really didn't want to upset his mother with stories about the Blackfeet and although he may leave out many details, he figured she had a right to know the truth of his life as a trapper and mountain man.

As the sun was rapidly heading for the western horizon his mother stopped him and said, "We best save that story and the rest for after supper when your father and sisters are home." His mother looked at Jacob and told him to kill three of the young roosters and they would have fried chicken for supper. Fried chicken was one of their favorite foods and they didn't get it very often or their farm would be without eggs. Both Jacob and Albert jumped up, smiling that they would gladly go catch, kill, and clean the six-month-old roosters for a dinner of their mothers chicken fried in a hot skillet of lard.

Before she headed to the house she told Benny they would set a pallet in the kitchen for a bed but Benny said, "No Ma, we'll set us up a lean-to out here by the creek." Neither of them much fancied the idea of being inside for the night, "we'll be just fine out here."

She looked at him and said, "Nonsense the skeeters and chiggers will eat you alive."

But Benny just smiled and said, "We'll be fine they can't go through our buffalo robes."

While his mother left for the house and his brothers for the chicken coup, Benny and Little Dove led their horses down the creek just a little ways to the old swimming hole. It took them less than an hour to have a lean-to setup and a bed made inside. The horses were hobbled and happy on the plush green grass along the creek and Little Dove looked up at Benny as he gazed across the growing fields of the farm he had wanted to get away from most of his life. She could tell he was happy to be here but there was something else in his look that she wasn't sure what it meant. Finally, he turned to her and took her in his arms and said, "You were right Little Dove, I needed to come back here and see my family again but I miss the mountains already."

She hugged him tight and simply said, "Me too."

The day had been very hot and humid compared to the dry air of the high mountain valleys of the Rockies. They were both pleased as they walked back toward the cabin when a slight breeze started to blow along the creek.

As they came out of the trees along the creek in sight of

the cabin. Benny could see his father with a bucket at the well washing after a long hot day delivering the mules. Benny hurried straight toward the well, Little Dove nearly running to keep up. Mathew Lambert looked and hurriedly dried off as his oldest son approached. He smiled and nearly shouted, "Benton it is really you?" They hugged and while they held one another his father said, "When you disappeared from working the river I was afraid you were dead."

Benny, feeling bad now, pulled away and looking his father directly in the eyes said, "Pa, I'm so sorry. It happened so fast, I had a chance to go west and I took it. I didn't have time to think about it or plan it, I just left and Pa, it is what I was supposed to do."

Mathew Lambert just stared into his son's eyes and nodded then said, "I suppose it was son, I guess I knew from the time you was waist high you weren't ever gonna be no farmer. Now let me meet this pretty young lady with you."

Benny introduced Little Dove to his father and just as they were going into the house Benny's sisters returned from the Trumbull's. Mrs. Trumbull had been helping them sew new dresses for Jacob and Bess's wedding. She was the best seamstress in this area and was also making Bess's wedding dress. Benny was shocked at how his sisters had grown. When he left Rachael was just thirteen and Fae eleven, now at sixteen Rachael was a woman and Fae, fourteen with her hair down past her waist and sparkling blue eyes, was a far cry from the little girl he remembered.

They were more shocked to see their oldest brother than he was at how the two of them had changed. They were fascinated meeting Little Dove with her obsidian dark eyes and black hair that shined in the setting sun.

Dinner was set out on their large kitchen table that served as the counter as well. This was the first time in years her whole family was together and it brought tears of joy to their mother's eyes.

Benny's father said grace and Little Dove, although confused at first about what he was doing, understood by the time he was finished and smiled that these people thanked the One Above for their food. Fried chicken was another first for Little Dove and one she really enjoyed. It was like Benny had never left, with the boys bantering back and forth. Benny could see the joy in his mother's eyes and was once again grateful to Little Dove for pushing him to come back, even though it would only be for a short time.

After the meal was cleared and the girls had done the dishes, they all sat around the table with cups of strong coffee and listened once again to the stories of Benny's life in the mountains. Benny's told them of his life on the river and how he had disliked the rough men and knew just a few months after leaving home that working there was not the life he wanted. He told them of meeting men that were going west to get rich trapping furs that had invited him along, so he went. He told them of how the men he went west with were not trappers and how they struggled to survive, but then he met Grub Taylor and Ely Tucker. They were older, experienced trappers and mountain men and they had shown him how to trap, hunt, and survive in the Rocky Mountains. He told how they had become like family to him and Little Dove, and were the best men he had ever met. He was now their partner and right now they were at the Rendezvous on the Wind River not far from the Shoshone village where they all had lived last winter.

His mother asked again, "Is that where you met Little Dove?"

It was Little Dove that spoke up then. She told them how Benny had saved her from the Blackfeet that had attacked her village and tortured and killed everyone. That because of Benny she was alive that he could have left her behind and she believed most men would have but Benny saved her and took her with him. She told them he was a great warrior and their hearts were as one.

Rachael then asked, "Who are Blackfeet and why would they kill everyone?" Little Dove looked down and they all could tell the memory of that day was hurting her.

Benny said, "The Blackfeet are a tribe of Indians that live in the northern Rockies around the headwaters of the Missouri River and they are a curse for anyone that goes near their lands. They attack and kill anyone that is not one of them. The Crow and Shoshone, the Flathead and Sioux, and any white man foolish enough to get to close to them, the Blackfeet will kill them all.

Little Dove then continued, "Benny is a great warrior, he has killed many Blackfeet, like his friend the great white warrior Grizzly Killer who my people sing about around the fires at night. When he saved me the Blackfeet killed everyone in my village and the ones that were not dead they tortured them until they died. I was out gathering food and hid during the attack but then Benny found me. He was riding a horse from a Blackfoot warrior he had killed and he took me away from there and kept me safe."

Everyone around the table was in shock at Little Dove's words. Benny's mother had tears welling up in her eyes that her son had to kill someone. Benny looked around the table and said, "There are lots of dangers livin' as we do in the wilderness and a man must do what he has to in order to survive, but the joy of seeing land that no white man has ever seen before outweigh them dangers. I have the best friends a man can have both, Injun and white and I truly love my life in the Rockies."

His father didn't know what to say, he knew Benny had always needed more excitement than the farm provided and it sounded like he had sure found it. Mathew Lambert had been like Benny when he was young, and at that time St. Louis was just a small town and St. Charles was not much more than a stop on the river. He had hacked this farm out of the wilderness along Dardenne Creek and had raised his family here. He had come to Missouri from Tennessee in his late teens and had been in a couple of fights with Shawnee war parties. He could remember how the great Shawnee Chief Tecumseh had shot fear through every settler, until he had finally been killed in battle. Although he had fired his old musket during those battles, he had been fortunate enough not to know whether he had ever hit anyone or not. He didn't blame Benton for striking out on his own for he had done the same thing at about the same age.

Benny asked about the mules, and that brought a big smile to his father's face. His pa told him he had started breeding mules the same year that Benny had left home and there was such a demand for them they could hardly keep up. He told him that they have added to their broodmares every year and the demand grew bigger with more settlers moving in and the army starting to build forts west of here. He talked with pride in his voice when he said, "These big mules of ours, after the boys gets 'em broke to the harness and plow, brings top dollar and people have been coming from all around for 'em."

Benny smiled and nodded, very happy the farm was finally doing well and said, "Well the farm sure looks good, y'all's done a great job."

Jacob then said, "Benny you said somethin' 'bout a man called Grizzly Killer earlier. I heard some men down on the dock as I was pickin' up a load of oats talkin' 'bout him." Benny looked and nodded and asked what they were sayin', "Said they were in a roadhouse in St. Louie just yesterday and a man with a bunch of Injuns came in, said the proprietor tried to throw 'em out 'cause they was Injuns and that man and the Injuns cleaned house with the proprietor and the men that thought they were goin' to help. Said he had the biggest dog they'd ever saw with him."

Benny asked with a big smile on his face, "Did they say how many were killed?"

Jacob looked concerned as he shook his head and said, "Nobody was killed just had the hell beat out of 'em."

Their mother said, "I won't have any cursin' in this house and you know it, Jacob."

Jacob looked down at the table and said, "Sorry Ma."

Benny smiled, remembering she had even got after Pa for the same thing when he was young then said, "Grizzly Killer, Running Wolf, Red Hawk, and Buffalo Heart are the men we came back here with, along with their wives Sun Flower, Shining Star, and Raven Wing. The men in that roadhouse don't know how lucky they are. Grizzly Killer is known as the greatest warrior in the Rocky Mountains, either Injun or white and the great medicine dog can and will kill a man in a heartbeat to protect any of us."

Jacob looked in awe and he asked, "Did you say he is comin' here?" Benny nodded and said, "I expect him in the next two or three weeks." His mother then commented, "Sounds like he is a mighty violent man."

Benny nodded his agreement and said, "He can be Ma, but wait 'til you meet him. He is as nice, honest, loyal, and honorable as any man alive and he hates violence, but he will not stand for anyone harming his family or friends, he is only violent when he has to be but when he has to be he is very violent indeed. You see, we live in the wilderness where danger is all around you and the closest law is fifteen hundred miles away."

Then Fae asked, "Why would you want to live in a place like that?"

As Benny started talking they all could tell the love he had for the Rocky Mountains with their towering peaks and the wide open spaces. His face and tone in his voice showed them all, including Little Dove, that he truly loved the west even with all of its dangers. Pa smiled knowing now his oldest son had found both the adventure and the happiness he had left home looking for.

They talked well into the night, Jacob and Albert asking one question after another until Pa finally told them they still had a farm to run and they all better get some sleep. It had been a long but enjoyable day for Benny. As they crawled into their lean-to and under the robes that night, he held Little Dove close and thanked her for urging him to come back home, for this day alone had made the two-month long trip worth it.

Not long before the sun set, Charles and Emma came out to not only protest again about the lumber but to thank them all as well. Zach had already asked Running Wolf, Red Hawk, and Buffalo Heart if they would help for a few days in building the barn. They all looked forward to learning something new and were excited to get started. Zach asked Charles to show him how he would like the barn finished up.

That evening with all of them together, they made a large pot of stew, Emma showed the other women how to use the new vegetables and potatoes. They added plenty of the newly dried venison as well as the opossum to the stew. Henry laughed at the Indians for not knowing what an opossum or raccoon was asking, "Ain't any of ya never saw a possum or coon?" Zach shook his head explaining that opossums and raccoons didn't live out in the Rocky Mountains. He went on telling Henry it was just as strange for them to think you have never seen a mountain goat, or an antelope or seen mountains so tall that even the trees couldn't grow on top of them. Henry started to understand how different his world was living here than where these Indians came from.

After all the vegetables and meat were put in their biggest pot to start cooking, Sun Flower saw the pretty flower pattern dress Emma was wearing and she wanted to look that nice as well. All three women decided to put on the dresses that Zach had bought them. The Indian women not even considering they were doing anything that wasn't proper, got out their new dresses and standing in plain view of everyone slipped out of the doeskins standing there completely naked, trying to remember just how to put the underclothes on. Zach saw the shocked look on Emma's face and then Henry's as his eyes were about to pop out of their sockets and a smile was slowly forming on the face of Charles as he watched these three beautiful women dress.

Emma looked at Zach in total disbelief as he smiled and said, "They just want to look as pretty as you do, but they may need some help if you wouldn't mind." Emma jumped up and went to help, anything to get them covered back up.

After the women had their new dresses on she stepped back, seeing the innocence and natural beauty they had. It was plain for her to tell Raven Wing and Sun Flower were sisters although Raven Wing was just a little taller and looked a little more athletic, their facial features were very close to one another. Both Emma and Charles were a bit surprised to learn Shining Star and Running Wolf were brother and sister for those two looked nothing alike. Charles could see why Zach was attracted to both women, they were as pretty as any he had ever seen except Emma.

Henry didn't talk much the rest of the evening with the sight of three naked ladies burned into his memory, but he couldn't wait to tell his friends James and Willy what happened. He wondered, as they walked back across the pasture, if white women looked like that under their clothes too.

There were high scattered clouds and just after the sunset the fading light from its rays painted the clouds with colors from light pink to dark purple with blaze red-orange in between. It was a spectacular display that lasted but a brief couple of minutes before the color completely faded away. Once again the fireflies came out as they did the night before. At first they were seen along the edge of the woods but it wasn't long and they could see the glowing little bugs out across the pasture as well.

The night was warm and humid as they all went to their lean-to shelters for the night. Zach laid down on top of their robes but soon was forced underneath because of the biting chiggers. They were one thing he was very glad didn't live in the Rockies.

It had been a full day for them all and sleep came fast, although some of Jimbo's wounds were deep, he didn't act like they were bothering him much. The loud croaking of the bullfrogs along the small creek and the constant chirping of crickets, although different than what they were used to hearing were nevertheless soothing natural sounds that seemed to help them fall asleep. The warm humid air had made both Sun Flower and Shining Star move their naked bodies away from Zach as the warmth made the night too hot for sleep.

Sometime after midnight, Zach was awakened by Jimbo's warm wet tongue across his face. His eyes opened immediately and he could hear the deep-throated growl. He dressed quickly and had the others up as well. He watched Jimbo as he was intently sniffing the air facing downstream toward the river. Not knowing what the danger was, but trusting Jimbo completely he had the women take the babies and go upstream and into the woods until he knew it was safe. Then with a hand signal he had Jimbo head downstream.

No more than fifty yards out Zach saw a flash of light and hit the ground just as another flash from the pan of a rifle split through the blackness of the night, followed immediately by the muzzle flash. Zach heard the soft muffled moan come from Running Wolf as the second shot tore into his thigh. Running Wolf had sent Luna with the women for protection so she wasn't with Jimbo as he attacked the two men with rifles. The first man had just finished reloading when the big dog hit him from the side, knocking him to the ground and biting down on the side of his head, tearing flesh and skin away nearly scalping him. Zach flinched slightly as he heard Jimbo's vicious growl and the man's terrified scream. Jimbo didn't stay to finish the job, he took another bound for the second man. With his ramrod still in his barrel the man threw up his arms as two hundred pounds of growling dog jumped on him. This time the scream was from terror, even before Jimbo bit down on his arms but then the screaming from the pain was so loud it shattered all other sounds of the night. The arm that was up protecting the man's face was firmly locked in Jimbo's powerful jaws and the bones broke. He bit down, shaking his head trying to rip the arm from his body.

Zach had motioned Red Hawk and Buffalo Heart to move out away from camp to see how many men were attacking, while he crawled over to Running Wolf to see how badly he was hurt. The heavy lead ball had ripped open a nasty gash high in his left thigh that was bleeding a lot. Zach put pressure on the wound with one hand while he took off his belt with the other to place a tourniquet just above it. Running Wolf was pale but he helped Zach as he used the handle of his knife to twist the belt tight, slowing the flow of blood.

Zach could hear one of the men whimpering as Jimbo came back to him, then only minutes later Red Hawk and Buffalo Heart moved in on the two men after they were convinced no others were with them.

The first man Jimbo had attacked had passed out and Red Hawk assumed he was dead but the second one just had a severely damaged arm. Both bones in his lower arm were broken and the flesh around them had been ripped away and damaged so severely his arm would likely have to be removed after they got him to a doctor in town.

Charles and Emma had heard the gunshots and were dressed in no time. Charles had an old model 1803 Harpers Ferry rifle. He checked the powder under the frizzen then they headed out to their friends camp. By the time they reached the oaks where Zach had set up camp the women had the fire built up and Raven Wing was working on Running Wolf's leg. He had only been wearing his breach cloth when he was hit so there wasn't any buckskin or canvas cloth from his new trousers in the wound.

Emma had Charles run back to the cabin for a clean sheet to make bandages and as soon as he returned, he and Zach saddled up to ride into the city to find the sheriff. It took them over an hour to find the on-duty deputy, but when they told him what had happened he went to another deputies house for more help and then to the doctors. The deputies drove a buckboard while the doctor had a single horse drawn Dearborn type carriage. Zach and Charles led them out to the pasture alongside the Dodds farm.

They could see the fire blazing through the darkness long before they reached the

Dodds pasture. The women had built the fire up much

larger than normal to provide more light for Raven Wing. She had finished bandaging Running Wolf's leg and was now doing what she could for these two men that had caused all this. Although she wasn't sympathetic to either of them, in fact she was only trying to keep them alive for Emma, None of the Indians understood why or what it meant when she said they must stand trial for what they have done.

The other man they had thought was dead moaned as Red Hawk and Buffalo Heart dragged him in close to the fire. His wounds although were severe and he had lost an awful lot of blood were not as deep as his partners were. Raven Wing had taken sinew and a needle and closed up the worst areas of his torn scalp and was just wrapping strips of the sheet around his head when the doctor and deputies arrived.

After hearing what had happened the doctor wasn't any more sympathetic than Raven Wing was but he examined Running Wolf and then the two that Jimbo had attacked. After examining each of them he turned and asked Raven Wing where she had received her medical training, saying he couldn't do any more than she had already done. He then looked at the mangled arm and said, "Mr. that arm has got to come off, there's no way it will ever heal up. If not, in a few days it'll get to stinking and then the poison will get into your blood and you'll die. That might happen anyway but you got a lot better chance if we take it off now." The man was in shock and didn't say a word, finally the doctor said, "Either now or in the jail a few hours from now won't make much difference, I suppose we'll wait till morning."

One of the deputies said, "I saw a man that had been mauled by a bear a couple of years ago and even he wasn't torn up this bad." He looked at Zach and continued, "You say your dog did this to both men by his self?" Zach silently tapped his leg and Jimbo came out from under his lean-to to him. The deputy shied away as the big dog approached, after seeing him he had no more questions.

As the deputies were loading the severely wounded men onto their buckboard the doctor carefully took his time and examined the gunshot wound in Running Wolf's thigh. Once he was satisfied he turned back to Raven Wing and asked again, "Ma'am, where did you get your medical training, I have never seen an Indian that had this good of training before and I have lived on the frontier for over twenty years."

She looked at him knowing he was paying her a compliment and said, "My training was by Blue Fox the great Medicine Man of my people the Shoshone and from the One Above that helps guide and teach me each day." Dr. Hogan smiled then ask what was in the poultice she had applied over the sinew stitches and she told him. He did not recognize the name she called the plants but when she showed him he smiled, amazed this young woman knew as much or maybe more about the healing plants than he did after all his training and years of being a doctor.

The doctor asked her why she had helped the men that had attacked them and she smiled and pointed to Emma who said, "So they can stand trial and be hanged. Men that would bushwhack our friend's right here on our farm shouldn't get to die that easily."

Dr. Hogan turned back to Raven Wing and asked, "Is that why you saved them?"

Raven Wing answered, "I saved them because Emma asked me to, I do not know what a trial is." She then shook her head and said, "I would not have let them die, I would have cut their throats for what they did to my husband."

Her tone hadn't changed any and the matter of fact way she said it made both Dr. Hogan and Emma believe that is exactly what would have happened.

The deputies asked Zach if he would ride into town in the morning and tell the sheriff just what had happened but Zach shook his head saying, "We are going to be raisin' a barn in the morning if the sheriff wants to talk, he can come out here." Neither deputy was going to argue with this large mountain man. Zach then turned to the men lying in the back of the deputies' buckboard and said, "You two is mighty lucky it was my dog that got to ya first. Any of the rest of us would have killed you both and drug ya out into the woods for the crows and buzzards." He then turned and walked back over to the fire to see how Running Wolf was doing.

The deputies didn't doubt that what Zach said was true and just as they were pulling out of the pasture onto the road leading into town one of them said, "I sure wouldn't want that bunch after me." His partner silently nodded then looked back, making sure the doctor was right behind them.

The next morning when Zach, Red Hawk, and Buffalo Heart got to the barn, Charles and Henry were already there laying out what needed to be done next. Red Hawk and Buffalo Heart were quite impressed with the hickory handled hatchets, to them they were fine weapons not building tools. Unlike Zach's Cherokee tomahawk, these hatchets had a large flat surface opposite the blade for pounding in nails or stakes.

Charles left for his day's work on the docks, feeling bad he couldn't stay and help. Henry, for only being twelve years old, was a stout and steady worker. Building with lumber was completely foreign to Red Hawk and Buffalo Heart, but they both were fast and eager learners.

By midmorning, the women came to see what they were doing and before long they too were helping, handing up boards and nails to the men. As lunchtime neared, Emma had Sun Flower and Shining Star helping her slice ham and get lunch ready. She had been out to her garden which had many things now being ready to harvest. She pulled a bunch of radishes and green onions, cut some broadleaf lettuce, picked some cucumbers, and chili peppers and even found a few ripe tomatoes.

It wasn't long until they had a feast set up for lunch. Red Hawk and Buffalo Heart had gone back to camp and helped Running Wolf over to the barn, and to Emma's surprise Charles got home just as they were eating.

The garden fresh vegetables were a delightful treat for the people that had never even heard of them before. The radishes, chili peppers, and narrow green onions were a particular delight to the men. Emma showed the women how to make them all sandwiches with sliced ham lettuce and tomato, it was another first for the Indians. They had put boiled jerky and even slices of roast meat on a biscuit before, but this was the first time they had ever had multiple ingredients between slices of freshly baked bread.

About midafternoon, the sheriff and another deputy came to the Dodds farm and they all could tell he was in a foul mood. He hadn't liked Zach not coming into town to meet with him over such a serious matter and now one of the men the dog attacked had died and the other had lost his arm.

The sheriff being upset didn't bother Zach at all, he had done no wrong and he wouldn't let any man, regardless of his title, push him at all. The sheriff was a perceptive man and within moments of meeting Zach Connors, he knew he was dealing with someone that would not be intimidated. After the sheriff heard Zach's story and saw the wound on Running Wolf's leg, he knew the two men had been in the wrong but what he couldn't figure out was what they thought to gain by bushwhacking a mountain man and a half-dozen Indians. The women would have made a good prize but there are plenty of willing women in St. Louis, he felt there had to be something more. Finally, he asked Zach what he thought the men were after but Zach just shook his head and told him he had no idea.

DURING THE NEXT FEW DAYS AS THE BARN WAS BEING raised, the competition between Red Hawk and Buffalo Heart with the use of the hatchets became intense. Every minute they weren't working, they were throwing the hatchets at a stump or seeing who could chop through a hard oak branch the fastest. The competition got so spirited they all got in on the game and had started to bet on the accuracy of their throws. Red Hawk was feeling so confident he challenged Grizzly Killer to the best of ten throws. Zach had used his Cherokee Tomahawk since he was just a boy and it had become like an extension of his own arm. Running Wolf had seen the deadly tomahawk used in battle several times and he warned Red Hawk and Buffalo Heart not to bet against Grizzly Killer with anything they didn't want to lose. With the confidence of youth and several days of practice, Red Hawk bet his belt knife against Grizzly Killer's that he could beat him the best of ten throws.

The hatchets were heavier than his tomahawk and they all laughed at Zach's first throw nearly missing the stump, being way too low. Not only was the throw low but it hit handle first and Zach was afraid it might have broken, but the hard hickory held and a couple of throws later Red Hawk was starting to feel less confident. They were tied at five throws each but now Zach was comfortable with the feel of the hatchet and took Red Hawk's prize knife, beating him six of the ten throws.

Zach didn't need or want Red Hawk's knife but he knew it would be an insult to his proud young friend not to take it and he put the knife under his belt and would figure out a way later to give it back to him without it being an insult.

Building the barn was the first time Charles had ever worked side by side with Indians and it soon became clear to him why Zach Connors liked these people. Many people at the time and in the area believed the Indians were no better than dangerous animals that needed to be exterminated, or at least moved further west so the land could be used for farming. After only a couple of days Charles Dodds saw how wrong they were. These were people that loved and laughed, they were intelligent and hardworking, but more than anything he found them to be faithful and loyal friends.

At lunch one day, Sun Flower called Zach by his Indian name, Emma looked puzzled and asked him why they called him Grizzly Killer. Zach shrugged his shoulders and said that was just his Indian name. She could tell by the way the others looked at him there was much more to the story so she turned to Sun Flower but she lowered her eyes not wanting to say more than her husband had. Running Wolf smiled and said, "Grizzly Killer tell them the story or I will," but he was embarrassed at the notoriety that had come along with the name so Running Wolf told them from the beginning. He told them of the day they had first met and Grizzly Killer had set his broken leg, and of the fight with the Shoshone Warriors that were after him. He told of him killing the great grizzly bear alone and of then making a gift of the bearskin and most of the meat to another group of Shoshone warriors. He told of the fight with Black Hand to save Shining Star from Black Hand and the defeating of Thunder Cloud the Great War Chief of the Blackfeet. He told them of Jimbo the great Medicine Dog that Grizzly Killer had trained from a pup. The Indians believe Jimbo could read Grizzly Killer's thoughts and that the medicine the two of them shared was stronger than any other. He told them the Ute's and Shoshone had been enemies for longer than any man had been alive but Grizzly Killer had changed that, now they were friends. He told them that Grizzly Killer was known throughout the Rocky Mountains as the greatest warrior, either red or white, that lived.

Emma was staring at Zach as Running Wolf talked. His head was down, not being comfortable hearing the praise his partner was saying about him. Charles wondered if Running Wolf wasn't exaggerating some and Henry's eyes were wide listening to the stories. Red Hawk and Buffalo Heart then told of Grizzly Killer, Running Wolf and the women saving them from a war party of Arapaho's and how Grizzly Killer, Running Wolf, Sun Flower, Raven Wing, and even the great medicine dog had killed the warriors that were torturing them and had killed their friend Sees Far.

Grizzly Killer finally said, "Enough of the stories, we've got a barn finish."

Emma then said, "Zach, it sounds like you have done a lot in the years since you left."

Zach answered her by saying, "The Rocky Mountains are a wild and dangerous wilderness and I have only done what I had to in order to survive and to protect my family and friends."

RUNNING Wolf's leg was improving each day but because of the wound, he could only watch as the barn was getting closer to being completed. The many different vegetables that were being grown in their garden had fascinated the women and Emma had spent time with them in the garden, telling them what each different one was. They found it amazing that these things could be planted and grown without having to walk along the creeks and hillside sides looking for the wild sego lily roots, camas bulbs, or any of the other plants the women used to supplement their diet. Being late in July many of the garden vegetables were ripe and Emma gave the women seeds from tomatoes, corn, summer squash, radishes, and peppers for them to take back with them to plant.

Young Henry liked the company; he enjoyed working with the Indians and was amazed after hearing all of the stories about the wild and savage Indians, but these people were as kind and thoughtful as any he had ever met. After work each day, Red Hawk and Buffalo Heart would take Henry out into the woods to teach him to track and hunt. They taught him different ways to set snares and traps. They had fixed him up with a simple Indian saddle on one of their spare horses as they spent all their free time in the woods together.

Zach had learned during the course of the last week that Charles had dreams of planting tobacco and hoped one day to be able to expand his farm. With him having to work the docks, there hadn't been enough time in the two years since they had come to St. Louis. The land next to his was available, and he told Zach that he had nearly fifty dollars saved of the four hundred it would take to buy it. He then hoped to be able to farm and grow cotton and tobacco; that cash crops would mean that neither Henry nor himself would have to work on the docks ever again.

The barn was erected and they were just finishing up the roof when Zach told everyone the next day he was going to town. That night around the fire with just his friends and family, he told of his reason for going into the city and asked if anyone wanted to go with him. Although none of them wanted to go into the crowded city again they all liked what he had said.

Zach knew very well none of them were comfortable in the city but he was very pleased that his goal of giving them a glimpse of the world outside of their beloved mountains and how the world of the white man had been successful. He wondered about Benny and Little Dove, and if they would be ready to head back west in just another week or so.

The next day with Charles working on the docks and Zach riding into town, Red Hawk and Buffalo Heart took Henry once again into the woods. The day started out differently than most had, it was Henry teaching these two Shoshone braves. Neither of them had ever seen a turtle before and just out of camp they came upon two of them sitting in the sun on the side of the creek. Once again Henry was amazed that they didn't know what a turtle was. He had never been anywhere that turtles weren't common and in his mind the Rocky Mountains must really be a strange place. Today, Jimbo had gone with the boys after Zach had told him to stay behind and the turtles were a mystery to him as well. When he approached, the turtles pulled their legs and feet in and closed up their shells as he sniffed and pawed at them. Henry picked one up to show his Indian companions and tell them all about them. He told them his ma made really good soup out of them.

Zach rode directly to the bank where he had exchanged his gold and ask to see Mr. Chouteau once again. Mr. Chouteau was glad to see him and wanted to know if something was wrong at the boarding house; he paid for a week but stayed only one night. Zach smiled and told him nothing was wrong, in fact, they had been treated wonderfully but the city was too crowded for them to feel comfortable and they were staying at the Dodds farm just out of town.

Zach then told Mr. Chouteau the reason for his visit, he wanted to purchase the quarter section of land just north of the Dodds farm. Mr. Chouteau smiled, thinking a wealthy man was going to settle there and the bank would have another wealthy patron. Zach went on asking if he could set up a bank account in the name of 12-year-old Henry Dodds and if the land could be put in Henry's name. Although Mr. Chouteau told him it was highly unusual, it could be done. Zach was told it would take a couple of days for the arrangements to be made for the land and that it would be necessary for an adult to able to sign along with Henry on his account. Zach agreed and gave him Emma Dodds name.

Zach told Mr. Chouteau that the Dodds would not be willing to accept what he was doing as a gift, so it needed to be completed and then given to Henry and Emma Dodds two weeks from now. He gave Mr. Chouteau twelve hundred dollars, instructing him that after the purchase of the land to put the remainder in the account in both Henry and Emma's name. Mr. Chouteau told him it was highly unusual to pay for the land even before the paperwork was drawn up but Zach smiled and said, "If General Ashley trusts you with his money then so do I."

Zach left the bank and was about to mount up when a shadow fell upon him. He turned to see a very large man standing there, blocking the sun. With the sun right behind his head, Zach didn't recognize the face of Ben Beaumont and asked, "Can I do somethin' for you mister?" Ben stepped off to the side as he held out his hand to shake with Zach. The face then became familiar and Zach remembered the fights he'd had with the Beaumont brothers. He shook Ben's hand and said, "Looks like ya made it back alright Ben." Ben smiled and nodded saying it was a long hard trip but he'd taken Grizzly Killers advice and made the journey in just under two months.

Ben then asked, "Can I buy you a drink, I got somethin' ya need to hear and I don't much want to tell out here in the open."

Zach could tell by the tone of his voice that Ben was serious and said, "I'll follow ya."

Zach followed Ben to an out of the way tavern and then hesitated before going inside after the big man. Although he wasn't carrying his Hawken, he felt the grip of his belt knife as he entered. He wanted to trust Ben but there was just a hint of uncertainty in his mind. Ben ordered whiskey for two but Zach shook his head telling Ben and the bartender he never drank. Ben looked at him and smiled saying, "I never met nobody that didn't drink before."

Zach smiled and told him, "I've lived in the wilderness my whole life and the only place you can get liquor is at Rendezvous, I guess I just never got a taste for the stuff."

Ben said, "My pa drank all the time it seems like, least when he wasn't beatin' on one of us boys, so we started sneakin' his bottles, drinkin' by the time we was 'bout ten or eleven years old. Maybe that is why Cal and Bull turned out so mean."

Zach could tell Ben was having a hard time saying what was on his mind and finally asked, "What is it Ben, what's botherin' ya."

Ben looked him in the eye's and said, "I know most men would have killed me and left me out there to die but you helped me that day. Cal was bent on killing you so I feel I owe you. The sheriff let that feller yer dog attacked go, after the doctor cut off his arm. He figured shootin' an Injun wasn't no crime anyway. That feller's name is Isaac Marsden and he has been gettin' his friends talked into goin' back out to where yer camped and killin' yer dog. He says you got enough money on you none of 'em would have to work fer a year."

Zach asked, "Do know this for sure."

Ben nodded, and said, "Yeah, they tried to get me to go with 'em, and they is plannin' this fer tonight." Zach shook his head and Ben continued, "But that ain't the worst of it, one of the sheriff's deputies is some relative of the fellow the dog killed and he's got the sheriff and deputies already to string ya up."

Zach laid a ten dollar gold piece on the table and said, "Thank you, Ben, I could see that day along Black's Fork you were a good man, this drink's on me."

Zach left the tavern and mounted up on Ol' Red; he was deep in thought, figuring out just what to do. He knew it would be safest just to go back and load up and leave, there was really nothing left for him to do in St. Louis, other than he wanted to get Running Wolf a Hawken rifle if he could. His Pennsylvania long rifle was a nice accurate weapon but it was a lot heavier than a Hawken was. The thought of running from a fight didn't sit well with him, but he knew his own feeling were secondary to keeping his family safe.

He asked a man on the street if he knew where the Hawken Brothers' gun shop was and made his way there. Upon entering the shop, Samuel Hawken was helping a customer at the counter while his brother Jake was working on one of the newest cap lock actions. They had several rifles on display and Zach was looking them over when Jake Hawken came forward, still holding the lock in his hand. Zach was curious and asked about it. Jake told him it was a new firing system. These little caps fit over a nipple and then exploded into the powder when the hammer strikes the cap. Zach asked what made the spark, Jake Hawken tried to explain but even he didn't understand it well enough to explain to Zach. He told Zach they were just experimenting right now but someday he thought all rifles would have a caplock action instead of a flintlock.

Zach asked if there was any .50 calibers for sale and Jake Hawken smiled and said, "We just finished a .50 and we have a .54 that a man had ordered and can't pick up 'cause he was killed in an accident on the river." Zach had decided long ago the money he had sitting in a bank in St. Louis would never do him any good, so spending it didn't bother him a bit. He bought both rifles and the bullet molds, two dozen English Flints, a small keg of powder and twenty pounds of lead bars. If he had a fight coming up he had decided he was going to be well armed. It came to $98.50 and as Zach counted out the gold and silver the smile on Jake Hawken's face grew. Zach wasn't wearing his buckskins, he was dressed like most of the working men in St. Louis, but there was something about him that made Jake Hawken's think he was a trapper and he said, "Must have just brought in your plews." Zach smiled and nodded then carried out the supplies and hung them from his saddle. Jake and Samuel brought out the rifles. When Samuel saw Zach didn't have a scabbard for even one rifle he hurried back to the shop and brought out a pair that was custom made for their rifles. Zach smiled and handed him another $5.00 coin and the two brothers helped tie the scabbards onto his saddle.

It was mid-afternoon when Zach reached the Dodds farm, Charles had just gotten there and was starting to work on the barn door. He saw Zach ride into the pasture and waved. Zach waved back but didn't stop. Running Wolf was now walking on his own but he was slow and limped badly. They all could tell something was wrong when Zach stepped out of the saddle. He asked where Red Hawk and Buffalo heart were, and just nodded when Shining Star told him they were with Henry in the woods. He nodded and figured they wouldn't be back until evening.

He told them what Ben Beaumont had said and then added, "We can pack up and run but there is no way to know if Charles, Emma, and their children will be safe from men set on revenge." He then rode over to the barn and told Charles the same thing, then asked him to bring Emma and Charlotte out to their camp and together they would decide what to do.

CHARLES AND EMMA WALKED THROUGH THE PASTURE toward the oaks where Zach was camped. Charles was carrying Charlotte with one arm and his Kentucky long rifle in the other. Emma had a worried look on her face and showed even more concern when she saw the serious looks on of all the others. Zach went over what he had been told by Ben Beaumont again and it was Running Wolf that said first, "Grizzly Killer I don't see how we can run and leave the Dodds unprotected."

Zach nodded his agreement but Charles said, "It is not us they are after we should be fine."

As Zach looked at him and then Emma, he could see how frightened she was and he said, "You may be right, but do you want to take the chance of gettin' Emma and Charlotte hurt if you are not."

Charles shook his head and said, "So what do we do?"

Zach had been thinking about this as he rode from the city and said, "First thing is for you Charles, to take all of the women and children to safety. You know this country better than any of us. Do you have a safe place where you can take them?"

Emma spoke then, looking at Charles she said, "What about that place on the creek where we go for a picnic."

Charles smiled and nodded his head as he looked at Zach and said, "It is a clearing about two miles up the creek they will be safe there, I will get them set and be back."

Zach shook his head and said, "No Charles you stay there to protect them, I could have one of the boys stay with them but you have to live here after we leave, it would be much safer for Emma and Charlotte if you were not seen with us." Charles frowned but nodded he understood, he did not want to be seen as not being as brave or unwilling to fight to Emma, as the man she had waited so long for was.

Charles knew there was nothing between Emma and Zach anymore, but he could also tell by the look on her face that she still cared for him. He also knew Zach was right, they had to live here, and no one could think he had any part of what was going to happen tonight. Zach, looking at Charles again asked, "Does Henry have a gun of his own?"

Before Charles could answer Emma with a look of horror on her face, shouted, "He's too young, you can't expect him to fight."

Zach nodded and said, "You're right and I don't, but I want to know y'all are protected. Sun Flower and Shining Star both have rifles and Raven Wing has her bow, if both Charles and Henry have rifles I will know you are well protected and won't worry about it."

Emma felt foolish for the way she had reacted but the worry and concern was overpowering. Charles answered Zach and said, "Yes, he must have it with him, it wasn't in the house."

Zach brought up Running Wolf's horse and a pack

horse, then asked Running Wolf if he could ride. He looked at Zach and said, "Yes I can ride but I'm not goin' nowhere, somebody has to stay here and tend the fire and make camp look normal if you're plannin' what I think you are. You're goin' to need me right here in camp."

Sun Flower then spoke. "I am not leaving either my husband, you do not know how many men will come and I can shoot too. Our camp will look more natural if I am with Running Wolf." Zach shook his head, he knew his bold brash wife well enough to know that he wasn't going to win this argument. Although both Shining Star and Raven Wing wanted to stay, but they both knew protecting Star and Grey Wolf was their first responsibility.

As the women were fixing the evening meal, Red Hawk, Buffalo Heart, and Henry came back to camp. Henry was carrying two cottontail rabbits and three squirrels. As they walked in Buffalo Heart said to him, "Henry get them critters skinned and ready for the pot." He then saw the serious looks of everyone in camp and asked, "What has happened?"

As Henry was skinning and cleaning the rabbits and squirrels, Zach told Buffalo Heart and Red Hawk what had happened. The thought of battle excited both of the young warriors. They were young and felt invincible and although they had already proven themselves in battle against the hated Blackfeet and Arapaho, they wanted to prove both their bravery and skill in battle against an unknown enemy. Like most Indian cultures, these two young men had been raised to be warriors and they knew the greater their prowess in battle, the more important they became in the eyes of their village. They both wanted to be as great of warriors as Spotted Elk or Grizzly Killer and Running Wolf was, and they needed to fight to prove themselves.

Zach could see the excitement on the faces of his two young friends and tried to calm the excitement they both were feeling, but the thrill of an impending battle was running through their veins and finally he just said, "Boys we have to follow a plan and please don't kill if it is not necessary." They both nodded they understood, they both respected Grizzly Killer and both trusted him completely, they would do whatever he asked of them.

Zach could tell Charles was feeling left out, that they thought he couldn't handle a fight. He looked Charles in the eye and said, "Me and Runnin' Wolf are trustin' you to protect our families. It is the greatest responsibility and we would not ask that of any man we didn't know could do it."

Charles nodded he understood and the respect he had for this man that he had once hated and been jealous of grew even more. He thought back to Pottersville and waiting for Emma to finally agree to marry him. He had never met Zach Connors but he hated him, knowing he was Emma's first choice. Even though Charles knew Emma was his wife now, the feelings he had about Zach were difficult for him to suppress. Both Emma and Zach knew it and both respected him even more because he did.

As the sun set once again the color of the sky was spectacular. Although there were few clouds, just as the sun disappeared the whole western edge of the sky turned blaze orange and looking west Zach thought about the mountains and home. He felt so far away and he was ready to go back again.

He had been raised and learned many of his skills in the heavily wooded hills of Kentucky but the Rocky Mountains were now his home and he missed them. He hoped this journey had succeeded in showing his friends and family why it was important to learn the white man's ways. To learn that someday they must live among them, for Zach knew there was no way to stop the westward expansion of America. He didn't know how long it would take but he knew just in his lifetime the country had moved from the Appalachians to west of the Mississippi. He knew the Corp of Discovery led by Meriwether Lewis and William Clark had blazed a trail all the way to the Pacific Ocean. Men like William Ashley, Jedidiah Smith, William Sublette, and even himself were finding the routes and blazing the trails that would eventually lead settlers west. Just like they did in Kentucky, first would come the settlers, clearing the land and planting their crops, then the businessmen would come to sell to and buy from the settlers, and soon towns would be built and the wilderness would be settled. He hoped it didn't happen in his lifetime but he knew deep within himself it would and his children would have to be prepared for it.

Sun Flower broke his thoughts when she walked up beside him and told him their food was ready. Their supper was a stew that included the rabbits and squirrels that Henry had taken during his day in the woods with his new friends, and turnips, carrots, and potatoes from Emma's garden. Shining Star started to make biscuits like they always had but Emma showed her to leave out the baking powder and drop small spoons full of the dough into the stew. The dumplings were another first for them and they all enjoyed it.

As the light faded they all stayed around the fire in case they were being watched, they didn't want anything to look out of the ordinary. After full darkness they put their supplies under their robes to look like they were sleeping. Staying in the shadows, Charles took his family along with Raven Wing, Shining Star and their little ones into the woods roughly following the path of the creek. It took over a half hour but they arrived in the clearing safely. Running Wolf told Luna to go with them and told Charles to watch the wolf that she would know if anyone was coming toward them long before anyone else.

The moon was just peeking over the treetops when they arrived and with its light, Shining Star and Raven Wing could see this grass-covered meadow with the creek running along its side was indeed a nice place. However, the worry about the rest of their family made the beauty of the meadow meaningless to them all.

Running Wolf really couldn't move around at least not comfortably and so he sat by the fire with his bullet mold, turning narrow lead bars into .50 caliber round balls all evening. Zach presented the new .50 caliber Hawken to him. It was a full ten inches shorter than his Pennsylvania made long rifle and at least three pounds lighter, but since he had never shot it he chose the long one at least for tonight. By the time Zach was ready to sneak out of camp, Running Wolf had a pile of three dozen more deadly round balls ready to be loaded and fired. They hadn't had time to mold any of the larger .54 Caliber balls so the .54 Hawken stayed in its scabbard.

Zach threw more wood on the fire and waited for it flare up, then he stood there in its light, stretched and faked a yawn. Then as if he was going to bed, he crawled under his lean-to. He rolled out the dark side of it and slowly crawled through the grass into the woods. He had Jimbo stay in camp for now, he knew a simple whistle and he would be by his side within seconds.

A few minutes later Red Hawk and Buffalo Heart, doing the same thing Zach had done, met him out in the woods. Zach didn't know what to expect or when these people he truly believed were coming for him and his dog would be there. He wasn't sure why, but just like when he had first met him along Black's Fork, Zach trusted Ben Beaumont. Even though he had killed both of Ben's brothers, he sensed Ben was different and he was sure the men Ben had told him about were going to attack sometime before morning.

Zach figured if he was planning this attack he would try to surround the camp and attack from all sides. Besides Running Wolf and Sun Flower by the fire, there were only the three of them. He had to go back and get Running Wolf and Sun Flower out of camp without anyone that may be watching knowing it. Red Hawk told him he could do it and within fifteen minutes he was lying in the grass next to his lean-to, telling them both to slowly let the fire die down and go to their robes just like he had, and make their way into the woods. When Red Hawk returned, Zach handed him back his prized knife that he had won from him in a challenge saying, "You may need this, my friend." Red Hawk hesitated then smiled with a slight nod and put the knife back in its sheath on his belt.

When Running Wolf got to the edge of the woods Zach met him, his leg was throbbing with pain but as long as Zach had known his partner, he had never heard him complain. From where they were, Running Wolf was about forty yards from the fire and although it was rapidly dying down, the nearly full moon had risen over the trees and was providing enough light that anyone entering their camp would be an easy target.

Red Hawk and Zach were out in the tall meadow grass and as usual, Jimbo was right by Zach's side. Running Wolf was right where Zach had left him leaning against a tree while Sun Flower and Buffalo Heart had split up, one on each side of Running Wolf.

It was over two hours later that Jimbo's ears perked up and as Zach watched his big medicine dog he could see the hair start to rise on his neck and down his back, then the low growl from deep in his throat started. Zach moved his hand in just a half circle, telling Jimbo to circle behind the intruders and then wait. Zach put his hands to his mouth and the sound of a screech owl shattered the silence of the night. His call alerted his friends and family that the men seeking revenge were here. Within minutes he could see four men sneaking toward the oak trees where their camp was set up. Then another crept by only twenty feet opposite of him. That made five he could see and he wondered how many he couldn't see.

He wondered just what they were going to do, were these men of the caliber that would just kill everyone in their camp including women and children or would take their revenge out on Zach and Jimbo. Suddenly a cold calm came over him as he realized it didn't matter, these men wouldn't be sneaking in at night if their intentions weren't bad. He had instructed everyone not to fire first, to let the intruders make the first move. Now as he laid there in the grass, watching these five men he wondered if that was a mistake.

The five men Zach was watching stopped about twenty yards from the fire, which was now nothing more than glowing coals. He was about thirty yards behind them and although he could see Jimbo, he didn't believe his big dog was any further than a good leap behind one the men. Zach watched as they raised their rifles and as they did he saw just a glimpse of movement on the far side of camp and he knew then there were indeed others that he hadn't been able to see.

The bright flash of burning powder split the darkness and the sound of their rifles rang out through the warm humid air of the summer night. Zach waited to fire, he wanted to make sure where each and every one of them was. A moment after they shot the seven men charged the lean-tos, smashing their rifle butts into what they thought were the now wounded and dying. Zach fired and just as he did so did the rest. The men that had survived that volley knew they had been fooled and the four of them turned and ran, abandoning their dead and dying friends to their own fate.

One of them made it about ten feet when a Shoshone arrow with a tip made from barrel strapping hit him in the throat, the deadly iron tip lodging in his spine killing him instantly. Raven Wing had returned, leaving Gray Wolf with Shining Star, knowing if anything was to happen to her Shining Star and Sun Flower would raise Gray Wolf as their own.

Two of the bad guys didn't fare so well, Jimbo attacked just as one of them turned to run. The pain and fear could be heard in his scream but it lasted a mere moment. Jimbo's deadly jaws clamped down on his throat. Another man tripped and fell into the fire reaching out with both hands to break his fall and put them right into the center of the still glowing coals. The last made it nearly twenty yards out of camp when Buffalo Heart threw his new hatchet, hitting the scared and fleeing man directly in the face.

From start to finish the battle hadn't lasted more than fifteen seconds, and four of the seven men were dead, two others had severe gunshot wounds and the last one's hands were burned so badly he couldn't use them at all.

Zach stood watching for any other movement before slowly walking toward the fire. Although he had seen gruesome scenes before and had been forced to kill on many occasions, he hated having to do so. He knew that as long as there were men like these in the world he would do whatever he must to protect his family and friends.

BENNY AND LITTLE DOVE WERE AWAKE AT THE CRACK of dawn, listening to the birds in the woods welcoming the new day. Little Dove stood and stretched and Benny watched with delight as the dim light reflected off her naked body. She walked over to the edge of the swimming hole and just as Benny had done so many times as a boy, she dove into the cool water. A moment later Benny joined her and suddenly skinning dipping in the old swimming hole took on a whole new meaning for him.

As they dressed, Benny had her dress in her simple doeskin dress, knowing she would be much more comfortable than she was in the store-bought clothes. She smiled as she slipped the dress over her shoulders and felt the freedom of movement she was so used to.

Their horses were on rather long hobbles and had the freedom to reach the creek for water so with just a quick check making sure they were okay, they left for the cabin.

They could smell frying bacon and coffee as they approached the cabin and Benny could hear his brothers in the barn doing the morning chores. He noticed they had turned the big shire mares out into the pasture with the mules where there was ample grass, and Jacob was giving some grain to their donkey studs.

His mother was still cutting thick slices of bacon and Rachael was frying it in two large black iron skillets as Benny and Little Dove came inside. Since Benny had left home his pa had turned the fireplace in the cabin into a cooking stove by laying rock and mortar on the two sides and in front. He had purchased a flat iron plate to lay across the top and sealed it with mortar with an opening in the side to add wood. It had made cooking and keeping the family fed much easier for his mother and sisters, and still provided plenty of heat for the winter.

They all stopped what they were doing for a moment to greet Benny and Little Dove, and Benny noticed them all look at her dress. Rachael smiled as she looked at how much more comfortable she looked and said so. Little Dove smiled and asked, "Why do white women wear so many clothes? My dress is cooler and easier to move in."

Their mother laughed which caught them all off guard then said, "That is a question I would like to know the answer to myself." Both Rachael and Fae were shocked their mother would say such a thing for she was always making sure the two of them were properly dressed.

Bacon was another first for Little Dove, the salty smoky flavor was a delight and so were the grits flavored with the bacon grease. The hot biscuits were like the ones she had learned to make from Sun Flower, they tasted a bit different made with lard than hers did that was made with bear grease but she truly enjoyed the new tastes. There was a large platter of fried eggs and they ate their fill. Eggs were plentiful in the summer although the chickens laid year-round, in the summer they produced two or three times more than in the winter.

That day and the next several days, Little Dove spent most of her time with Rachael and Fae, the two of them were fascinated with their sister-in-law and Little Dove loved hearing them tell of Benny when he was younger. Benny worked the farm with his father and younger brothers. He could tell his brothers would be farmers, they were both proud of the farm and the mules they bred. Jacob was particularly fond of the mules and the big shire mares, he cared for them as if they were children.

Benny and his pa watched as Jacob and Albert harnessed two young two-year-old mules for the first time and was amazed at the tender manner they used. Jacob loved the mules and horses and they responded to him with, what appeared to Benny, to be a love of their own. Benny wondered if it was hard for him to sell them after he had raised and trained them. His pa answered that question by saying, "Yes and no, he does get attached to them but he takes great pride that the mules he trains go all around the country doing the jobs he has trained them to do." His pa told Benny that he believed if it wasn't for the mules, Jacob would have left the farm just like he had.

Benny felt the need to try and explain why he had left, but his Pa stopped him and told him there was no need that he understood. He then told Benny the story of when he left home and the feelings he had, it was something Benny had never heard before and made him feel so much better that his father understood.

As the two of them leaned against the fence and talked they watched the two boys working the team of young mules. His father asked Benny about his life in the mountains and about Little Dove. He had sensed that there were things Benny didn't want to say in front of his mother.

He told his Pa the story of his friend being killed in a drunken knife fight in St. Louis and that is why he left the river. He told of the long hard journey to the Rockies and of the four men he went with and they had turned out to be worse than most of the men on the river and then that first winter meeting Grub and Ely. Mathew Lambert could tell the love and respect his son had for these two by not only what he said but the tone in his voice as he talked about them, and he was thankful Benny had found good men to teach him an all-new way of life. Benny told of Ely getting shot by the very men he had gone west with and him tracking them down. He told his father about finding Little Dove trying to escape the massacre of her village by the Blackfeet. How she had seen her parents and everyone she had ever known and loved, tortured and killed. He told of Grizzly Killer, whose real name was Zach Connors, that he was from Kentucky and how he had become as good of a friend as Grub and Ely were. He told his Pa of the land and mountains and the Shoshone people all over again, and there was no doubt in the mind of his father that Benny had found a life he truly loved.

Mathew Lambert had always hoped his oldest son would take over his farm someday but now he understood that was never meant to be. Although he had known Benny was not a farmer by the time he was a teenager, he had always hoped he would change. Now he was happy for his son, he had found a life that truly made him happy. As he watched his two younger boys working with the mules he knew they would keep the farm going long after he was gone.

Little Dove had not understood what this wedding

everyone was excited about was, and Rachael explained it to her by telling her it was a ceremony that the preacher performed to marry a man and woman and make them husband and wife. Little Dove was still puzzled and asked, "What is a preacher?" The girls looked at one another not knowing how to answer her, it was their mother that after sitting down with them, told Little Dove the preacher was like their Medicine Man, that he taught them about God and how God expects every one of his children to live a good life. She told Little Dove about the Bible that the preacher taught from and how they believed all were God's children. Little Dove smiled as she started to understand and told her newfound family about the Shoshone belief in the One Above, the maker of all things.

Although Little Dove had never heard of the Bible or its teachings, because of her love of Benny and her belief that he and Grizzly Killer were good men, it was easy for her to believe this Bible must be good and she would stand with Benny while their preacher performed the ceremony, making them man and wife in the eyes of God. She smiled, believing that if the One Above and God were the same maker of all things, that she and Benny were already man and wife in his eyes.

That afternoon Bess Applegate and her mother came to the farm to see Jacob and make further plans for the wedding. Bess's mother, Anna Applegate was surprised and shocked that they were now planning a double wedding. She remembered Benny from church but she didn't understand how he or any white man could actually marry one of the savages that had killed her family back in Ohio. Margaret and Rachael were both glad Little Dove was with Benny right now as they tried to reassure Anna Applegate that Little Dove was not a Shawnee and she was anything but a savage. Bess didn't know what to say, she didn't want her mother's hatred of Indians and what had happened when she was a child to ruin her wedding. She also didn't understand why her special day had suddenly become something totally different, either.

Bess had never met an Indian before and could remember the preacher saying over and over in church that we were all God's children and she didn't understand her mother's hatred. Bess knew her mother's family had been killed by the Shawnee but Anna Applegate had never told anyone, not even her husband, about the horrible memories she had when a Shawnee raiding party had attacked her family's farm.

Her voice was shaky as she told them about what had happened that day so long ago. Their farm was just a mile north of the Ohio River in Hamilton County, just west of Cincinnati. She was just 10 years old and was out throwing feed to the chickens when the Shawnee came to the farm. Her father met them and they seemed friendly enough. They were showing him some furs like they wanted to trade, when suddenly two of them grabbed him and another scalped him while he was still alive, then they cut his throat and laughed as he bled to death. This was the first time in her life she had spoken of that day and the memory so long suppressed was what had festered into a blind hatred of all Indians.

Once she started talking she felt she had to continue, it felt like a heavy weight was being lifted from her. She told how her mother ran out of the cabin toward her, but the Indians caught her and beat her ripping off all her clothes and when they were done with her they scalped her as well. Anna was shaking as she stared blankly forward as if she was watching it happen all over again. She told them she could still feel the heat from the burning cabin on her face and could see the arrow-riddled body of her brother lying in the dirt as he had run to try and help their mother. She told of hearing the screams of her baby sister as she was trapped inside the cabin. She told them of how the Indians just ignored her like she wasn't even there and she never understood why they killed her family but never harmed her.

Bess was horrified by what had happened thirty years before and in tears seeing the pain her mother was in. She hugged her and could feel the trembling and suddenly the tears started. It was the first time Bess had ever seen her mother cry, in fact, it was the first time Anna Applegate had cried over that horrible day.

Little Dove had come back to the cabin and had been standing just outside the door and had heard everything Anna Applegate had said. It brought back her own memories of the Blackfeet attack on her village. She understood more than any of the others what Anna Applegate had gone through. Little Dove stepped through the door and they all turned and looked at her. She could see the searing hatred in the eyes of Mrs. Applegate, even through the tears that were still flowing freely from them. She nervously stepped toward her. Bess, still holding her mother could feel her body tense as Little Dove knelt on the floor before her.

Little Dove started to speak to her and told her that she too had seen her parents killed by Indians, that the Blackfeet had staked her father to the ground and started fires on his feet slowly burning him to death, that her mother's head was caved in with their war clubs and everyone she had ever loved was killed that day. She told her of how Benny had saved her from the Blackfeet.

As Little Dove talked, Bess could feel her mother start to relax. This was the first time in Anna Applegate's life she had ever heard an Indian speak English, and for the first time started to realize they had feelings just like any other people. With the burning hatred she had held inside of her throughout her life, she had never believed any Indian was capable of human emotion. Now this pretty dark-haired young woman before her spoke with the same feelings that she had. She could see the tears well up in Little Dove's eyes as she told them all of that day on Ham's Fork, how it was the worst day of her life and yet without that day happening she and Benny would not have found each other.

Anna Applegate had feelings now she did not understand. It was like her own words and tears had started to release the hatred she had held on to so tightly her entire life. She felt sorry for this Indian woman kneeling before her, and before today that would never have happened. For the first time in her life she knew she was not alone in the pain she felt and because of that, she was drawn toward Little Dove. Anna reached out to Little Dove and held her tightly. She had emotions she never felt before, even with her husband and her children. None of them could possibly know the way she felt, but the Indian woman did and that made her feel close to her.

Bess did not understand the way her mother felt, she had never before seen her like this. Not only was it the first time she had ever seen her cry but now she was holding on to this Indian woman she had never met before like she was one of her own children.

A moment later, she released Little Dove and they both wiped the tears from their eyes. Little Dove and Anna had shared something that neither one of them understood but the closeness they felt for one another was a bond they both would feel for the rest of their lives.

The house was quiet as they all felt that the tension was

gone. Anna was embarrassed, she had bared her deepest feeling before these people that up until today had been only acquaintances. She had shared with them things she had never even told her husband but in doing so a great weight had been lifted from her. She felt as if she had been reborn.

Bess had always loved her mother and she knew her mother loved her but she had always believed she was a hard stern woman. Today however, she saw a side of her mother she had never known existed and she had learned the reason for her hardness.

For the next week, these women spent time every day together as they planned the wedding. In Bess's mind, her mother had become a different person, the hard edge she always had was gone and she seemed happier than Bess had ever seen her. Bess's father John had noticed the change and thought it was just the excitement of the wedding that had her feeling so happy. It was only Anna that truly knew, the hatred she had always held had kept her from knowing real happiness throughout her life and that hatred was gone. It had been lifted from her by the act of someone she had just met, to whom her hatred had been directed, an Indian woman from a land she would never see.

ZACH SENT JIMBO FOR SHINING STAR AND THE DODDS while Red Hawk and Buffalo Heart removed the bodies from camp. The man with the burned hands was just sitting there by the fire in obvious pain, a look of both terror and regret on his face. One of the wounded men had been hit high in the shoulder and couldn't move his arm, the other was lying unconscious and at first, they thought he was dead. As Red Hawk and Buffalo Heart went to move him he moaned and a closer look revealed his only wound was a crease in his hair. The lead ball had knocked him out but did very little damage, there were only tiny beads of blood seeping slowly from the shallow furrow that the ball had plowed across his skull. As he came around he had a pounding headache and was confused for a couple of minutes, before he realized just how bad a situation he was in. Then the confusion turned to fear as Zach tied his hands behind his back.

Raven Wing had dropped her bow now the fight was over, and had gone out to help Running Wolf come back to the fire. Sun Flower was with him and with the sisters on each side of him they were back in camp in just a couple of minutes.

Sun Flower built up the fire to provide light and the man with burned hands scooted away from its heat. Raven Wing brought their pouch of bear grease and offered to put it on his hands. At first he shied away from her, but as she was backing away he changed his mind and held his severely burned hands out.

Sun Flower and Zach helped the one with the shoulder wound over to the fire. Although the bleeding had nearly stopped, he had lost a lot of blood and was pale and weak. He tensed, and she could see the fear in his eyes, but there was also something else behind it. Raven Wing sensed it more than she could see it and it caused her to pause, she wondered if she should help this man or kill him. What she sensed was evil, and a deep hatred of her and her people. She turned to Zach and said, "Grizzly Killer, this man has evil in his heart, he will kill any of us if he gets the chance."

Zach didn't question what Raven Wing had said, he just walked over, pulled his pistol from under his belt and pressed the barrel to the man's temple and said, "Mister, it would be a lot less trouble to kill you right now than it is to treat that shoulder, which do you prefer?"

At that moment the fear was overpowering and he dropped his head and with a shaky voice said, "Help me." Raven Wing still wasn't sure she should as she pulled her knife and started to cut the shirt away from the ragged wound.

Jimbo came running back into camp as Zach started to question the man he had tied up. He asked his name but no response, then he asked why they had attacked them. The man just stared forward, then Zach bent down and said, "I got all the time in the world but I don't think you do."

Zach saw a flash of uncertainty in the man's face, then trying to be tough he said, "You go to hell you stinkin' Injun lovin' squaw man."

Anger flashed in Zach's eyes but his demeanor never changed. He turned around to Red Hawk and Buffalo Heart and said, now speaking Shoshone, "Will you two stake him out?"

As they walked forward, the man now in panic yelled at Zach, "What are you goin' to do to me?"

Zach turned and said, "Mister I ain't goin' to do nothin' to ya." Then turned toward where Raven Wing was working on the bullet wound in the other man's shoulder, he knelt down and started asking this man why they had come out here and attacked their camp. He was in shock from the wound and all Zach got from him was a blank stare.

As Zach stood back up, he saw Luna was back with Running Wolf and then the smile on Shining Stars face as she walked in and saw everyone was alright. The look on Emma's face was one of pure horror as she saw Red Hawk and Buffalo Heart just finishing staking the obstinate man to the ground. Charles didn't say a word but turned Charlotte's head into his shoulder as Emma asked Zach, "What are going to do to that man?"

Zach, with a very matter of fact tone, said, "We are going to find out why so many men came out here to kill us tonight and apparently he needs a little encouragement to talk." Then looking at Charles he said, "It would be better if you and Emma took Henry and Charlotte home."

Charles asked if he needed to go after the sheriff but Zach shook his head, saying, "From what I was told I believe he already knows and will do nothing about it anyway. All you have done is rented us this pasture in trade for lumber, so no one can say you had any part of this. We will be leaving tomorrow or the day after and if the sheriff or anyone else wants to come after us, we will be a long ways from your family." Charles nodded, and Zach as well as Sun Flower saw a sadness cross Emma's face but only for a moment before she turned toward her husband and they walked the quarter mile to their cabin.

Zach walked back over to where the man was staked to the ground and asked, "Do you feel like talkin' now," but the man just stared at Zach with hatred-filled eyes. Zach nodded that he understood and turned to Sun Flower, once again speaking in Shoshone, asked her to build a fire between his legs. Sun Flower didn't hesitate as she brought small branches and twigs they used to start their big fire and piled them up well above his knees. Zach again knelt down and said, "Mister if you've ever seen this done you'd know it ain't pleasant. All I want is information as to why you came out here after us and who put you up to it. You tell me that and all of this will go away and in a few days you will be back home."

Although the man didn't seem to have the fortitude he did just moments before he said, "You ain't gonna do nothin', you're a white man."

Zach turned to Sun Flower and nodded. He watched the man straining to see what was happening as Sun Flower brought a burning branch from the fire and started the pile of twigs between his legs on fire. Zach told him one more time he could stop this at any time. As the flames grew and he could feel the heat start to get intense on his inner thighs and manhood, panic set in and almost in a pleading voice shouted out, "If I tell you they will kill me."

Zach, in his calm voice asked, "Just what do you think that fire is going to do to you?"

Another minute and his trousers were starting to smoke and he shouted in sheer panic, "Okay it was Virgil Hathaway, he wanted y'all dead, said we could have all the money."

Zach asked, "What money?"

The man, now nearly, pleading said, "Put out the fire, I'll tell ya anything."

Zach nodded again and Buffalo Heart kicked the fire out from between his legs and as he did he looked at Red Hawk and said, "He is no warrior, only a man with his manhood burned."

At that, they both laughed and Zach still kneeling by the man said, "I'm waiting or do you want them to build the fire again? If they do it will not be put out."

He then told Zach that Frank, the man that died from the dog attack was Virgil's cousin and it was Virgil that arranged the attack tonight. He went on telling Zach that Frank saw all the money he had when he bought the wood from the boatyard and that he and Daniel thought they could take it from him. He told Zach that Virgil was a deputy to the sheriff and that was why he didn't come out himself. "He told us all we could have all the money after we killed you and the Injuns."

Zach understood then that he hadn't been nearly as careful as he should have with that much money, and once again he remembered the dream years ago, when his father appeared to him and had told him he had never learned of the treachery of men. He stood up and stared out into the darkness and thought about what his pa had said in that dream, and he knew it was true, it seemed to him he would never learn. Zach did understand that he had always trusted men until their actions proved they couldn't be trusted and that is the way he preferred to live. He believed the world would be a very unhappy place if one doubted and suspected everyone they meet. He didn't have a suspicious or treacherous mind and he decided right then and there he was not ever going to change his outlook.

Zach believed in justice, he knew some would consider it the same as revenge, but he did not. Justice was making one pay for their actions; revenge to Zach meant getting even with someone for your own gratification. For this attack on his camp he would demand justice for the man that had set it up, and had caused all this death and mayhem. He was a deputy sheriff and Zach already knew, in this case, the law would not deliver justice for these men.

By daylight, the bodies of the dead had been loaded onto pack horses and buried miles away in the thick woods west of the city. The three survivors were still in camp and wondering just what this big mountain man and Indians were going to do to them. So far Zach figured none of the three wounded men had associated the Dodds with any of the actions he had taken against the men that had attacked them and he wanted to keep it that way. Once again speaking Shoshone, he asked Red Hawk and Buffalo Heart to take the three of them out into the woods, far enough they could not see or hear what was going on in camp.

As Red Hawk cut the rawhide from the stakes that had the man staked to the ground, he sat up and carefully touched his legs and groin. The burns were not serious but they were blistered and uncomfortable enough that he would not be walking far or riding a horse for a few days. The one with the shoulder wound was now alert but weak from the loss of blood. Zach figured the one with burned hands would not have the use of them for many days, maybe even weeks. He looked at the three of them in the eyes before they were marched away and said, "If you want to stay in these woods forever like your friends, all you have to do is to not listen to me. It will much easier for us to kill you all than to keep you alive." Zach could see they needed no further convincing.

Red Hawk and Buffalo Heart preferred spending their time in the woods and gladly marched the three wounded men nearly a half mile and into a small clearing they had found. Zach had Jimbo go with them, for he was going into the city one more time. He wanted to check with Mr. Chouteau at the bank before they left for good.

AT THE BANK, Maurice Chouteau showed Zach the deed to the land recorded in young Henry's name and the bank book, also in the name of Henry Dodds, with Emma Dodds in control of the money until Henry became an adult. When Zach asked how much he owed him for taking care of it all, Mr. Chouteau told him that was already taken care of from the funds he had provided.

Zach told him that he and his family were leaving the next day, going back to the Rocky Mountains and he doubted he would be in St. Louis again. Disappointment showed on the face of the banker, he had really hoped Zach Connors and his money would stay. Zach asked him to wait a few days before delivering the deed and bank book to the Dodds, and he smiled and assured Zach that he would do it personally.

Zach rode Ol' Red back down to William Ashley's warehouse to say goodbye to his old friend but General Ashley wasn't there. The man there told Zach that Mr. Ashley had to go to a meeting that he was going to become a congressman and represent the people of Missouri back in Washington. Zach didn't know much about government and had no idea what a congressman did, but he was sure if William Ashley wanted to be one, he would be a good one.

As he rode north along Front Street back toward the Dodds farm, with the busy docks and mighty steamboats pumping smoke out of their twin stacks, he thought of cool clean air and the quiet surroundings of Black's Fork and home. It had been three months since they had ridden down the trail leading away from the dugout that he and his pa had built when they first found that spot. It had been in the early fall after the very first Rendezvous in 1825, and he missed it. He missed the cool crisp air of the high country and the afternoon thunderstorms as they rolled through the high peaks. He missed the yipping of the coyotes and howls of the wolves echoing in the canyons.

Zach had no regrets about what had happened to the men that had tried to attack them. They got what they deserved, but he was still worried what might happen to Emma and her family if Virgil Hathaway still wanted revenge. Zach was tired, he hadn't slept at all the night before but he wasn't going to rest until he was sure the deputy was no longer a threat. He knew he couldn't just walk into the sheriff's office and he had no idea where Virgil lived, so he kicked Ol' Red into a lope and just a few minutes later, rode into their camp.

He only spent a moment greeting his wives and little girl, then whistled just as loud as he could. A few minutes later as he was watching the woods, movement caught his eye as Jimbo came at a dead run to him. He remounted his big mule and told Jimbo to find Buffalo Heart and then he followed the dog as he led him right back to the small grove where Red Hawk and Buffalo Heart were holding their three prisoners. Zach's eyes were red from the lack of sleep and he was in no mood to be trifled with. The three could see that. He pulled his large skinning knife and then said, "I am only going to ask this once and if I don't get an answer I am goin' to start skinning you one at a time." He hesitated for only a moment just, long enough for what he had said to sink in and then asked, "Where does Virgil Hathaway live?" His question was directed at the one that had told him about Virgil last night. He was naked from the waist down, sitting in the cool grass. It had been so painful for him walking with his trousers rubbing against his blistered groin and legs he had taken them off just after they entered the woods.

He looked at the knife Zach was holding and then at the look in his eyes and he had no doubt about what Zach had just said. He didn't hesitate, he told Zach that Virgil lived up on Spruce Street just before you get to Chouteau's Pond. He told him he couldn't miss it, it was the last house on the street. Zach asked if he lived alone and was told yes, his wife had left him.

As Zach rode away, the prisoner with the wounded shoulder said, "Yah know Abe, Virgil will kill ya if'n he finds out it was you." "Yeah maybe so but he's gonna have to find me first and when that Grizzly Killer gets done with 'em I don't figure he'll be findin' nobody," Abe replied.

Zach slept most of the afternoon but was saddled up and back in the city before dark. He located the last house at the top of Spruce Street, then just waited. Zach had always been a patient man when hunting and that was just what he told himself he was doing now. He didn't have to wait for all that long before Virgil rode up to the house on an almost black gelding and then continued on to the small corral around back.

Zach followed him around the house, staying in the shadows and out of sight. He was now wearing his buckskins and had his Cherokee tomahawk in his belt on one side and his knife on the other. He had left his Hawken in its new scabbard on Ol' Red. As Virgil came out of the corral, Zach stepped out right in front of him. Virgil was startled but only a moment later he realized whom he was facing and said, "So you're that Injun lovin' bastard with the big dog, well thanks fer comin', now I don't have to come and find ya."

Zach smiled as he said, "Mister you and that thievin' cousin of yours have caused a lot of trouble for me and I'm here to put a stop to it."

Virgil defiantly responded, "I'm the law here you bastard, I say when it stops, not you."

Zach looked him directly in the eyes and said, "You may think you're the law here mister but I live by the law of right and wrong and this time you are wrong."

Zach's fist struck so fast Virgil never even saw it coming. He cursed several times as Zach let him get back to his feet, but now Virgil had a very large knife in his hand. Trying to catch Zach off guard he lunged forward, but Zach jumped out of the way. As Virgil turned to face him again he saw a completely different man. Zach was in a slightly bent forward position with his knife in his left hand and the deadly tomahawk in his right and said, "You sure you want to do it this way?"

Virgil was now livid with anger and nearly shouted, "I'm gonna gut you just like a hog being butchered." He struck out again with his deadly knife. There was no doubt in Zach's mind that the man had killed before as he knocked the knife away. Virgil too knew the man he was fighting was also skilled with his knife. Virgil's next lunge was his last and as Zach's blade blocked the lunge of Virgil's knife, he brought the tomahawk around with all his force, burying it nearly to the handle in the side of his neck.

Zach pulled his deadly tomahawk free and shook his head in disgust. After he loaded Virgil's body onto his horse, he mounted Ol' Red and led the black horse carrying Virgil's body out into the dark woods way west of Chouteau's Pond, he told himself justice was served. He buried him in a place that he figured would be hard to find, then let the horse go, knowing he would find his way back to his corral. Zach then rode Ol' Red through the dark woods around the west side of the city and eventually back to camp.

ZACH WAS QUIET WHEN HE REACHED CAMP, AND THEY all knew by his silence that he'd had to kill again. Sun Flower and Shining Star both knew their husband well enough to know how he hated to kill, but both were thankful that he had the strength to do whatever he must to protect the people he cared about. It was that strength that had made Zach Connors become known as Grizzly Killer and one of the most respected men west of the Mississippi.

They loaded up and were ready to leave by the time the warm summer sun showed itself over the thick woodlands that made up the eastern horizon. They left the horse that Henry had been riding and one other of their Pawnee captures there in the pasture, so Charles and Henry would both have riding mounts. They rode up to the cabin to say farewell to a dear friend and her family, Charles, Henry and little Charlotte.

Emma was silent and everyone could tell she was emotional about Zach riding out of her life once again. She had fought with her own feelings ever since she first saw him standing outside her front door a couple of weeks ago, and she wondered if she could really love two men, because that was the way she felt. He was riding out of her life again, only this time she was not expecting him to return and she felt an emptiness inside as she watched him ride away. Henry was excited about having a horse of his own and although, Charles was very appreciative of Zach's generosity, he also believed it was because of his feelings for Emma, and because of that he was glad to see him go.

Abe and the other two wounded prisoners had realized no one was watching them as the darkness of the forest faded with the coming dawn; they had no idea the mountain man and his Indian friends had left for good. The three of them, as quietly as they could, snuck away through the thick woods, hoping the two Indian braves that had been watching them would not be back until they had made it into the city. Herb Frasier was still weak from the loss of blood from his shoulder wound and was being helped by Jules Caron. While Abe Heckle, who was still naked from the waist down and walking rather awkwardly with his legs far enough apart that the blisters from the burns would not rub, just walked away, leaving the other two.

Zach rode along the river road with Running Wolf beside him. Jimbo and Luna were both running out ahead and both seemed mighty happy to be on the trail once again. Although Zach knew the sheriff wouldn't know for sure what happened to his deputy, he knew he would be the one suspected of the disappearance. Not knowing for sure how corrupt the sheriff himself was, he wondered if the three men they had left in the woods would go to the sheriff immediately. If they did Zach wanted to be far enough away that they wouldn't be followed.

They crossed the Missouri River on the ferry at St. Charles and followed Benny's directions out to the Lambert farm. Just out of precaution, after they crossed the river they stayed out of site. If the Sheriff of St. Louis was going to follow, Zach was going to make it difficult for him.

They could have reached the Lambert farm late that afternoon, but Zach led them off the road out into the woods to camp for the night. If they were being followed he did not want to bring trouble to Benny or his family.

Zach had learned, to live in the wilderness a person must always take every precaution possible to survive, and now he figured that was true whether you were in the wilderness or in the city. The dangers of civilization might not be the same, but there were dangers no matter where you went. Zach, as well as his friends and family, had learned they preferred the dangers of the Rocky Mountains to the crowded streets and dishonest men of St. Louis.

Even though there was no sign of being followed, Zach stayed camped in the woods for two more days with them all taking turns watching the road. The fact was the sheriff wanted no part of what his deputy had planned and following the mountain man and several Indians was the last thing he ever thought of doing. In fact, he never even went out to the Dodds Farm to ask any questions. He knew the men had got what they deserved.

After the two days, Zach was finally convinced he wasn't being followed so they packed up and rode on to the Lambert Farm. From where the road crested the low ridge, Zach could tell by Benny's description they had found the place. It was a lot larger than he expected but there was no doubt this was the place.

IT WAS Little Dove that first saw the group of her friends while they were still nearly a quarter mile from the cabin, but there was no mistaking the mountain man riding his big red mule and the huge dog and white wolf out in front of them. She yelled for Benny with an excitement in her voice that brought everyone running from the cabin and the barn to see what was wrong.

Jimbo came running up to Little Dove with as much excitement as she had but when Benny's mother and sisters saw the size of Jimbo they all backed up toward the door of the cabin. She hugged Jimbo and accepted his licks on her face.

Benny and Jacob came running from the barn and Jacob slowed when he saw the size of Jimbo. Jacob was still holding his pitchfork and when Jimbo saw Benny he ran toward him. Jacob stepped back putting the pitchfork out to protect himself as Jimbo jumped up on his older brother. He stood there in disbelief as Jimbo had his front paws on Benny's shoulders, licking his face. Jimbo's head was actually taller the Benny's.

Benny laughed with joy that his friends had arrived then turned to Jacob and said, "Brother, this here is Jimbo, the Big Medicine Dog." Jacob slowly put down the pitchfork and stepped forward after he noticed the wagging tail and friendly look in the eyes of the big dog. Jacob had always had a way with animals, because they had always sensed the love he had for them and Jimbo was no different. When Jimbo jumped up on Jacob it caught him off guard and he went over backward. He had to cover his face with his hands as Jimbo's wet tongue went to work licking him. Benny laughed and laughed and in just a moment Jacob was laughing as well as he hugged the big dog then tried to get back up.

Zach whistled and Jimbo instantly left his bewildered new friend and ran back to Zach's side. This was indeed a happy reunion and as they all were introduced, Jacob noticed two things: first the beauty of these Indian women and then Ol' Red. There was a special place in his heart for mules and had been ever since his pa had brought the first donkey stud to the farm to breed to his big shire mares. He reached out to the big red mule and Zach warned him that Ol' Red didn't cotton much to strangers. Jacob ignored the warning and step forward anyway; Zach was truly surprised when his mule started to nuzzle Jacob's hand. Zach helped Running Wolf step out of the saddle for his leg would not support him just yet. Benny was concerned and even though Zach tried to play the incident down, Benny kept questioning until they all got the picture of what had happened. Benny's mother had been skeptical after hearing the stories Benny had told them about this man they call Grizzly Killer, for he sounded like such a violent man. Now she had met him and heard him tell of the violence they had just left in St. Louis, she believed just as Benny did, that Zach was not violent by choice.

Star and Grey Wolf were a joy for Margaret as well as her daughters and she could hardly wait to have grandkids of her own. They had made cookies that morning and the two toddlers each took a cookie and were as happy as they could be.

Albert and their father were out in the woods cutting poles to enlarge the horse corral, just days before Mathew had made a trade for four more shire mares. The Lambert mules were in such demand now they were making more money by selling mules than they were on the cotton and corn crops. He figured their future was in the mules and he was determined they would raise the best.

Benny and Little Dove took them along the creek to the old swimming hole where their lean-to was set. It didn't take long and they all had a comfortable camp set.

It was nearly the end of July and the air was hot and muggy, the cool water of the swimming hole was just too inviting to resist. They were all naked and in the water except Running Wolf when Mathew and Albert each brought in a big load of corral poles being drug by two of their mules. Albert couldn't wait to meet Grizzly Killer and when his sisters told him how big Jimbo was he couldn't wait to go meet them, so they all walked along the creek to the swimming hole.

Jimbo and Luna heard them coming long before they could be seen and ran to meet them. Both Albert and Mathew stopped dead still when they saw Jimbo and this beautiful white wolf coming toward them and the girls laughed at them as the huge dog came wagging his tail.

Running Wolf was sitting there on the bank, wishing he could get in the cool water, he heard the laughter and said, "Sounds like someone is comin'." They all stopped to listen and could hear the Lambert family walking along the trail and started to get out of the water. Albert was in the lead at seventeen years old, he came into the opening of their camp just as Sun Flower stepped out of the water. He stopped so suddenly Jacob ran into his back nearly knocking both of them down. When Jacob looked up, Sun Flower was standing by the fire completely naked and Raven Wing and Shining Star both carrying their little ones stepped out, followed by Little Dove and Zach, Benny, Red Hawk and Buffalo Heart. By that time all of Benny's family was standing there with their mouths open and their eyes the size of saucers. Margaret was trying the get her children to turn around and not look but Mathew just burst out laughing and said, "Looks fun maybe we all should take a dip." He walked on in as everyone was getting dressed.

Margaret had been told how lovely these women were but never expected to see them like this. Rachael and Fae had both turned red and were nearly giggling but Albert was still as a statue as though he was in shock. That was the first time he had ever seen a woman naked and that sight would be burned into his memory forever. Jacob would never admit it to anyone but he had talked Bess into skinny dipping a couple of different times this summer but she was shy and he never got a good look at her out of the water.

They had all noticed the large crystal around Sun Flower's neck as she had walked up out of the water. Although Sun Flower was no longer sick and the queasy feeling was gone, she didn't exactly feel like her old self and refused to take the healing crystal off.

Although Zach wasn't embarrassed himself, he fully understood how this must look to the Lambert's. Benny however was bright red with embarrassment. He was trying to put on clothes faster than he ever had in his life.

Margaret would never admit it, as she watched these people get dressed she wished she had the same kind of freedom they had. She could tell these women had no idea they were doing anything wrong and she longed for that type of freedom herself. She also knew that white society would never allow that and she wasn't sure she would be able to do what they were doing, even if it did.

Benny couldn't look his mother in the eye but his father came right to him as nothing had happened and said, "Well son, ain't ya goin' to introduce me to your friends?" Mathew shook all their hands, followed by Albert. His face started to turn red again when he looked into Sun Flower's beautiful dark eyes but he recovered and said, "Very glad to meet you, Ma'am."

After the introductions had been made, Benny looked at his ma and said, "Ma, it was hot and well, the Indian people just ain't the same as the whites. They all go swimming and bath together and never think nothin' of it."

His mother smiled at him and he nearly went into shock as she said, "At times I wish we could be more like them." Benny looked up now and saw a completely different side of his mother, one he would never have even guessed existed.

After they were dressed and the introductions were finished, Margaret asked Sun Flower about the crystal around her neck. They all sat around the little fire and listened as Sun Flower and Raven Wing told them how the mountain had given Raven Wing the healing stone and how it had helped with Sun Flower's sickness. Margaret looked deep into Sun Flower's dark eyes and asked her about the sickness and how she now felt. At first Margaret had been concerned about a disease but as she listened to Sun Flower she began to smile and said, "My dear, it sounds to me like you are going to have a baby. That sounds like the way I felt with Albert." Sun Flower was in shock hearing that and she slowly turned and looked at Zach. Margaret continued, "I felt different with each and every one of my children, but it sure sounds like you are pregnant."

Sun Flower was speechless as she thought, could this women she just met know more than her sister? Her emotions were going wild as she thought about having Grizzly Killers child. Margaret could see both the disbelief and hope in her eyes and continued, "I have had six children and each one was different but I knew I was pregnant,

I know the signs. With Benny I was sick every morning for over two months. With Rachael I never did get sick but with Albert I felt just like what you described."

Sun Flower didn't know whether or not to smile, hoping she was right. She could feel her heart racing with the possibility that she was carrying Grizzly Killer's child. She looked at Raven Wing, and although she had thought the same thing she hadn't wanted to get Sun Flower's hopes up in case she was wrong. She knew how bad Sun Flower wanted this, but now she nodded her agreement to her younger sister. Tears filled her eyes as she looked again at Zach and the smile on his face made her heart beat even faster. She stood and went to Margaret and hugged this woman she had just met. She didn't know how but in her heart Sun Flower knew Margaret was right she was finally going to give Grizzly Killer a child.

She touched the crystal still hanging around her neck, then silently thanked the One Above, maker of all things for this crystal. She believed it was the reason she was finally going to give Grizzly Killer a child.

THE WEDDING WAS NOW JUST three days away and Little Dove and Benny had explained to their friends that his mother wanted them to get married in the church with Jacob and Bess. Zach understood that completely, there had been times over the last few years that he had wondered if he would ever be able to talk a preacher into marrying him to both Sun Flower and Shining Star. That thought no longer mattered to him, he firmly believed the good Lord had led him to both and that in his eyes they were indeed married.

Since the wedding ceremony was for the white people,

Little Dove was planning on wearing one of her store-bought dresses, but Benny asked her to dress as her people would. He was proud she was Shoshone and he wanted her dressed as one. In fact, he had gone into St. Charles one day with his father for supplies and had brought back some bright blue cloth and a whole bottle full of glass beads. Once Sun Flower, Shining Star, and Raven Wing understood that the wedding was a very special ceremony, they all pitched in and the day before the wedding they had a dress that would be the envy of any Shoshone woman.

Benny had wanted to surprise his family at the wedding, he wasn't sure what he was planning would be alright with everyone but it was his life and he was proud of it. With everyone's help, he was going to be dressed as a Shoshone warrior when they showed up at the church.

He knew it would cause a stir among everyone there and because this day was planned as Jacob and Bess's wedding he talked to them both about his plans. At first, Bess had been opposed to sharing her wedding day with Jacob's brother who she barely remembered. She hadn't wanted him or his Indian squaw to have any part of that day, but after she had listened to Little Dove speak to her mother and how after her mother was a much happier woman she was glad now and even looked forward to have her and Benny part of her wedding. The dark force of hatred she had carried with her since childhood had been lifted from her and everyone around her could see she was much happier now. Bess would be forever grateful to Little Dove and now looked forward to her and Benny being married alongside Jacob and herself.

Bess knew it would cause talk among many of their friends at the wedding but she knew that talk would happen regardless of their dress. Just the fact that a white man was marrying an Indian would cause talk. She hadn't known Benny and Little Dove long, but she had grown to love and respect them both. Both Jacob and Bess said they would be proud to stand next to them in their traditional Shoshone dress. To the rest of Jacob's family, it would be a surprise.

THE MORNING OF THE WEDDING WAS BUSY FOR THEM all, their little church was nearly five miles away and it had to be made ready for the wedding and the reception and dance afterward. They had let Preacher Adams know that it would now be a double wedding. The preacher had told nearly everyone else and they were all curious about who Benny was marrying now that he had returned home.

The little church was filled to capacity that afternoon as Jacob walked in wearing a new suit that Benny bought him. There was whispering and an excited buzz among the women, how handsome of a young man Jacob was. Next, Benny walked in dressed in the finest buckskins he'd ever had. The women had decorated his shirt and leggings, befitting the warrior they knew he was. Zach smiled, thinking if it wasn't for his light hair no one would be able to tell he wasn't Shoshone.

Now the little church was deathly silent, not a sound could be heard as Benny walked down the aisle and took his place beside his brother. A minute later Running Wolf, Red

Hawk, and Buffalo Heart followed by the three beautiful Indian women all dressed in the best Indian dresses they had with them came in. Everyone in the church strained to get a look at the Indians and wondered just what was going on. Some of the looks they were getting were hostile and they could tell just their presence had some people nervous.

Margaret Lambert and her family were sitting in the front row and although she also was surprised by Benny's dress, she now understood more than ever that he was proud to be living among these people. She stood and walked back to where they had set down, taking Running Wolf by the hand she helped support him and led them all to the front row to sit with her family. Benny's eyes welled up at that gesture and knew then that his choices in life had been fully accepted by his family.

The preacher walked up to the front of the church, and a moment later Bess, holding a bouquet of daisies and her father's arm, started to slowly walk down the aisle. It was the first time Jacob had seen her dress and he thought right then, she was the most beautiful thing he had ever seen. Right behind them Little Dove and Zach stepped in and started down the aisle. She was dressed in a fully beaded and fringed dress of soft doeskin. She had a sash of the bright blue cloth Benny had brought her tied around her waist and pieces of it tied in her hair. Sun Flower, Raven Wing, and Shining Star had spent all morning getting her ready, and Little Dove had never in her life felt as special as she did now. Zach too was dressed in his buckskins, Shining Star had cleaned them to the best of her ability for there wasn't time to make a new pair. She had also painted a Grizzly Bear's Head on the back of his shirt. As usual, he had his grizzly claw necklace around his neck and the silence in the church was deafening as Zach left Little Dove standing next to Benny and took his place sitting between his wives. Rachael had taken Star from her mother and they all waited for the preacher to start the ceremony.

The preacher himself was pleased Benny was getting married in the church and that he had brought his Indian friends as well. It was his job to spread the word of God and if to some degree he could make these Indians believe, then he had done his job. He had no idea they did believe in God, even if they didn't call him that, and they were a very religious people.

He started out the wedding and Little Dove was listening very carefully to his words. She wanted to understand this ceremony that was so important to Benny's family. The preacher got to the part where he asked the congregation, "If anyone has a reason why these men and these women should not be wed to speak now or forever hold your peace."

A man near the back shouted, "A white man shouldn't marry no Injun." Everyone in the church tensed and Zach started to rise but Benny's mother put her hand on his leg, telling him to stay seated as Benny's Pa stood. He was not the only one he saw rise, across the aisle Anna Applegate stood.

Mathew followed her down the aisle as everyone in the church tensed. Bess was shocked, she had no idea what her mother would do. Anna looked calm and she walked up the man that had spoken and said, "Paul Meyer, why did you come to the wedding today?"

He looked at her a little embarrassed and confused and said, "I wouldn't have if I'd know some savages would be here."

Anna reached out faster than he had expected and slapped him across the face and Mathew said, "Paul, now is a good time for you to leave."

Paul looked defiant as he said, "I'll leave when I'm ready!"

Staying very calm Mathew said, "Paul, you will leave now one way or another."

Everyone in the church could hear every word that was said, and a half dozen men stood to back Mathew up. He was well respected and liked, and everyone knew Paul Meyer as a troublemaker. Paul looked up to the preacher and said, "Are you gonna let 'em throw me outa your church."

The preacher responded, "This is not my church, Mr. Meyer it is the Lord's, and there is no room in it for hate, for the Lord taught us to love our neighbor, he didn't say that neighbor had to be like us." Paul Meyer left humiliated and headed to a tavern he frequented, in disgust. Even though Paul Meyer was much older than Bess Applegate he had always dreamed of having her for his own, though he had never tried to do anything about it.

Before the preacher started up again Little Dove apologized to Bess for the trouble, thinking she was the reason. But Bess smiled at her and reassured her there was nothing to apologize for.

It took only minutes for the preacher to finish the ceremony and when he said you may kiss the bride Little Dove was surprised that Benny grabbed her, pulled her close and kissed her standing there in front of everyone. Although it didn't seem to bother Benny at all, she was embarrassed, she was always much more reserved until they were in private.

Outside in the churchyard, there had been two whole hogs roasting since midnight and nearly everyone that attended had brought some food item. It was a feast and party for the whole community, with some coming from nearly twenty miles away. It didn't matter whether it was a wedding, christening, or funeral, these people supported one another and they all loved the chance to get together and celebrate. It was hard and lonely work living isolated on a farm and to get away from that and celebrate anything was a great release for all of them. Two men had brought fiddles and another a banjo, and everyone ate, laughed, and danced until well after dark.

Margaret took her daughters along with Sun Flower, Shining Star, and Raven Wing back to Jacob and Bess's new cabin the men had built on the far side of the fields and got it ready for their wedding night. They lit the coal oil lamp and Sun Flower started a small fire in the fireplace. The girls giggled, knowing what their brother and Bess would be doing as they helped their mother make the bed. With the money from one of the mules they had sold, they had ordered two windows for the cabin and now they opened them both, letting the gentle breeze blow through cooling off the warm air inside.

The bed was made of logs and Margaret had sown the mattress by hand out of canvas and then they had all helped stuff it with straw. Margaret remembered her own wedding night, she believed that was the very night Benny had been conceived. She hoped for grandkids, but she also thought it best for Jacob and Bess to learn to care for each other, before they had a child to care for.

THE SUN WAS WELL above the horizon and the temperature was rising rapidly before anyone stirred on the farm the next morning. Benny and Buffalo Heart took over for Jacob, making sure the horses and donkeys were all fed. There was plenty of grass in the pasture to keep the mules happy through the summer months. That afternoon a violent thunderstorm developed and it hailed harder than any of them had ever seen. Some of the hail was as big as a silver dollar and even Jimbo and Luna hid in the lean-tos until it stopped but it rained so hard they couldn't see across the field to Jacob's cabin for over an hour.

All of them were homesick for the mountains, even Benny was ready to head back west. He wondered how Grub and Ely were and how they had faired at the Rendezvous. He thought to himself how glad he was to have made this trip back and to know his family was now prospering on the farm. For his family as well, to know he was doing well and was happy in his new life, but the Rocky Mountains were now his home and missing all of his friends, he longed to get back there.

The rain let up well before dark and that evening over supper Benny told his family they would be leaving, going back to the Rockies the next day. Benny's family hated to see them leave, his mother had tears in her eyes but his father understood. Benny was a man on his own now, he wished he would have been happy and made his life on the farm, but he knew now his son was living the life he was meant to live.

That night when they got back to their camp by the swimming hole, they again went skinning dipping one last time under the partial moon. After their swim Zach, with Jimbo by his side, went out to Ol' Red and their horses. They were now well rested and had regained the weight they had lost from the two months of continuous travel and now they had to do it all over again. Zach wasn't looking forward to the long trek back across the barren plains, but other than no trees and no mountains, the traveling every day wasn't all that much different than his life in the Rockies. Whether he was trapping or exploring new country it seemed they were always going somewhere. It was the excitement of seeing new land, country that had never been explored before that was so appealing to Zach and Benny and men like them. It was the freedom to go anyplace anytime or to stay where you were that had made the life of a mountain man so enjoyable to those that needed that freedom. Now Zach knew they were leaving, he was feeling excited to get back to his beloved Rocky Mountains.

He was concerned for Sun Flower, would another two months in the saddle hurt her or the baby? The women all assured him that they have been having babies on the trail since time began, Sun Flower would be no different.

At daylight they were all up breaking camp. The ground was still moist from the rain of the day before. By the time they were loaded up and ready to head west, Benny's mother and sisters had a huge feast prepared. Thick cut slices of cured and smoked bacon, Johnny cakes with thick sorghum molasses, fried eggs, and biscuits. They all ate until they were stuffed and after came the tearful goodbyes. No one said anything about it, but they all seemed to know this was probably the last time they would ever see one another. The entire Lambert family watched them ride up over the little ridge toward St. Charles and the ferry and then out of sight.

THE FOLLOWING DAY after his work was finished at the bank, Maurice Chouteau took his single horse carriage out to the Dodds Farm. Charles and Henry had just returned from unloading a steamboat up from New Orleans. They had no idea what the banker wanted to talk to them about and then they were stunned into complete silence when Mr. Chouteau handed young Henry the deed to the quarter section of land adjacent to their farm.

Henry didn't know what a deed was or what it meant. Charles stated, "I don't understand." Although Zach hadn't told Mr. Chouteau to keep his name a secret, the banker wasn't sure he wanted it known either, so for now, he just said, "I was given the funds and instructions to make this transaction in the name of Mister Henry Dodds, I'm not sure I have the liberty to say more."

Henry looked at the paper again and then looked up at his father asking, "Pa, what is a deed and what does this mean?" Charles was speechless, he had no idea what to say.

It was Mr. Chouteau that smiled at young Henry and said, "Well son, that piece of paper means that you own the land right here next to your farm. It is a full 160 acres and it is all yours, and I have something else for you as well." He slowly pulled out the bank book but before handing it to Henry he asked, "Do you know what a bank book is young man?" Henry, looking puzzled shook his head. Mr. Chouteau continued, "In this little book is a record of money that is deposited in my bank by individuals, when they want to take money out of the bank they bring this book and we mark in it how much to take out and that person gets the money, and this book has your name on it."

Henry again looked confused and asked, "What's deposit mean?"

Mr. Chouteau smiled and said, "It's just a fancy word for putting your money in the bank." He continued to explain," Henry since you are so young, this money that is now in the bank in your name is also in the name of your mother."

Henry looked up at Emma and then at Mr. Chouteau and said with a big smile on his face, "She ain't my real ma, my real ma died. She's my new ma though and me and Pa both love her a lot."

Emma had tears in her eyes and running down her cheeks, not only from what Henry had just said but also because she knew there was only one person that could have done this. Maurice Chouteau handed Henry the bank book and he opened it up and showed Emma. She gasped when she saw there were six hundred and twenty dollars on deposit at the bank. She looked at Mr. Chouteau and said, "This all came from Zach Connors didn't it?"

When Mr. Chouteau nodded Charles said, "We can't take this, not any of it. You have to give it all back to him."

Mr. Chouteau looked at Charles and said, "Mr. Dodds, Mr. Connors told me that you would not accept this from him. I believe that is why it is all in Henry's name. He also has left St. Louis and I believe he is now well on his way back to the Rocky Mountains. He said he didn't believe he would ever return. Mr. Connors is a very wealthy man, not only has he done very well trapping furs he has found gold somewhere out in that wilderness and as he explained to me, money has no value out there, for there is nothing to buy. They trade for what they need. From what William Ashley has told me about him, Mr. Connors, who is known as Grizzly Killer by everyone across the great-plains and Rocky Mountains is one of the best trappers and mountain men there is. He said men like him could never live and be happy in the civilized world. So you see Mr. Dodds, the money, and the land is your son's and your wife's. Even if I wanted, I couldn't return it."

Charles Dodds was stunned, as was Emma. They thanked Mr. Chouteau over and over and walked him out to his carriage. As he sat down and picked up the reins he said, "Most days the banking business is plain and fairly boring. But on days such as this, my job is truly a pleasure."

FOUR DAYS LATER THEY WERE NEARLY A HUNDRED miles west of St. Louis. The thick woodlands were starting to give way to grass-covered prairie. The first couple of days on the trail west had been quiet, no one was very talkative as they thought about everything they had seen during their stay in the land of the white man.

That night after they had finished their evening meal, they talked about their experience in St. Louis. It was Running Wolf that said, "I was young the first time I ever saw a white man. General Ashley was leading his brigade down the See-Kee-Dee and stopped to trade for horses to go back north over the mountains. I went with Grub and Ely and several others to guide them for several months and they taught me to speak their tongue. The next time I saw a white man was when Grizzly Killer found me with a broken leg and a Shoshone war party was trying to kill me. After that, it was at the Rendezvous in Willow Valley that I saw them. I believe Grizzly Killer is right, every year there are more and more white men coming into our land. Most are good people but many are not. I believe, like Grizzly

Killer, they will keep coming and we must learn to live among them." They all nodded their agreement and reflected on what that might mean for the future.

Three days later they could see the small town of Independence before them. Zach didn't know how they had missed it while they were coming east, he figured they must have been further south past this area. He had been told while in St. Louis that a town had been built on the river about a week's ride to the west just before the Missouri made its big turn back to the north and now, here it was right in front of them.

They rode right down the main street and Zach stopped in front of a small general store. At that time Zach knew of no settlement further west. Because of that, Independence was being used as the jumping off point for anyone heading west, whether they were heading up the Missouri River or across the prairie to the Rockies or further south to the Spanish territory. Independence was small and Zach was surprised by the supplies the store had. He bought more flour, sugar and cornmeal, and as much salt as he figured they could carry, as well as some small barrels to put it in. They had run out of bear grease and he didn't know if they would see a bear until they returned to the mountains, so he bought enough lard to get them through. He bought potatoes, carrots, and onions to last them a couple of weeks, knowing they wouldn't keep any longer than that. The store had several bolts of canvas and he purchased several yards of it. It was much lighter and easier to cover their supplies with than the heavy bulky buffalo hides.

After his experience in St. Louis with the men that had seen his money pouch, he made certain no one in Independence had any idea he was still carrying nearly fifteen hundred dollars in gold coins.

They rode out of Independence, staying out on the prairie nearly a mile away from the river, yet following its course and just before they camped for the night, they saw a small herd of young buffalo bulls. Since they hadn't had fresh meat in several days, they decided while the women set up camp they would try for one.

Zach hadn't had a chance to try his new .54 caliber Hawken and he was curious if it really had more power. While the others all rode way out around the dozen animals, Zach was crawling through the tall brown dried out grass hoping to get close enough for a shot. He stopped and watched the buffalo for a moment and smiled, he knew this is the way he was meant to live. His wives and child waiting for him to make a kill so they all could enjoy the fresh meat.

Running Wolf's leg, although it was healing, wasn't quite ready for a buffalo hunt and he sat his horse over a half mile away, watching. Buffalo Heart, Benny, and Red Hawk had ridden out around the small herd and then started to move toward Grizzly Killer. It wasn't long and the buffalo knew something was wrong and started to move away from the three riders and right toward where Zach was hiding in the tall grass.

Zach had told Jimbo to stay with Running Wolf while he was stalking the buffalo and as the dozen young bulls started to move the big dog whined and the hair down his back stood on end. Running Wolf had just opened his mouth to tell Jimbo to calm down when the dog took off at a dead run toward his master.

Zach fired as the first two-year-old running bull was about eighty yards out. He could tell, as the new Hawken kicked back into his shoulder, the rifle had more power and was pleased as the buffalo fell not moving at all. Zach was reloading as another of the young bulls looked his way and a moment later charged right at him.

Benny and Buffalo Heart both saw what was happening and urged their horses into an even faster run, trying to reach Grizzly Killer in time. Zach stopped loading as he saw the charging bull. He had to drop the rifle and dived to the side as the bull lowered his head to ram him. If his reflexes would have been only a blink of an eye slower, Zach would have been ripped apart by the deadly black horns. The bull missed his body as he jumped head first to the side but one of the bull's horns caught Zach's moccasin, ripping it from his foot and tearing a nasty gash from his ankle to the bottom of his foot.

Zach ignored the pain, he knew this cantankerous bull was not finished. As the bull slid to a stop and turned back toward Zach, he was snorting and stomping the ground, but just as he lowered his head to charge again Jimbo attacked him from the rear. His powerful jaws biting into the bull's hind leg. The furious bull now spun toward the dog but Jimbo's reflexes had him well out of the way. The bull, now confused, looked back at Zach and then at Jimbo. He could hear Benny and Buffalo Heart's horses fast approaching and the other buffalo on a dead run out onto the vast prairie. He turned and ran off after his rapidly retreating companion's with Zach's moccasin still hanging from his horn.

After making sure the buffalo was no longer a threat, Jimbo ran right to Zach. His heart was pounding fast and hard and as the adrenalin rush started to fade, he sat down on the grass to see the damage to his foot. By then Benny and Buffalo Heart were both kneeling in the grass next to him and a couple of minutes later Red Hawk and then Running Wolf, leading Ol' Red, got there.

Zach's foot was bleeding and sore, the skin was ripped

open in a three-inch long tear. The men tied a strip of softly tanned antelope hide around it to stop the bleeding. They carried the soft strips of leather for just that purpose and then they helped Zach mount Ol' Red. Him and Running Wolf went back to camp so Raven Wing could treat Zach's wound while the other three gutted, skinned, and butchered the downed Buffalo. Zach had been worried about the new rifle he had dropped but its landing in the tall grass had done no damage at all.

Zach turned white and had beads of sweat forming on his forehead as Raven Wing stitched the nasty wound closed. He had been sewn up several times, but this was the first time on a foot and was by far the most painful. His wives were on each side of him holding his hands until Raven Wing was satisfied the tear was properly closed. Sun Flower then got hot water and a coffee cup as Raven Wing opened her medicine kit to mix up a poultice to keep the wound from becoming red and inflamed.

They stayed camped on the prairie for an extra day, not only to give Zach's foot time to start healing, but also to dry and cure as much of the buffalo as they could. Zach had them take the cornmeal out of the eight-gallon barrel and fill it nearly half full of water. He then had them add a lot of salt to it. After the salt was all dissolved they cut inch thick strips of the buffalo meat and filled the barrel with it. Zach wasn't sure how long the meat needed to soak in the brine or how long it would last afterword, but he knew salt pork kept for a long time even in the heat of the summer and he hoped this would too.

They stayed camped there at the big bend of the Missouri for two full days before following the river north toward the Platte. Six days later they reached the spot where the Platte River empties into the wide Missouri.

They were all amazed at how much smaller the Platte was now than only a couple of months earlier.

They ate the potatoes, carrots, and onions every day until they were gone, although the onions lasted much longer than the others. After that, the women would search the river bank and along the creeks that fed the Platte, looking for edible plants and roots each day. Zach's foot was still tender, but he was once again wearing moccasins and walking almost normal. Running Wolf's leg was nearly healed as well, and now he also was walking without much of a limp. They stayed south of the Platte, deciding not to cross until they figured there wasn't any chance of the quicksand that had caught them on their way east.

They pushed ever closer to home each day, for the next two weeks, until they crossed the South Platte. After that, the river was much smaller and they crossed to the north side. So far they had not seen any of the Pawnee that Zach was expecting to encounter as they traveled through the heart of their land. They hadn't encountered the massive herds of buffalo either, but there had been enough along the creeks and river to keep them fed.

A couple of miles past the confluence of the South and North Platte was where they crossed to the north side and set up camp, even though it was still only midday. Running Wolf wanted to let the pack horses rest for the remainder of the day and they needed fresh meat.

Zach took Ol' Red and Jimbo to do a scout south of the river. He crossed the river and headed southwest, roughly following the South Platte while the others went hunting to the north. He rode to the top of one of the thousands of rolling hills, staying just below its crest just in case someone was out there. His eyes strained as he looked west across the vast empty prairie as he tried to see any sign of the beloved mountains he knew were out there. They were there alright, just too far away to be seen. He longed to stand on the bank of Black's Fork and watch Ol' Red and the horses frolic in the big meadow. He could close his eyes now and see the towering peaks that reached to the sky just south of their home. He thought to himself that a man that loved seeing new country as much as he did shouldn't be homesick but that was what he felt like.

As he studied the barren prairie lands all around, he realized how deceiving this land could be. It looked nearly flat but with its rolling hills blending one into another as you looked out across the vast distance, Zach knew there could be large Indian villages or massive herds of buffalo behind those hills and a person would never know they were there. He looked down at Jimbo and he too was intently looking, but his gaze was down into the river bottom. Zach figured the South Platte was a little over a half mile below them, but as he watched his dog he became more and more convinced something was down there.

Zach was now studying the tree and brush line along the river looking for any movement or anything that may be out of place, but after several minutes he hadn't seen a thing. Jimbo had been with Zach since he was a pup and Zach knew his big dog well enough to know something was there and that something was probably watching him. Not wanting to lead a party of Indians, whatever tribe they may be, back to his loved ones, he decided to go down to the river and see just what had caught Jimbo's attention.

He checked the prime in the pan of his new .54 caliber Hawken as well as his pistol and then proceeded with extreme caution. He rode Ol' Red down the gentle slope toward the tree line of the South Platte. Jimbo had stayed only a few feet in front of Zach all the way down, and as they approached the trees and brush along the river, the hair started to rise down the center of his back.

Zach stepped out of his saddle and just dropped the reins, Ol' Red knew not to wander. Zach silently patted the big mule's neck then carefully stepped into the trees and underbrush along the river. It was about the third week of August and the wild plums and berries growing along the river were ripe. He slowly moved forward with all of his senses on high alert. Jimbo was just a step ahead of his master, he hadn't started his deep low growl but all of the hair down the center of the back was standing up his ears were straight forward and every muscle in his body looked tense. Zach was sure something or someone was there and he knew he must find out who or what was making Jimbo nervous.

They were moving very slowly, Zach knew very well an arrow, lance, or even a deadly lead round ball could come at him at any time, but he had to know or he couldn't return to his camp tonight. They were nearly a hundred yards from Ol' Red when suddenly and with no warning a big silver tipped grizzly stood up from a stand of wild plums he had been feeding on. The massive bear was only fifty feet in front of them. Both Zach and Jimbo froze. Zach wasn't even sure he was breathing as the big bear sniffed, testing the air trying to determine what the strange smell was.

Zach knew that a bear's eyesight was poor and he didn't think the large grizzly could tell for sure where he and Jimbo were, but their ability to smell was even better than Jimbo's was. It would not be long before it had zeroed in on their scent. If the bear charged Zach knew he could fire before it got to them but he had never seen just one shot stop a grizzly. If he fired and wounded the bear it would more than likely mean both of their deaths, just like it had with his pa those years ago.

The bear's nose stopped moving around and Zach heard the familiar huffing as the large male grizzly stared right at them. He dropped down on all fours and charged. Zach rapidly brought his Hawken to his shoulder and set the rear trigger, but the charging bear stopped about twenty-five feet away. Jimbo's teeth were bared and his hair was standing on its end but he never made a sound. Zach could hear his own heart beating in his ears as he kept the front sight centered on the big bear's shoulder. He was hoping if he had to shoot, the shot would break the bear's shoulder and at least slow him down enough that they might get away. The bear swung his mighty paws across the ground throwing dirt and debris for several yards out as he snapped his powerful jaws together continuously warning Zach and Jimbo not to mess with him.

After two full minutes of that terrifying display, which seemed like a lifetime to Zach, the bear just turned and walked away, disappearing into the thick brush. Zach turned and made his way back to Ol' Red just as fast as he could with Jimbo right on his heels. He would never know why the big bear did not charge, but as he rode back toward camp he said a silent prayer, thanking God he had not.

THREE DAYS later the sky was dark and threatening, the wind was blowing in gusts that were hard enough to sting their faces. Flashes of lightning could be seen to the south-west and they all knew the approaching storm was going to be violent. Zach moved down close to the river where there were a few cottonwoods and called a halt so they could better prepare for the coming rain, then decided just to wait it out where they were.

They hurriedly set up their lean-tos with the openings away from the wind and settled in to wait out the storm. He figured they were only two or three days from Scott's Bluff and from there he knew they would be able to see Laramie Peak. Although they would still be a hundred miles away, it was the start of the Rocky Mountains and it was now starting to feel like they were getting close to home.

The ground started to rumble and as Zach looked out to see what was making the roar, he saw a white wall of hail was coming right towards them. As the hail moved over, it was replaced by a hard rain. Moments later, as they laid up under the buffalo hides of the lean-tos, they could feel the ground trembling again and they could hear a different type of rumble. It was getting louder and the ground was now shaking. The hard rain had slowed to only a drizzle and as they watched, over ten thousand head of stampeding buffalo came over the low rolling hill to the north. Zach figured they were running away from the violent storm and stinging hail, but he worried that they were right in the path of thousands of the stampeding beasts.

Zach hoped the few trees and river would stop the running mass of buffalo, each one weighing up to a ton, and it did. As the buffalo reached the river they stopped running, the stampede was over. Within the next little while, the massive herd started to graze all around them.

The storm, as violent as it was had lasted only an hour, but now there little hastily created camp was surrounded by ten thousand buffalo. Zach and his wives just laid there under the lean-to, watching. After the stampede, there were several calves that still wanted to run and they were kicking their hooves in the air and bucking. Others had their heads together trying to push one another, practicing for when they would become dominant bulls, fighting to keep their harem of cows.

Zach was holding Star, their little blue-eyed daughter, and they all were smiling with delight as they watched her pointing her little fingers at the running and playing buffalo calves. Shining Star leaned down next to her and whispered, "I pray my little one, you will remember the land of your father and you too will be free to show your children Where the Buffalo Dance."

Lane R Warenski lives in a log home in Duchesne County, Utah, where he has an unrestricted view of the highest peaks in the mighty Uinta Mountains. He was raised being proud of his pioneer heritage and with a deep love and respect of the outdoors. Ever since childhood, following his father, Warenski has hunted, fished, and camped the mountains of the West. Whether it was the daily journals of William Ashley and Jedediah Smith or the fictional stories written by the great storytellers like Louis L'Amour and Terry C. Johnston, throughout his life, Warenski loves reading the history of the first explorers that came west, most of whom never dreamed they were opening this wild and rugged land to the pioneers and settlers that followed.

CPSIA information can be obtained
at www.ICGtesting.com
Printed in the USA
FFHW020026171218
49890345-54490FF

9 781641 193436